GW00643720

SUSTAIN

New York Times and USA Today Bestselling Author
TIJAN

DEDICATION

This book is dedicated to my readers!

Thank you for always supporting me,
and I hope you enjoy this one as well.

PROLOGUE

Breathe, little girl.

I could hear my mother's voice as she whispered into my ear again. Plates had been shattered. The kitchen table was flipped upside down. Doors were ripped off their hinges. With each crash and roar coming from the other room, my little fingers had dug into her arm. That was the night he left.

I thought nothing could get worse for us.

I was staring down the barrel of a gun now.

I'd been wrong.

CHAPTER ONE

They came in when we were sleeping. They were silent until our bedroom door was kicked open, and a loud male voice shouted, "Police! Police! We have a search warrant!" They flooded into the room. It felt like a stampede was entering, as the floorboards jostled and the bed shook. I sat up, dazed, but Elijah was already up. He kicked off the bed sheets, grabbed his jeans, and ran to the window. "Freeze! Stop right there and let me see your hands. Freeze!"

A strong hand grabbed my arm, and I was yanked upright. I soared through the air and hit against the far wall. It all happened in the blink of an eye.

Thud.

I can't believe this is happening, I thought while in the air, right before I crashed into the wall with that thud. Elijah and I had been at a rave three hours earlier. The night had been filled with techno music, neon lights, and sweat that came from too much dancing, too much sex, and too much fun. And now this—I wanted to curse. I wasn't dumb. What was happening before my eyes brought back all my brother's warnings.

"He sells drugs, Bri."

Braden had been so sure. I had been *sure* he was wrong. I had laughed at him and walked away, shaking my head, but a part of me had wondered. The money I found in boxes and bags that were stuffed everywhere. The chest he kept a lock on and refused to tell me what was inside. The nightly visits from people who were never allowed inside the house. After the first few fights, I stopped asking, because the truth was, I didn't want to know.

Living in Grant West allowed me to live in that denial. Our town wasn't a large city, but we had a large university and two technical colleges. The population swarmed tenfold during the school months, and because of all the newbies in town, the locals formed a tight unit.

Sometimes they mixed with us. That was inevitable, especially at bars and sporting events. We tried not to associate with outsiders, but I knew one person that did. Elijah. All those college parties he dragged me to, only to disappear as soon as we walked through the door—those college students were his customers.

I groaned.

Idiot!

I was pulled from my thoughts when the cop pushed me face-first into the wall. He kicked my legs open, wrenched my arms behind my back, and slapped handcuffs onto my wrists. I winced as the cold metal cut into my skin, but ignored the pain and twisted my head to the window to see Elijah on the window frame, poised to jump.

The cop closest to Elijah yelled, "Elijah Turner, get on the floor!" Elijah stopped and spun around to face the room. His crystal green eyes jerked to mine, and his shoulders heaved up and down. The scratch marks I had left a few hours ago stretched with each breath he took.

So much passed between us in that look.

He had lied to me, but I had let him.

Everything was tuned out. The police were still yelling for him to stand down. Their guns remained aimed right at him, but he was looking at me.

He had lied to me. We were over, repeated in my mind over and over again.

Then I saw a shift in him. An apology flashed in his gaze, and I knew he was going to jump. I twisted in his direction. "No!"

The officer slammed me back into the wall. "Stay." His knee pressed into the back of my thigh, holding me in place, and he pushed down on my handcuffs, making them bite into my wrists, but I didn't feel it.

Please don't, Elijah, I silently pleaded with him.

He read my unspoken message and took a deep breath in resignation. He was going to surrender. Relief flared through me. I was pissed at him, but jumping would have made things worse. I still cared about him.

The police sensed the shift in him and moved in. They dragged him from the window, pushed him to his knees, and handcuffed him.

Once he was in custody, they took him first, leading him out the door. I was next. A female officer took my arm and led me out of the bedroom, into another room. As they did, I could hear drawers, boxes, and books being dumped onto the floor from Elijah's room.

The officer searched me. My clothes were brought in, and she searched them, too. She went through the pockets of my jeans, checked my shirt and my bra before tossing it to the guy in charge of me. My flip-flops were next. The bottoms were inspected. They were looking for a secret compartment in anything. When nothing was found, she returned my clothes, and I was allowed to re-dress.

When I was taken out, I saw police officers searching all over—other rooms, the bathrooms, and the living room. Even the stair rails. Someone tossed my bag to the female holding my arm. It was unzipped, and the front pockets were pulled out; they had searched it. Another cop came over to us with my wallet. I watched her rifle through everything before she pushed it into the main compartment of my bag and zipped it back up. She said to the cop, "That's hers. She might need it." She met my gaze then. "We took your phone. It might have evidence on it."

I hissed as I was yanked forward again. That was my phone, dammit.

Looking around for Elijah, I saw him in the second cruiser parked outside. When he turned to me, I pulled my gaze away. This was his fault. I had heard the rumors, but I had trusted him. I turned my back on a lot of people because I chose to believe my boyfriend. Elijah had never lied to me before, but this was one big-ass lie.

The cop led me to a different cruiser, and I was pushed into the backseat. Her hand covered my head until I cleared the door. Once inside, she popped into the front seat and turned up the heat. It was then that I realized how cold it was. The clock on her dashboard said it was 4:17 a.m., cold for the little clothing I was wearing. She didn't say anything before she left again, shutting her door, and I was alone.

I was numb.

I was shocked.

I was livid.

I kept playing out the image of the cops bursting through the door. Elijah. This was his fault. No, it was mine. I should've listened to my brother. *No.* I was going back to my boyfriend. This was all his fault. Well. Check that. Ex-boyfriend now.

Hell. I was tired, too—tired and wired at the same time. My chest was moving up and down at a rapid pace. My skin was crawling, but I wanted to curl under a blanket at the same time. I understood why criminals looked crazy on those cop shows, if this was what they were feeling.

Then the cop came back and got inside. "Your name is Brielle Masterson?"

She was cold and brisk. Well, whatever. I watched those shows, too. I knew to keep my mouth shut. Plus, even though I was pissed at Elijah, I wasn't exactly being flooded with warm feelings for these officers. It was dumb and immature, but I kept my mouth closed. That was my middle finger to her.

She turned around to face me and held up a file. "It doesn't matter if you don't tell us. We know who you are."

How?

She arched an eyebrow. "We have your phone, Brielle."

Oh. Well. Color me foolish, except—gritting my teeth—I still didn't care.

The officer added, "Do you have any idea why we're arresting you and Mr. Turner?"

I said nothing. I could be stubborn. My brother would testify to that. I wasn't guilty of anything, so I wasn't worried, or I didn't think I should be worried. The cop kept talking, but I tuned her out and caught a glimpse of myself in the rearview mirror. I was surprised at the hard mask looking back at me. My face looked etched in stone, but there was anger boiling under the surface. *Damn straight. Thanks a lot, Elijah.* Wrinkling my nose, my dark hair was a mess. I hadn't showered since the day before, so it was greasy. I reached up to smooth my hair out, at least to look a little presentable, but it was pointless. My hair had a mind of its own.

The cop was watching me with narrowed eyes. When I saw that, I turned away, and my chin rose in defiance. She sighed. I caught movement from the corner of my eye as she put the file down on the passenger seat. "Look," she started, "I don't know your full story. You have a juvie record, I see. Some fights when you were younger. It says you took on a group of girls. Another time you assaulted your boss at Dairy Queen."

I snorted. The pervert thought breasts were on the menu...*my* breasts.

She kept going, "You are going to be processed, and you'll be booked. You don't have any drug-related charges. I'd hate for this to be your first one. If you cooperate, you can make it all go away."

My gaze jerked to hers.

"Tell us what you know about Elijah's drug circuit." She smiled at me, though her eyes remained flat. Her tone sounded so friendly. I rolled my eyes. I grew up being poor. My mom worked the night shift, so it was Braden and myself. Our dad left when we were six, and we had to learn to fend for ourselves. We fed ourselves. We dressed ourselves. We figured out what things we needed for school. Mom tried, but she was usually a zombie. I wasn't an idiot, and this cop wasn't going to fool me otherwise.

She was saying, "...the more you help us, the more we can help you."

I slumped down in the seat and took a deep breath. It wasn't going to happen. I was now in a waiting game. Glancing out the window, I wondered how long this would take. Braden's band played at Rowdy's last night, so that meant they might still be there. Even if it was another hour from now, they could still be in the basement. It was where they practiced, but it was where they partied, too. I'd try Rowdy's number when I was released. Because, you know, they'd have to release me if I wasn't guilty.

"Fine." The cop held up her hand in surrender. She turned back around to face the front. "I hope you're ready for this. You're going to be interrogated just like every other criminal we arrest."

Except I wasn't a criminal. They'd figure that out sooner or later. As she pulled out onto the street, I closed my eyes to try to get some sleep, or at least to calm down more. My heart was still racing. When we got to the police station, the wired feeling was fading, and the exhaustion was taking over. When I was taken into an interrogation room, I eyed the table and had visions of just lying on top of it and going to sleep.

"How long have you been dating Elijah Turner?"

Instead, this was what I got.

"Do you sell drugs for him?"

No answer.

"We know you graduated two years ago, but we know he's got students from the high school selling for him. Is that what you do? Do you recruit students at your old high school?" She laid a file onto the table.

I closed my eyes. The questions were giving me answers, not the other way around.

"There are witness accounts placing you and Elijah at a rave last night. Drugs were sold at that rave. Your boyfriend's drugs. If you were a part of it, come clean now. Brielle." She gentled her tone. I opened my eyes to see a soft grin on her face. "We know a rival organization is moving in. Are you helping both sides?"

What was she talking about? I wanted to ask. No, I wanted to demand.

She leaned across the table toward me. "The time for you to start talking is ending. We have people talking. Don't think we don't. They are going to name you as an accessory to this whole thing. We can protect you, Brielle, if you help us. We can keep you safe. Elijah will have no idea you were a part of this."

I wanted to flip the table over. Then I wanted to leap over it and run out of there. Instead, I took a deep breath and hunched further down in my seat. She was going to keep talking, no matter what she threatened.

"Oh." She started laughing, stood up, and walked in a small circle. "Do you want a lawyer? You think your mom can pay for one? I read your file. Your whole history is in there. Your daddy left when you were little. Your mom's working two jobs. You didn't go to college.

How come? My guess is that you stuck around to help your mom?" She opened a folder and skimmed her hand down it, stopping in the middle. "It says you work at the nursing home, but you quit recently. Is that what you're going to do all your life? Are you going to get another job?"

"How is that any of your business?"

"You make shit money. With what we have on you, a public defender won't get you off. You're looking at jail time, Brielle. Jail."

I wanted to laugh at her. For what? For picking the wrong guy and ignoring my brother's warnings? Yes. If that was a crime, take me away, Officer.

Someone knocked briefly on the door, and a new guy came inside. Looking in his older thirties with his blond hair combed back, he was dressed in jeans and a shirt. He was also wearing a GWPD vest. After he nodded to the woman, she left and he turned to stare at me. Nothing was said for a minute, and then he slowly sat down in the chair across from me and folded his hands together, resting them on the table between us. "My name is Detective Williams, and I am here to tell you what we know. You can decide whether or not you want to participate in this investigation or not. Now." He leaned back in his chair. With one finger, he slid a picture across the table toward me. "That's a picture of a girl that overdosed at a rave last night. What Officer Sonya said is true. We do know you and Elijah were there, but we can't connect you to the girl. However, we do know that your boyfriend oversees Grant West. Someone else runs Grant East. Are they the ones moving in? Wait, that's another discussion if you decide to help us. We don't know if you're a part of it, and because of that, yes, you will be released in a moment."

My head perked up.

He shook his. "I want you to know everything before you leave, so sit back. We would like you to help us, and we can hold you a whole hell of a lot longer without officially arresting you if we need to. But we're not going to do that as a sign of good faith. Call me a hopeless romantic, but I have a feeling you won't be able to not help when we're done."

That was stupid of him. I leaned back in my chair and settled in. No matter what he said, I wasn't a narc. "You're not from around here, are you?"

His eyebrows moved forward before flattening back into place. "Why do you ask?"

"You recently moved here?"

He didn't reply, but he didn't need to. His mouth flattened. "I don't know what that has to do with this, but here are the facts. A girl overdosed. She is in the hospital, and she may never wake up." He pointed to the picture. "Do you know this girl? Did your boyfriend sell drugs to her?"

I didn't know her, and I had no idea if Elijah did or not. Until this morning, I hadn't even wanted to admit he was a drug dealer.

I remained silent, and after another two minutes passed in silence, he stood up and a disgruntled sound came from him. It sounded like a groan mixed with a gurgling bark. "Fine. We have nothing to hold you. Elijah has been adamant that you have no part of his organization. He's insisting we release you before he will comply, so with that said, you are free to go."

I shoved my chair back and stood. "Can I get my phone?"

"No. That stays with us."

"I thought you said you were letting me go?"

"You're the girlfriend of a known drug dealer. We have every indication that he might've used your phone to set up deals. Your phone stays with us."

They think he used me? Used my phone? My jaw squared, and I stalked down the hallway. Leaving didn't take long. They never fingerprinted me. No paperwork had been filed so the only thing I waited for was my bag. As the cop moved to hand it to me, he held it a moment. I glanced up to see him staring at me. It wasn't a crude stare—not like a lot of the guys in school or Elijah's friends. It was in a way that my mom used to look at me. His eyebrow raised as he said, "Dump the bad boy. He's not worth it, and in the end, he'll just take you down with him."

He let go of my bag.

"Thanks," I muttered under my breath, pulling my bag on my shoulder as I headed to the front of the station. Little did they know it was already over. I was an idiot, but I was a single idiot now. Then I stopped and turned back to the clerk. "Can I use your phone?"

"What number?"

Oh, this would not make me look good. "Rowdy's."

His nostrils flared.

"Just call. My brother's band practices in the basement. They'll still be there. They'll answer."

He did and it wasn't long before I heard someone answer. He straightened and his hand scratched the back of his head. "Yeah, hello. This is Officer Malley. I've got a…" He paused and held the phone against his chest. "What's your name?"

"Bri."

He held the phone to his ear again and continued to frown at me. "A Bri here. She reassures me that her brother's band uses your basement to practice…" He stopped, and after another moment, he nodded and hung up. "The owner's sending someone to pick you up."

I nodded and headed outside to wait. I didn't want to stay in there. If I did, who knows what could happen. They could change their minds and take me in for more questioning. I knew they probably wouldn't, but I didn't want to chance it. Visions of my bed were taunting me, jumping all around in my head and laughing at me as I sat on the curb and waited for Braden.

Twenty minutes later, my brother's truck slid to a stop in front of me. Grabbing my purse, I didn't see who was behind the wheel and said, "I know you guys played tonight and figured you'd still be partying, but I was nervous you would've passed out or with some girl…" Then I saw who was staring back at me and forgot what I was about to say. "Fuck me."

Luke Skeet. His dark brown hair fell over his forehead, but he ignored it. A hint of dark humor entered those grey eyes of his, and he shook his head. "No, Bri. All those nights I crawled into your bed, fucking was the one thing we never got around to doing." His eye twitched, and his hand tightened its grip on the steering wheel. He skimmed me up and down. "Pity about that."

I tried to stop my body from reacting. I did, but I failed. He was still gorgeous. My body grew heated, and I swallowed, already feeling my pulse quickening. Until three years ago, Luke Skeet had been my neighbor and best friend. I had made avoiding him into an art since Luke was still my neighbor and still friends with my brother. Oh yeah, he was in my brother's band, too—the band I helped form when we were in middle school.

All of that ended when I found his bloody body lying unconscious on his kitchen floor. It was the same night I started dating Elijah.

CHAPTER
TWO

I didn't move to climb inside the truck. I couldn't. My throat was dry, and my arms wouldn't reach out to grab the handle. I couldn't look away from him. "What are you doing here?"

Wearing his signature tattered jeans and a simple white T-shirt, he looked delicious as he stared back at me. For a moment, just one moment, it was like when we'd been best friends. He was gazing into me, reading my thoughts, just knowing me. It was only the two of us. The world had melted away. I had missed this feeling. I licked my lips, and his gaze darted down to them, lingering there. Then he rolled his eyes, leaned back in his seat, and raked a hand through his brown locks. "What's the problem, Bri? You called Rowdy's for a ride. I'm your ride." The corner of his mouth curved up, and he chuckled. "Wouldn't that be fun?"

I flushed. Swinging the door open, I climbed into the passenger side with a sigh. "Why didn't Braden come?"

Luke shifted the gear into drive and pulled away from the police station before he answered. "Because he was busy, if you know what I mean."

Meaning my brother was with a girl. My twin brother had a pretty boy face. He looked young with soft skin, round cheeks, and dark brown eyes like mine. Girls loved him.

"You guys were still partying?" I looked down at my lap. I didn't know why I had asked that. I knew the answer.

Luke drove the truck out into traffic and glanced at me from the corner of his eye. "We had a gig last night." He turned the wheel, heading through an intersection. "And can I ask what you were arrested for?"

"I wasn't. I was taken in. Elijah was arrested. They let me go."

His lips pressed together in a flat line.

I could feel his disapproval and flushed again. It'd been so long since I'd been alone with Luke. I'd forgotten how powerful his presence was. Every sensation I had was on overdrive. I felt assaulted on all ends, from head to toe. My body remained heated, and my throat felt parched, like I was in a damn desert. His voice was soft, deep, disapproving, and seductive all at once. I shifted in my seat, trying to get more comfortable, but the smell of pine, sweat, and cigarette smoke filled the cab. I hated cigarettes. I hated smoking, and I knew Luke didn't smoke. He was just around it, but damn, when it was mixed with his own smell, it was intoxicating.

What was I doing? Even though I hadn't said the words to Elijah, I had already broken up with him in my heart, and the first guy to pick me up was turning me on? Literally?

Stop it, Bri. I cursed at myself.

Before I realized it, I found myself saying, "It's over with him."

Luke didn't say anything; he only glanced at me again.

As he turned into Rowdy's parking lot and parked, he turned the engine off and pulled the keys from the ignition, but he didn't move to get out. I looked back at him. So much had changed. Too much had changed. That thought kept repeating, over and over again in my head.

I bit my lip, and his eyes turned away. He rested a hand on the wheel and asked, his voice rough, "What do you want me to say?"

"What do you mean?"

"To Bray."

"I thought you said he was with a girl."

"He is." He turned back, and just like that, as soon as our eyes met again, I felt as if I'd been punched in the stomach with the look he'd given me. The kind of punch—the kind that's so shocking—that robs you of all your breath, and for a moment, you can't think or move. That was how I felt as he kept going, "I'm sure they're done by now, but he's going to ask why you're here and why I brought you. Do you want me to keep quiet?"

"Elijah and I are done. I didn't do anything wrong." *Except not listen to everyone.* "It's going to come out eventually." A different thought came to mind. "Is Emerson in there?"

Luke chuckled, and the smooth sound of it washed over me, acting like a caress. "You mean our bass guitarist? The guy who's always down for partying? Your cousin?"

I rolled my eyes. "Yes, the cousin that hates me."

"Yeah, he's in there, too."

Well, this was going to be fun. "Okay, let's just get this over with." I opened my door and got out. Luke did the same on his side, and we headed across the parking lot together. As we entered the bar, I heard my cousin yell out over the microphone, "All hail our lead singer, Luke Skeeet!"

A couple of girls giggled.

Then I heard. "What the hell?"

Coming from outside, I was blinded for a moment by the rising sun into the dark bar. Expecting them to have moved all the equipment down into the basement, I was surprised to see everything was still on the stage. Then I saw my cousin. He'd been sitting behind the drum set, but he was standing now, glaring at me.

"What are you doing with her?"

I flicked him off. Different day. Same routine.

"Fuck you, Bri."

The other middle finger went up, and I forced a fake smile. Since I started dating his best friend, Elijah, Emerson turned from loving me like family to hating me like we were blood enemies. It was a switch that happened over night, and after three years of his attitude, I stopped wondering what I'd done and just went with it. We were hostile, at best, but sometimes it got worse. I waited, wondering if this was going to be another night that would be another 'worse' situation. I was prepared and ready to fight.

Luke ignored him and glanced around. "Where's Braden?"

Emerson was a few inches shorter than Luke. Whereas Luke was six feet, broad shoulders, and lean with a trim waist, Emerson had a stout build. He was solid and muscular. The other difference was that Luke had a mop of brown hair, usually brushed aside and ruffled to look messy, but it worked for him. He was gorgeous with chiseled cheekbones and a face that belonged in magazines. My cousin had stopped trying to grow his hair out. Instead, he cut it all off and maintained a buzz cut, almost bald. His cheekbones were set too close to his eyes, his mouth was small and usually in a scowl, at least around me, and tattoos adorned his neck and body.

Grudgingly, Emerson answered, his glare moving away from me, "He headed home. Why?" After tossing the sticks onto the floor, which had me wincing, he jumped off the stage. Shoving his hands into his pockets, he came over closer, his beady eyes fixed firmly on me. "What are you doing here, Bri?"

I didn't look at him, but I felt Luke glancing sideways at me.

Here we go. "SWAT came in this morning."

Emerson narrowed his eyes.

I added, "Elijah was arrested. I was taken in, too." My lips were suddenly dry. "A girl overdosed at the rave last night. They're trying to pin it on him."

A deep growl came from the back of his throat. "Tell me you called someone to bail him out."

I didn't, but I didn't tell him that.

Emerson took my silence the right way, and another growl burst from him. "Are you kidding me, Bri? What kind of girlfriend are you? At least call his—"

"His what?" I cut him off. "His mom's probably passed out in her own vomit, and you know he's got no one else that he trusts. His roommate won't leave his basement, and I refuse to call any of his drug people. I don't even know who they are."

He clipped his head from side to side. "You're unbelievable." He looked at Luke. "I gotta bail him out. We have another gig tonight?"

Luke nodded, watching me the entire time. "Yeah."

"Do we need to practice beforehand?"

"Yeah, I want to practice that new song."

"Fine. I'll be here at eight."

As they talked, Emerson pulled out his phone and wallet. He thumbed through his cash, taking inventory, and when his frown deepened, I assumed he didn't have enough. I shook my head. "You're wasting your time. His bail hasn't even been set."

"Whatever." He seared me with another dirty look, pressing some numbers on his phone and lifting the receiver to his ear. "I can still start calling for a bond." As he moved around me, we heard him say, "Yeah, hi. I need the number for a bail bonds—" He shoved through the door, and it slammed shut behind him.

Luke didn't say anything. He was only watching me. Always watching me. I needed a moment to center my thoughts. Rather than looking at Luke, I looked around the bar. Rowdy's was a dingy, hole-in-the-wall, dive bar. There was nothing flashy about the outside. A simple sign was the only thing that hung outside to attract customers, and it was more to show where the entry door was. The inside had a stage in one corner with a small dance area. Tables and bar stools filled up the middle, and the back had pool tables with booths lining the walls.

The clientele had always been vast. They ranged from blue-collar workers to those down-on-their-luck to local college students. One dollar tap beer helped bring in those students, while Friday nights' DJ brought in the dancing crowd. Saturday nights showcased local bands with Luke and my brother's band playing the majority of them.

The floor was swept clean. The bar stools were sitting on top of the counters, and the chairs were turned upside down over the tables. Rowdy's office was closed, and I couldn't see a light from underneath the door. Only a handful of girls remained in the bar. A few were leaning against the stage, looking tired. I had a hunch they were waiting for Luke.

"You need a ride somewhere?"

"Don't you want to stay and socialize?"

Luke shrugged. "Those girls were staying for Em. I was heading out when the phone rang."

So, Rowdy hadn't answered. Knowing that Luke had been going home anyway but still came to get me, made me pause. I didn't want to think about how that made me feel. *Fuck, Bri. You were with Elijah only a few hours ago.*

"Yeah, can I get a ride home?"

A doom-and-gloom feeling settled on the bottom of my stomach, but as I followed him out of the bar and to his truck, I couldn't deny the spike in my pulse either.

———— ———— ————

When Luke dropped me off at my apartment, I went inside and leaned against my door. My insides were swirling. So much had happened, but I didn't want to think about it. I couldn't. 'Keep forward. Deal later.' That'd been a quote I loved and I needed it that day. So, I literally moved forward, showering and collapsing in my bed, but after waking a few hours later with nightmares of cops breaking down my own door, I figured the 'deal later' would need to be much, much later. It was close to dinner time, so to keep pushing everything out of my mind, I headed for my mom's house. Braden would hear about my escapade soon enough, but I wanted him to hear it from me.

My stomach grumbled as I went in through the back door. I needed to get some food, but instead of the expected aromas of dinner being made, there was nothing. The kitchen lights were off; only the hallway light was on. My mom rushed out, dressed in scrubs with her identification tag that said Sharon Masterson hanging around her neck. She'd recently showered and her hair, normally light blonde, looked dark as it was twisted up in a bun. She was slender, my size and height. Braden always complained he hadn't gotten the tall gene from our dad. Both of us got our darker looks from him, though. Dark hair. Tan complexion, but I was thankful that was it. There were so many other attributes we could've gotten from him, like being an abusive asshole. Being 5'11" was going to be Braden's curse instead.

"Oh, honey." She grabbed her keys from the kitchen table and came over to kiss me on the cheek. Patting my shoulder, she grabbed a water from the refrigerator. "How was your night?"

I watched her grab a gait belt and asked as she looped it around her waist, "Is that a trick question?"

"Huh?" Her forehead wrinkled. Searching her pockets, she bit down on her lip and started looking around the kitchen. "I need a pen. I always forget my pens."

It was on the tip of my tongue to tell her. Elijah. The raid. Luke. I didn't. I wasn't sure what she'd say to me. Our mom had never been a big disciplinarian. She let us make our own mistakes. She had to, though. She was too busy working to know half the times when we did get in trouble.

"There's food in the fridge, if you need to eat something." She hurried to the door, but turned and used her back to open it. "Oh. Can you wake your brother up? He's napping, and since you're here, can you give him a ride to Rowdy's? He asked for a ride earlier."

I nodded. *Yep. Sounds good. I'll tell you about the SWAT raid later… maybe…* By the time she rushed out the door, I knew I wasn't ever going to tell her. I'd tell her about Elijah. That'd be good enough. She liked him, but was wary after Braden shared his suspicions of him. Thinking of my brother, I went to wake him up.

An hour later, on our way to Rowdy's for his practice, I told my brother the news. He exclaimed, "This is awesome!"

Had I heard my brother right? "It's awesome I was taken to jail today?"

"No." Braden faltered. "You said you were done with Elijah, right?" Braden scratched the back of his head. When his hand left his head, the hair behind his ear remained standing up. It worked for him. He was dressed in a simple black shirt and jeans like mine, except his were baggy and hung low on his hips. With a few leather bracelets on his wrist and his new tattoo, he had taken on the rocker bad boy look.

I didn't know what to say. Hearing Braden say those words, that I was done, sounded alien to me.

The longer I stayed quiet, the more his grin slipped until it turned into a look of alarm. He turned squarely in his seat until he was facing me and raked a hand through his black hair. "Brielle, tell me you're not going back to him." He shook his head. "You told me you believed me earlier. You came in my room, kicked my bed, woke me up, and apologized for being a dumbass over the years. You said you believed me. You can't take it back."

I tried to shake my head, but my neck muscles had stiffened. We were done... We were done... I needed to keep telling myself that.

"Bri!"

I jerked out of my thoughts, realizing I had a death-grip on the steering wheel. "What?"

"You *are* done with him, right? I'm not going to shut up until you actually say the words."

"Yes." It came out hoarse, like I'd swallowed a boulder that was stuck in my throat. I coughed and said again, my voice much clearer, "Yes, I'm done. I'm sure Emerson told him already, anyway."

"For real, real?"

"Yes!"

"Good." He jerked back in his seat, a sound of relief coming from him. "Elijah's not a bad dude, like in personality and stuff, but the guy's messed up in other ways. For one, he sells drugs." He gave me a grin. "I can't believe he was able to hide it from you this whole time."

"Yeah." A lump formed at the base of my throat, blocking my oxygen for a moment. As my brother kept talking, so carefree now, pain sliced through me. With each word he spoke, the pain in my heart grew. Shit. Elijah and I really were done. Three years and now—that's why it didn't feel real to me. It felt like I was mad and just avoiding him for a weekend.

Braden continued chatting, excited to have his sister back. I could go to their practices, I could help with the band, I would have free time to hang out with him, blah, blah, blah. He kept going as I sat here, feeling as if someone was slapping me over and over again.

"Shut up."

Braden stopped. "Huh?"

"Just..." *Was there a nicer way to say this?* "Shut up, okay?"

"Why?"

"Braden." I closed my eyes for a second, wanting to just disappear and take a breather. I opened them again, but couldn't look at him. "I loved Elijah. We're over. Do me a favor and stop rubbing it in. I *literally* just told you."

He was silent for a moment. "He deals drugs, Bri."

"I know." My voice rose in volume, and I flinched, grabbing hold of the steering wheel like I was going to be ripped out of the car. "I know. I'm not going back to him, but it's hitting me for the first time here. For real. I just..." *need a minute*. I needed a minute.

"Okay." He started to get out, but paused at the door.

I lifted my top lip, hoping for a reassuring smile, but when he frowned even more, I knew I had failed. Raking my hand through my long hair, I shook my head and tried to stir my thoughts. Now that we were here, I was tempted to head inside Rowdy's and start drinking. There was a burning sensation in the middle of my chest, and the more reality was sinking in, the more painful it was becoming.

One of Braden's eyebrows arched from confusion. Then he gestured behind him, toward the bar. "Come inside."

"What?" I started to shake my head. Luke would be in there. Emerson, too. "No, no."

"Yeah. I know I got all excited before, but you should come in. You shouldn't be alone right now."

My head moved back. I harrumphed. "I won't be alone. I have friends..." I didn't. I'd had a couple of female friends in high school, but most of them had only used me to get to Luke or Braden. The others, who might've been genuine friends, had stopped hanging out with me. Well...I stopped hanging out with them. It'd all been about Elijah and his slightly creepy friends.

He snorted. "You have mom."

I gritted my teeth. "Braden."

"Stop it, Bri. I know you're hurting. I can see it in your eyes. I'm sorry for being an insensitive jerk brother. Let me be your brother now." His tone gentled. "Come inside. We're not twenty-one, but I'll make sure you get all the booze you want."

I rolled my eyes, laughing a little. After Luke's dad took off three years ago, the owner had given him a job doing whatever needed to be done around the bar. In the last few years, Luke had stopped working there, but the basement had been renovated for their practices. It was soundproofed and the manager, who took over most of the operations, didn't mind having them down there. They could practice all they wanted since it never interfered with the bar itself.

"Come on." Braden shut his door and rounded to mine. Opening it, he leaned inside and plucked the keys out of the ignition before I realized what he was doing.

"I don't think I can handle Emerson tonight."

"Nah." He pulled me out, shut the door, and threw an arm around my shoulder. "It's Emerson that won't be able to handle you tonight. I mean it. You can do whatever you want, even play drums."

He meant it as teasing, but at those words, my chest tightened again. I'd been a part of the band when they formed; half of my name was in the title, Braille. Damn, I hadn't touched the drums in so long. Feeling the beat, pounding it out, making everyone else feel it, too, opened a whole new yearning I had tried to bury with so many other things inside me.

Three. Damn. Long. Years.

"I can't."

Braden studied me as he walked inside. "Yeah, well, we'll see." He held the door open for me. The basement stairs were in front of us, and I started down, but paused and glanced toward the bar area. Luke was heading toward us. He paused, too. Once he saw me, our gazes collided, and I tore my gaze away, hurrying downstairs.

Braden stayed back, saying his hellos to Luke, and then their voices grew quiet. I kept going, knowing they were talking about me now. Before I hit the bottom step, I heard Luke say, "Yeah, that's fine with me." I stopped listening and moved into the main basement area.

Emerson was already there, tuning his guitar. He glanced up, his eyes sparkling, but when he saw me, he gave the same reaction as earlier that morning. He straightened, lifting the guitar strap and placing it onto the floor. "No. Get out."

"Fuck off, Em." I shot him an annoyed look and went for the bar. It was more of a bookshelf cut in half and positioned so it was sticking out of the wall. A run-down refrigerator was behind it, sitting in a corner of the room with a freezer next to it. The other side of the room was where they set up the equipment on a make-shift stage made from crates and recycled doors. The rest of the basement had three couches and two dark green lounge chairs spread all over. Each couch had a cushion that was ripped at the bottom and flayed armrests.

Braden and Luke walked down the stairs, and it wasn't long before my brother said, "Yes. She's here. Deal with it."

"No!"

"Suck it up, Em," Luke spoke.

Reaching for the bourbon, I froze. That was a new development. I might've been the poster child for avoiding Luke, but for him to speak up for me? And against Emerson? That was a new development. I shot Braden a look and saw he was surprised, too.

Luke added, "She's practicing with us. We've been talking about bringing in a fourth person, anyway."

Emerson snorted. "I thought we were talking about your friend, Gunn, not her."

"That's enough," Braden piped in. "It's decided. *I* decided. Bri's joining the band. We were better with her, anyway."

"No! Come on, guys."

"Well, let's not get too hasty." Luke was trying to keep the peace, but what he said earlier was still ringing in my ears. They were considering a fourth person? After I quit, Braden took over my spot on the drums, and Luke played guitar as well as sang. They never replaced me, and knowing now that they were considering it? It hurt.

Screw it. I was playing. Needing a little liquid courage to steady my shaky hands, I grabbed the bottle of bourbon and poured myself a shot. After tossing it back, I turned and held out my hands. Braden was beaming as he held out the drumsticks. I took them as I passed him by and sat in my old seat.

Once situated, Emerson rolled his eyes at me and held his hands in the air. "I'm not playing with her. Sorry. No way." He headed for the door.

"Emerson," Luke called after him.

"I'm out. I need to go see if they let my best friend out yet." He hurried up the stairs, his feet pounding on them until he shoved out the door, slamming it shut behind him.

"Let him go." Braden went to the bar and poured himself a shot, too. After he emptied his glass, he picked up the guitar Emerson had left behind. "Call Gunn. He can fill in."

I could feel Luke's gaze on me. Instead of staring back at him, I examined the drums more thoroughly, adjusted the stool an unnecessary amount of times, rested my chin on my chest, and fiddled with the drumsticks. The longer he remained silent, the more I fidgeted with the drumsticks.

Was he rethinking this? Is that why he's so quiet?

"Fine. Gunn's practiced with us enough. We shouldn't have too much of a problem, but don't get too excited. We both know Emerson will come back tonight. He storms off, but he always comes back."

"Fine. Whatever." Braden was firm. "We should use Bri, anyway. She'll remember most of the material, and she'll pick up the new stuff tonight. She's good. She's the best."

"Yeah." Luke didn't sound too happy about it. "We'll see."

When he left to call Gunn, I let out the small breath I hadn't even realized I'd been holding. Looks like I was going to be Drummer Extraordinaire for the night. I had to admit, I was looking forward to it—anything to keep my mind off Elijah, and Luke, too. Sneaking a look under my eyelids when Luke took his place at the microphone later, I realized I hadn't taken into account how it felt to play music with him again.

CHAPTER
THREE

Gunn arrived within thirty minutes. He was a large man, and when I said man, I meant man. We were all twenty and twenty-one, but Gunn looked to be in his thirties. Like Emerson, he was sporting a bald head, but unlike Emerson, he was taller than Luke. He was big, just big all around. Height. Weight. Muscles. When he came down the stairs, I wasn't sure if he would be able to fit through the doorframe, but he did. He ran a hand over his head, giving Braden and me a wave before ducking his head back down. That was the most interaction I had with him.

Luke called out the songs and did the countdowns. There weren't a lot of hiccups during practice. I was rusty, but I could get through a set. By the end of practice, I was breathless. My pulse was racing, and I was drunk without touching another sip of alcohol. I'd forgotten how a good set on the drums felt like great sex. I was buzzing, and I didn't want to stop.

"Fuck, yeah!" Braden held a fist up as he went around the stage. Luke gave him a shaky grin as he stretched his hand out in the air. Braden pounded it with his, then went to Gunn. He pounded his fist with Gunn's head lightly and circled to me. As he held his hand over the drums, I hit it softly with one of my sticks, and he shook his head. "This is what it should always be like, Luke." He winked at me before turning back, lifting the guitar strap over his head. "I love the grumpy bastard, but Emerson's full of drama ninety-seven percent of the time. Today's no different."

When I stood, my legs were even a little wobbly.

Braden saw my reaction and pointed at me. "See. I never get like that from drumming. That says something."

Luke stiffened. "Braden, come on."

My brother shrugged a shoulder. "I'm not saying we kick him out;

I'm just advocating bringing her in." His hands went up in surrender. "That's all. I love my cousin. I've kicked ass for my cousin, but," a dark cloud came over his face, and his eyebrows bunched together before he continued, "whatever. I'm just looking out for my sister, and on that note, I want to drink. I'm heading upstairs."

"We go on in a couple hours," Luke called after him.

Braden was already halfway up the stairs. "I know."

After he left, the room was suddenly very quiet, very awkward, and very tense. Gunn had put Luke's guitar to the side and seemed to be waiting, standing there. So was Luke. Both were watching me.

I raised a hand to the ceiling. "Uh, I'm sure Emerson will be back. So, no worries. That's all I'm saying." My tongue swelled, doubled its size, and I couldn't talk around it. "Yeah, so." I pointed upstairs again. "Braden's a little heated right now. I'm going to make sure he doesn't get into trouble, or worse, get naked."

I was halfway to the door before Luke said, "Braden's not wrong, but he's pushing this because of Elijah. You know that, right?"

Elijah. There went another punch to my gut. I turned around.

Luke stood there, a hand resting on the microphone stand, and my god, he looked lethal. A serious expression filled those eyes, an intensity clung to the set of his shoulders, and his lips were set in a firm line.

I tugged at the collar of my shirt. "I know. Braden wants me in the band. He thinks I'll get bored and go back to Elijah."

"Will you?"

Luke's words were so soft, I almost missed them. My senses were already in overdrive, but he sped them all up again. That was the power he had over me. Shit. I'd forgotten why I had avoided him all these years. It had become habit to stay away from him, but man, I turned around. I needed to not look at him. "I don't think I can anymore."

Too many memories were threatening to spill in my mind, all about Luke, so I hurried upstairs and joined Braden at the bar, sliding onto the empty stool beside him. He slid a beer over to me and held his hand up. "Another, barkeep."

His second beer was placed before him, and the girl leaned forward. "I don't give a shit what pretty boy band you're in, I'll boot your ass out if you call me barkeep again." She was thin, tall, and had long straight blonde hair that fell past the middle of her back. She had a heart-shaped face and dark eyes. Straightening, she skimmed a hard eye over me and nodded. "I'm Kelly."

"Bri." I pointed a thumb next to me. "The idiot's my brother."

"The idiot can be all nice to me in the morning hours, but when it comes to—" She stopped. "You know, I'm not even going there. Be nice or I'll tell everyone you have a tiny dick."

"I don't." He sat back, as if offended, but the wicked gleam in his eyes told me otherwise. He liked this one.

"They don't know that."

He groaned, picking up his beer to take a sip. When she left to help another customer, Braden watched her go, his eyes trained right on her ass. "See that, Bri. Don't walk like that. Ever." He turned to me, lifting his beer in a salute. "A public service announcement courtesy of your former womb-mate."

I took his beer away from him. "You should stop drinking. That's my public service announcement."

"Why?"

"Because you're worked up. If you drink any more, you're going to get drunk, and Luke will get mad at you."

He took his beer back. "I play better when I'm drunk. I think he'd thank you."

Then I looked over his shoulder, and a new ball of tension formed in my stomach. This wasn't going to go well. "Yeah, well, you shouldn't drink for another reason."

"Why?"

I nodded behind him. Emerson was coming through the door. He paused at the bouncer, said something, and threw his head back to laugh. He was in a good mood. That meant I probably wouldn't be by the end of the night. Then he looked behind him at the door that was held open by someone, but I couldn't see who it was.

An arm appeared first. As they walked inside, a tattoo on the inside of his arm was visible, and I knew who it was. That ball of tension doubled in size. I wanted to smack myself in the forehead. I should've known. There was only one person who made Emerson forget to be an asshole…most of the time.

I said, "Because Emerson's back." And so was Elijah, but he wasn't my brother's problem. He was mine. Just as I thought that, Elijah's green eyes scanned the bar and landed right on me, like he knew the exact location I'd be.

It was done. For real. Judging by the guarded look in his eyes, he knew it, too.

"Oh hell," Braden muttered. "Are you going to be okay?"

I felt my head moving up and down. "I think so."

Then Elijah was right in front of me, and without a word, I slid off the stool. I led the way, knowing he would be right behind me. Luke and Gunn were coming up the stairs. I opened the door that connected the basement stairs to the bar. Luke paused at the top of the stairs, drawing to his fullest height as he saw who was behind me. I felt Elijah's hand touch the small of my back, and all the nerves in my body jumped.

Luke's gaze fell to his hand, and just like that, his grey eyes turned dark. I shivered at the anger shining in his eyes. I looked away and walked outside of the bar. Elijah followed behind me.

Once outside, he leaned against the building and put a cigarette into his mouth. Exhaling, he said, "You with him now?"

I folded my arms across my chest. "No."

He paused, narrowed his eyes at me, and then shook his head. "I should've remembered who I was talking to. Always such a coward."

"Fuck you."

That got a laugh from him as he put the cigarette into his mouth again. Then he murmured as the smoke left him, "I don't get you. It took one night, and you were my girl, but Luke—shit. How long have the two of you been dancing around this? You screwed him already?"

Rolling my eyes, I turned away. He was hurt, and he was lashing out. This wasn't the normal Eli, but I understood it. So be it. I guess we were just jumping right into it.

He let out another cocky laugh. "You did. I can tell." He pointed the cigarette at me. "Did you ever cheat on me with him?" I shot him a look, but he shrugged. "Yeah, yeah. You knew Emerson was going to tell me. He told me you called Luke and showed up with him. Thanks for that. I really enjoy being dumped by my girlfriend through my best friend."

My jaw tightened. "I don't date drug dealers."

"I'll ask again. Have you been fucking him the whole time?"

I scowled. "No. Why don't we talk about you and the lie you've been telling me? How long have you been dealing drugs? How long have you been lying to me about that?"

"Like you didn't know," he taunted me. "You knew. You just didn't want to deal with it. Like me, I guess. I'm asking again. Were you with him while you were with me?"

"No," I folded my arms tighter over my chest. "I'm not a damn cheater."

"That's up for debate."

His gaze bore into mine. I wanted to look away, but I didn't. He was gauging my response, and then his shoulders slumped down. As he took out another cigarette, he said, "I don't get the two of you. I saw that look just now. I remember how tight you used to be. You want him. He wants you, always has. Are you really that scared of losing him?"

I flinched again, but lied. "What do you mean?" I knew what he meant.

"Stop jerking me around. This is me. We're now exes, Bria—"

"I'm not Bria anymore."

He sighed, rolling his eyes. "Yeah, whatever. Bri. Bria. Brielle. Whatever." Cupping his hand over the cigarette, he lit it and took in a deep drag. "Are you *together* together?"

"It's none of your business."

He laughed at that, but the sound bordered on being bitter. "It's not, but I'm curious. I'm roadkill on the Luke and Bri Road."

"Stop, Eli."

He didn't comment, but started laughing again a moment later.

"Every girl I'm going to screw this week will be a one-time deal. They won't be the same. No, Bri." He drew in a breath and let it back out slowly. "You're going from a three year deal to that. Skeet's been crawling into your bed since you were nine, whether or not you two were screwing. He's always been just *there*."

"Are we done? Are we officially broken up now?"

I felt the shift then. Looking up, I saw the rage barely blanketed in his eyes; this was the same guy who was going to jump out of his second-story window and run from the police. It was like someone had snapped a whip. A shiver ran up my back as I remembered how dangerous Elijah was known to be. He had never been with me. I knew he wouldn't, but this was that guy now.

He spat out, "You think this is a joke? That I'm here out of the goodness of my heart? You left me in there, Bria—Bri—Bria. You left me in there all day, and I get out to hear this shit. It was only a few *hours*." His voice rose.

"Stop, Eli."

He tossed his unfinished cigarette and rounded on me, raising his voice as he continued, "I feel fucking used. This whole time, why weren't you with him? It's obvious you love the guy…"

I couldn't listen to another word; I'd had enough. I started for the door, but he grabbed my arm and yanked me back. "Stop," I snapped before shoving him away. He backed off, holding both of his hands in the air with a snarl on his face. "Shut up, Elijah. You can't say a word."

"About what?" His anger went down a notch, but it was there. It was right under the surface. He crowded me, looming over me as my back hit the wall. "You're going to preach to me now?"

"Better than you mocking me."

The corner of his mouth lifted into a half-grin. "You think you're so badass, Bria. You're not. You're a little girl that was broken a long time ago."

My head went down, and my voice lowered. "Stop it."

He didn't. "Your dad left you guys. You blame yourself, for some stupid reason. It wasn't you that pushed him away. No kid sends a parent off…" He frowned as he trailed off.

"Except *your* dad took off and *your* mom's a mess."

"Shut up."

The tables had turned. I moved from the wall, facing him now. My jaw hardened. "Your mom's a joke. Your best friend is an asshole, your roommate is a shut-in, and your girlfriend..." I gave him a sickening grin. "Scratch that. Your *ex*-girlfriend has officially left you."

"Stop, Bri."

I snorted as my voice rose. "How many nights a week do you scrape your mom off some bar floor? How many afternoons do you find her in her own puke on the kitchen floor? However you want to spin it—that I'm a broken little girl, whatever. Fuck you. You're just as broken. It's why we were together."

"No, it's not."

I stilled, hearing the softness in his voice.

He murmured, "I did care about you." The green in his eyes grew warm. "I do care about you."

I sighed and rolled my eyes. "You want me to feel sorry for you? Why? Because I dumped your ass? You sell drugs for a living. Everyone told me, but I didn't believe them. I turned my back on my family and friends for you." *Liar*, a voice inside my head called me. "It's because of you my cousin went to rehab last summer, wasn't it? You're the one who sold him the drugs. He never said who it was, but it was you."

"It wasn't."

"It was." I knew it. It made sense now. At the thought of it, my anger started to rise again. "What kind of friend are you? Giving drugs to your best friend? To your girlfriend's cousin?"

"I didn't sell him drugs!" He pushed me back before I realized I had crowded him.

I blinked at his hands that had forced me away from him. Then a laugh gurgled up from the bottom of my throat, and I bent over and clutched my stomach, unable to stop laughing. This was what we did. We fought, and then we screwed. We never had a real relationship. Who was I fooling? I had no reason to feel guilty for breaking up with him. It was time to move on. It was time I became *better*.

"Stop it." He had grown quiet again. His head hung as he shoved his hands into his pockets, and his shoulders hunched forward. "I didn't come here to fight with you, whether you believe me or not."

"You and me." I shook my head, everything growing hard inside me again. "We are not good together."

He let out a deep breath.

"You know it, and I know it."

"Yeah." His eyes were haunted once more. He looked away, straightening from the wall. "I have to go. Take care…Bri."

He moved around me, but I grabbed his arm and wheeled him back around. "What's going on? What are you doing?"

A different Elijah looked down at me. The passion wasn't there. The cold anger wasn't either. Instead, he looked at me with politeness. I let go of him as if his arm had burned me. I backed away, but asked, "What's going on?"

"'What's going on?'" He flashed me a smile, though his eyes were dead. "This is when we break up. There are no ties anymore. You don't have to feel guilty for wanting to screw the guy you love now. We're done."

"Eli, don't do anything stupid."

"Like what?" With a mischievous glint in his eyes, he added, "Like sell drugs for money?" He started walking backwards, moving away from me, and he touched two of his fingers to his head in a salute. His lips twitched, mocking me. "Not your problem anymore, Bri. See you around."

A scream built inside me, twisting its way up from the bottom of my feet and gaining speed with so many damned emotions attached to it. It wanted to rip from me, to let loose all the frustration, all the sadness, pain, bitterness, everything with it. I didn't let it out, though. I swallowed it and shoved it right back down, and then, smoothing a hand over my pants, I went back inside.

I'd deal later.

CHAPTER
FOUR

Braden was waiting for me, leaning against the wall just inside the back door with his arms folded over his chest. When I came back into the bar, he straightened, and his arms dropped back to his sides. "You okay?"

"Uh." *Not really*. It felt as if an invisible hand had punched a hole in my chest and then wrapped around my heart. "I'll deal." Luke was on stage, warming up with Emerson. The two grinned at each other, and, man, that hand squeezed around my heart almost painfully. Then my cousin saw me and sobered instantly. He glared at me.

Luke followed Emerson's look to me. Our eyes caught and held. "Bri?"

"What?" Braden had been waving at me. "Sorry. What?"

The corners of his mouth dipped down, and he saw Luke, too. "I don't know, Bri. I don't know. You *just* broke up with Elijah."

That hand just kept squeezing. "Don't worry. It's not going there."

"Right."

He didn't believe me, but I didn't care.

"Subject change, please." I nodded at Emerson. "Am I right to assume I won't be playing tonight then?"

He sighed. "I guess. Will you stick around? I meant what I said. I want you back in the band. Stay. Hang out with us. Luke wants you in. I can tell. He just needs some hint from you, you know."

"Yeah." I didn't even know what I wanted, though. There was a reason I'd been avoiding him for the last three years. Braden patted the empty stool at the end of the bar, and I slid on it and rested my hands on the counter. "Barkeep. That's her name, right?"

He patted my shoulder. "I wouldn't use that term."

Kelly came over, shaking her head. With a half-grin, she poured a beer for me and slid it over the bar. "Here you go, and just so we're all clear, your sister can call me that, but you, buddy, you better only be using that term as a safe word."

I liked her.

Braden cocked his head to the side. "Safe word? I didn't know that was a possibility."

She chuckled, wiping her hands on a towel before resting a hand on the counter. She gestured to the stage. "I'm not saying it is. Aren't you needed up there?"

He winked at me, but beamed at her. "It's more fun here."

"Get up there, Rock Star. You need to work all these single females into a thirsty frenzy. Sales go up the second you and that heartthrob singer of yours start crooning those notes."

I *really* liked her. Catching the adoration and a hint of something more in the depths of my brother's eyes, I shoved him away. "Hurry. Get up there and keep bringing in the cash, Brother."

Tap, tap.

Luke leaned closer into the mic. "We need our drummer." He was watching us. "Any day, Braden."

A crowd had already congregated in front of the stage, and they all turned. A few waved their hands in the air. "Come on, Braden!"

"Yeah, Braden!"

"Come on, Hot Stuff."

"#hotdrummerneeded."

Someone laughed and added, "#hotdrummerneededinmypants."

That sent another round of laughter around the bar. My brother saluted my beer in the air, then hit the bottom back of the counter and chugged the entire thing.

The crowd responded with whoops, wolf whistles, and cheers.

He pumped a fist in the air and hollered, "Let's do this!" Then he pressed the empty glass to me and headed through the crowd, jumping onto the stage in one leap.

"Hey."

I turned.

Kelly had leaned closer. She glanced toward the back door. "I saw you head out there with Elijah Turner, right?"

I nodded. "That was my boyfriend."

"Good guy."

My eyebrow went up at that. "He's a drug dealer."

She winked at me, handing a glass to a customer. "Good guy, just misguided at times."

I snorted. "I'd like to think that." But I did. Elijah had good in him. He just . . .wasn't for me anymore. I shook my head. "Okay. I need a drink now. Braden took my beer."

"Not a problem." She gestured around the side of the bar. "We're going to get slammed. Your brother's band brings in the crowd, and we're down a girl. If you help out later on, if we're in a pinch, you can drink for free."

"I don't know how much help I'd be if I did drink for free."

She laughed before moving farther down the bar. "You'd be surprised how sober you get when twenty people are shouting orders at you. Think about it, but help yourself until then."

Shit. Free beer? Maybe I had come to the right place to deal with my break up. Laughing at my lameness, I slid off the stool to grab my first one. Braden hit the first beat on the drums, and Luke began singing. I went back to my seat, but as Luke kept singing and I kept hearing the band playing, that void reopened.

I'd need a second drink. Soon.

They took a short break ten songs in, and when they hopped back up, Luke's voice came over the microphone. I heard the crescendo starting from Braden's hands, and then Emerson joined in, building the bottom note.

I was going to be gutted by the end of their set. I wanted that. I wanted to be up there, creating the tension and setting the rhythm as Luke's voice cast its spell.

"Hey, Bri." Kelly came over to my end of the bar. She signaled around to the growing crowd. "You mind hopping in? You can do the beer. It's not hard."

"Yeah." I stood and heard Luke's words behind me. *"Leaving my body, leaving my heart, leaving my soul, bloody and broken —"* My knees were unsteady, and I shook my head, clearing my thoughts. Taking position behind the beer taps, I faltered.

He was singing about that night.

I had no idea he had written a song about it. They never asked to practice this song while they were in the basement.

"Two tall tap specials!" a waitress yelled from the side.

I jerked my head in a nod and reached for the tall glasses. Luke's haunting voice sounded over the crowd's growing buzz. "*She healed me up, cared for my wounds. Then left and ripped them open once more. Broken. I was left broken.*"

"Hey!"

I came back to reality at the waitress's voice and saw the beer was overflowing. Cursing, I switched the glasses and glanced at Kelly. "I'll cover the loss."

She waved it off. "No worries. We all do it. I don't normally advise this, but have a couple of shots. You won't be drunk, but it'll help tune out whatever you need tuned out."

"Yeah." I poured two shots of whiskey and downed them, and it wasn't long before Luke's voice couldn't infiltrate my wall anymore. After that, I got lost in filling orders.

Two hours later, Kelly nudged my arm. "We're doing last call now. I think we should be good."

The place hadn't emptied. It had just gotten more packed. "You sure?"

"Yep, I'll take over here. Crystal came in. She's the shot girl. That helped us."

"Oh, okay."

"Hey."

I had started to walk back around, but paused and looked back at her.

She gestured to the garbage cans, which were overflowing, forming piles around the bins. "I know it's a shit job, but do you mind taking those out? You'll get a portion of the tips, too."

"I thought my payment was free beer?"

She laughed. Braden hopped onto a stool at that moment, and her eyes darkened. She said to me, while eyeing him, "That payment's not good enough for how much you helped tonight. Doing the garbage seals the deal. Anytime you want a job here, you got one." Then she focused on Braden. "You guys sounded good up there tonight."

He winked at her, leaning forward with his elbows on the bar. "Something extra was up Luke's ass tonight. He sang his heart out."

They both glanced at the crowd still standing in front of the stage. Luke was talking to a guy as a group of girls swarmed in behind him. Drunken, glazed eyes stared at him in hunger. Most of the girls had their hair matted with sweat, but they tried to look sexy, standing in their best seductive pose, waiting for Luke's attention.

"No kidding," I murmured to myself and went to the garbage bins. While pulling them out, I was rougher than was needed. When I hefted one bag out of a bin and set it down to reach for the second bin, Emerson shot past me.

"Hey!"

He glanced over his shoulder, an apology on his lips, but seeing me, they formed into a scowl. He turned back around and shoved out the door.

"Ass." I rolled my eyes and finished pulling the bag out of the second bin. "Anything else before I take these out?" I asked Kelly who was laughing with one hip resting against the bar. My brother's gaze was firmly on her breasts.

She was still laughing as she shook her head. "Nope, that's it. Thanks again. Your tip will be waiting for you. We tally them all up and split evenly."

I nodded, tightened my hold around both bags, and started pulling them down the short hallway and through the back door. Dragging both toward the dumpsters, I heard someone yell out from behind me.

Turning around, I saw three guys in a scuffle at the corner of the parking lot. I started for them, abandoning the garbage bags. As I got closer, I saw that it was two guys holding a third guy against the wall. They were tucked in the back corner of the parking lot where, of course, the garbage dumpsters were located.

"Best damn luck in the world," I muttered to myself. Now what? I had no intention of going anywhere near that fight.

"Where's the money?" One guy reared back and delivered a punch to the guy's stomach, causing him to double over and clutch himself.

I'd need to get security to clear that up. As I left the bags where they were and started back inside, I heard a snarl back, "I told you. I'll have it after tonight." Oh hell. I stopped and turned around. That was Emerson, the great and unconditionally loving cousin of mine. Still. Security. That wasn't technically me helping him, just doing my duty as a Good Samaritan. They could clear the fight, but then I heard the scrape of a bat being dragged over the ground.

Security might not get here quick enough. They were on the other side of the bar. I'd have to fight the crowd just to get to them.

"I told you—" Emerson was saying again when the first swing came, connecting with his stomach. He bit off his sentence and folded over.

I couldn't believe I was doing this. We were going to get killed.

I surged forward, moving faster. "Hey!" I yelled, now running for them. They stopped their assault on my cousin and assessed me. I guess they figured I wasn't too much of a threat, because the second guy wrapped his arms tighter around Emerson, bracing him for another hit.

I could already hear Braden's voice in my head, to get my ass away from this, but my feet weren't moving back to the bar. Apparently, I felt some sort of loyalty to my cousin. Huh. Who knew? Weaving around the last car, I stopped just out of their reach and yelled again, "Let him go!"

Emerson's eyes were wide. I wasn't sure who was more surprised, he or I. Either way, I was there. I rolled my shoulders back, and my chin rose. I knew how to fight. Although those times had been taking on girls or when I was in a scrap with Braden and Luke when we were younger against whomever we had a problem with back then.

I'd never fought a grown man before. I was so screwed.

"Or what?" The first guy, the leader I assumed, stepped toward me. He rubbed his hand at the side of his mouth. When he moved into the streetlight, I saw there was blood on his knuckles. He was tall with bland features. His thick eyebrows sat over eyes that were set deep in his face. His small mouth, which was too close to his very large nose, gave his face a permanently pinched look to it. "What are you going to do?"

The guy holding Emerson pushed him to the ground and started toward me. It happened so fast. Emerson hopped back to his feet, looked at me for a split second, then rushed around both men and grabbed my wrist. He tried to pull me behind him to the bar. I went with him, but my other arm was restrained. I jerked backwards, out of Emerson's hold.

He stopped and braked between a row of cars as he looked at our new predicament. They had me, and he was the free one now. The indecision was clear. Then he started shaking his head and cursing.

Was he…no way…and yes, he did. I watched, my jaw falling to the ground, as my cousin sprinted for the door.

Asshole!

I didn't have time to plot my cousin's murder. Bringing my arm up and around, I forced the guy to break his hold. He had to let go, or his wrist would've broken from the angle I forced his hand to move. As soon as I was free, I scurried away, treading backwards. Both guys tilted their heads to the side as they watched my every move, and they both wore the same menacing expression. The leader, whom I nicknamed as Thing One, was tall and thin while the other, I called him Thing Two in my head, was shorter and stout. He was built similar to Emerson.

"I almost feel sorry for you, girly. You came to help that piece of shit, and he left you?" Thing One laughed.

Thing Two raked his beady eyes down my body while running a hand through his greasy hair. "She looks nice and ripe. Too skinny for my normal appetite, but still a good ride." He wet his lips, winking at me. "Is that what you came out here for? I bet you like it rough, huh?"

I had a knife. Elijah always made me carry one, but I didn't think I could do much damage with it. I didn't want to get close enough to them. "You guys might want to stop and think about this."

"Oh, yeah?" Thing One laughed. The sound was sickening. "Or what? Honey, you came out here. Your friend abandoned you to us. Maybe that's his way of paying me back?" He turned to his friend.

"What do you think? Maybe we'll let Emerson off the hook if we can get a good night from her?"

His friend shrugged, his eyes darkening with lust. "Sounds good to me."

"Yeah." The leader started to reach for my arm. "Sounds good to me, too."

I braced myself. This was really happening. Reaching into my back pocket, I started to pull the knife out when a body shot past me, took hold of Thing One, and slammed him against one of the garbage bins. Someone growled, "You're dead, asshole," and another thud as a second body shot past me, too. Thing Two was punched and tackled to the ground.

Luke had Thing One pinned against the bin with a hand to his throat. His features were tightened and strained as he delivered a punch to the guy's face. Once he let him go, Thing One fell to the ground and tried to block Luke's blows, but there was no stopping Luke. He hit him again and again in the face, then kicked him in the stomach. The quick assault stunned the guy. He didn't fight back, just tried to recover and block any more hits.

Emerson was attacking Thing Two. After delivering a couple of kicks of his own, he stopped and looked at Luke. Both guys weren't fighting back, so Luke and Emerson stepped back toward me, shielding me. Luke pointed to the back door of Rowdy's. "Em, go and get that garbage. Bring it over for Bri."

Emerson nodded and went back.

"Bri?" The leader looked up. "Brielle Masterson?"

Luke seared me with a look, then stepped in front of me to completely shield me from the guy's view. "Yeah, asshole. You think we're bad? She dated Turner. What do you think he'd do to you?"

The guy coughed some blood out and pushed himself to a sitting position. "We didn't know, but it doesn't change the situation. We're not scared of Turner."

Luke clipped his head from side to side. "Doesn't matter. Go near her again, and I'm sure you can test that theory—that you're not scared of him."

Emerson came back with both garbage bags. He tossed both into the bin and closed the lid. Ignoring the two guys on the ground, he swept past me and said to Luke, "If she wants in, I'm fine with it." Then he said to me, "We're even with this."

He didn't wait. He left, heading to the street instead of back to the bar.

Luke said to the guys, "Get lost. I mean it." Turning, he took hold of my arm and began guiding me back to the bar. Once we were through the back door, he glared at me. "What were you thinking? If you see two guys hiding by the garbage bins, you don't approach them by yourself."

Emerson hadn't told him.

I didn't even groan. I should've known better. Cousin of the Year was not an award he'd be winning. Ever. "I…it's done. Whatever."

He cursed under his breath, then went around me, and opened the basement door. Before going down, he glanced back. "Are you really done with Turner?"

I nodded, feeling pinned in place by his piercing gaze.

"Luke?"

A girl waiting for him at the bottom of the stairs. Of course, he'd have a girl waiting for him.

He ignored her and said to me, "Elijah deals drugs, and that brings problems. We have enough problems of our own. We don't need him around, so if you're really done with him, you can join the band. We have a gig out of town next Thursday. You have until then to decide."

He didn't wait for my answer. He went downstairs, took the girl's hand, and led her back into the basement.

What a perfect ending for the night. I had a sudden urge to start my own bar fight.

CHAPTER
FIVE

The first thing I noticed when I stopped just in front of the porch steps was the blood dripping from the soles of his shoes that were hanging out the door. The second thing I noticed were the dark, tattered jeans. I recognized the shoes, but the jeans sealed it. I knew without a doubt it was Luke.

The bag I'd been carrying fell to the ground, and I couldn't move.

He was dead.

"Bri!"

I woke with a gasp, then saw a shadow of a large man standing above me and froze. It was him. He'd come back for me. Blind fury kicked in, and I launched at the shadow as I let out a blood-curdling scream. "No!"

The shadow ducked and shoved me back onto the bed. He pinned my arms to my sides and got in my face. I saw his lips move, but couldn't hear what he was saying in my panic.

He couldn't be back. He couldn't. I kept trying to hit him, but he was holding me down.

Braden was yelling, pulling me out of my dream. His voice wafted back and forth. "Bri...Stop...me..."

"What's wrong with her?"

He looked to whoever had spoken from the doorway, but I couldn't see. It wasn't a voice I recognized. He scowled at them. "I told you to wait outside."

"I need to use the bathroom. You wouldn't let me use the one at the bar, remember?"

"Shit. Yeah, go and use hers."

I was still gasping for air, but saw a girl disappear toward the hallway. I heard a door close a second later. When Braden realized I had stopped fighting, he released my arms and stood back. "Holy crap. What was that?"

I shook my head and shoved him aside. Then I sat on the edge of the bed and put my head between my knees. Deep breaths in and out. I hadn't thought about that day for so long.

"When did you start having nightmares again?"

The toilet flushed from my bathroom. I held out an arm, pointing at the hallway. "Who was that? And what the hell happened to Kelly?"

My brother visibly grimaced and bit his lip before running a hand through his hair. "Uh. Her name's Crissy." The bathroom door opened and he raised his voice towards the hallway, "You can head to the kitchen. I'll be out in a minute."

I smacked him in the stomach. "And I repeat, what about Kelly, and why is that girl using my bathroom?"

"Uh." He cursed under his breath and sat beside me on the bed. "Come on, Bri. I'm not exclusive with anyone. I like Kelly, I do, but I don't want a relationship."

I heard his condescending tone and glared. I shot back, "What's wrong with a relationship? You could do with some maturing."

He gave me a 'duh' look. "I'm in a band."

"So?"

"So. I'm. In. A. Band." He shook his head. "Come on. For real. You don't get that?" His shoulders rolled back, and a cocky expression flashed over his face. "I'm hot shit. Why would I want to get a ball-n-chain?"

I stared at him, waited ten seconds, and then smacked him on the back of his head.

"Ow." His hand moved to where I hit him, and he cradled it. "What was that about?"

"I'm going to have to apologize to my future boss because my brother's a man-whore douche nozzle. That's what that was about."

"Your future boss?"

"Kelly offered me a job."

His eyes got big. "No way. You can't. Em and Luke said they okayed you to join the band."

"No." I shook my head. A big yawn came over me, and I reached for my phone. "Braden, why are you in my apartment at three in the morning? I'm tired. Leave me alone." Nudging him off the bed, I pointed to the door and yawned again. "Go. Leave. Take your Kelly-replacement-because-you're-afraid-of-commitment girl with you."

"Oh." His cheeks puffed out, and he raked a hand through his hair. "You're going to hate me, like really hate me."

Why did I get a sudden doom and gloom feeling after hearing those words? Ignoring my gut, which told me to push him out the door and lock it, I folded my arms across my chest. Dear Lord. I would probably need His help by the end of the night, judging from the sudden nervous look on my brother's face.

His laugh moved up an octave, and he shifted, his hands going behind his back. "Uh, I need your help."

"That's established. The 'with what' is not."

He rolled his eyes. "Come on, Bri. Don't be snippy."

I lifted an eyebrow. I was waiting.

"Okay, okay. Paul called me. You know Paul?"

"From Shifter?" I named another local band.

"Yeah. He said Emerson's at his party, and he's in bad shape. He wants us to come and get him out of there."

I sighed. Goddamn, Emerson. "Yeah," I mumbled as I started to look around for a sweatshirt. I'd need to put on jeans, too. "Is he drunk or high? I need to know what to prepare myself for."

"He's drunk."

I heard the hesitation in my brother's voice and looked up, fixing him with a stare.

He shrugged. "And high."

"All right." I shooed him out of the room. "Get lost. I need to change."

"You'll come?"

"Yes." Ducking my head, I pulled a sweatshirt on and grabbed a new pair of jeans. These were faded and ripped, like all my others. It was my trademark look. "Get out before I change my mind." As he did, I grabbed my shoes. With Emerson, who knew what situation would happen. Having to run away or chase someone down was realistic for us. It'd been like this all our childhood. Emerson did something or said something, and the rest of us had to fight for him. I didn't know why Elijah hadn't been called, and I didn't want to ask Braden either. He'd scowl and say this is family business. When I was ready to go, I headed for the kitchen and found Braden waiting with his girl.

She had long black hair that fell to the middle of her back with white streaks running through it. Her jeans were like mine, and she was wearing a black tank top. Her boobs were pushed up to high heaven, and her lips were plump. We didn't run in a wealthy crowd, and this girl didn't look like she had money for Botox, but I was pretty sure she had way too much injected into her face. She would've been pretty if she had gone with a natural look— less makeup, less Botox, less cleavage, and less white streaks, but I didn't say a word. I never mixed well with ninety-eight percent of other females.

"We ready to go?" I asked, grabbing my keys.

"Hi, I'm—" Crissy held her hand out, but Braden stepped in front of her.

He pushed her arm down and nodded to me, saying, "Yep. We're all good."

Ignoring the puzzled look she gave him, I swept past them and headed for Braden's truck and took shotgun. When Braden and the girl realized what I was doing, he started laughing. The girl paused. A soft "Hey," left her, but Braden hushed her before going to the driver's side. She had no choice but to take the backseat. When she got inside, I waited, but she was quiet. Good. No fight there, but then I saw another one coming.

Braden started the car and pulled across the road...right into Luke's driveway.

"What the hell?" I sat forward in my seat.

"What?"

My brother's tone was too innocent. My eyes narrowed. "Stop with the bullshit. Luke?"

"This is what we do. This is our crew."

Frustration like no other rose within me. This *had been* our crew. Emerson got in trouble. Braden, Luke, and I went to help him, and after dating Elijah, I knew he got called quite a bit, too. This wasn't our crew anymore, but it didn't matter what I said. Luke was leaving his house, and he braked when he saw who else was in the car.

His mouth tightened, but then he went to the other backseat door. So he hadn't known either.

I hissed to Braden as the door was opening, "We need to talk about how things have changed from three years ago to now."

He rolled his eyes. "Get over it. We need all the help we can get. Paul said some other guys were at the party—guys he didn't know. He asked Emerson about them, but Em was adamant that he needed to leave them alone." When Luke shut the door, Braden looked up in the rearview mirror. "Hey, man."

"Hey." Luke glanced at me. His tone was cautious, but resigned.

Lovely. I was glad we were on the same page, at least.

He glanced at Crissy. She held up a hand. "Hey there."

Luke narrowed his eyes and didn't respond to her. He asked Braden, "Was he high or drunk?"

Braden answered Luke, "He's both and Paul said there are some other guys there who will help us get him out." *If this became a bigger problem than a four—I doubted the girl would help—three-person job.*

"We might need them." Luke's tone was ominous.

Crissy was looking among all of us. "Uh, should I be worried? Is this guy violent or something?"

Braden opened his mouth to answer. I beat him to it, saying, "Or something. He's an asshole when he's sober, so take a guess what he's like when he's drunk."

"Oh." She shrank back in her seat. "Not good."

That was putting it lightly.

"Okay. Shut up." Braden turned on the radio. "I know no one's happy about this, but we have to. He's—"

"—family," I finished for him. "I know."

He looked up and met Luke's gaze in the mirror. An unspoken message passed between them. My jaw hardened. I didn't want to guess what they were thinking. Falling silent, the rest of the ride was like that until we pulled up to Paul Montrose's house. He was the lead singer of Shifter, a punk rock band with whom we were all friendly. We got out and headed up to the two-story home that looked like it belonged in the suburbs and not on the edge of Grant West. With a natural reserve behind it and a candy warehouse across the street, Paul hosted a lot of parties here because of the privacy. He had no neighbors, and a lot of his friends were in bands. A stage was set up in the backyard where we could hear someone playing. The music had blasted us as soon as we turned down the road.

Paul came out the front door, holding a beer. He was close to six feet, with a lean build like Luke's, and dark blond tussled hair. I always liked Paul. Sometimes there was jealousy among the bands, especially if someone left one for another, but not with him. He was even-keel with everyone. As we crossed the yard, he waved. "Thanks for coming."

I held back. Paul had called Braden, so I expected him to talk for us, but Luke moved forward. He asked, "Where is he?"

Paul gestured to the second floor. "Wessler and Nix got him to a bedroom up there, and we're trying to keep people from going up there. He tried starting a couple fights. After the third one, we'd had enough. He was scaring a lot of the girls, too, and he's got these friends here. I don't know how to get them to leave, but I don't want to call the cops. Because, you know." He put his fingers together and pretended to smoke a joint. "Anyway. You can use this way to get him out." He walked around the side of the house. There was a side porch and stairs that wound up to the second floor, leading to a door.

"How is he?" I asked. If Emerson had passed out, this would be much easier.

"He's..." he hesitated, "...a handful."

A handful for Paul was a nightmare for the rest of us. "That's probably putting it nice."

"Yeah. Well." He shrugged, taking a sip of his beer. "I wanted to call Elijah, but Emerson kept saying in the bedroom we couldn't call him, so sorry, guys. I know this must be a pain." Stepping back, he took another drag from his beer and waved again. "I'll let you guys deal with him, but I'm here if you need help."

"Thanks for that, Paul, and thanks for calling us and not..." Luke grew quiet. There was no one else to call. Emerson didn't want Elijah called, so we were it. Realizing that, Luke motioned to Braden instead. "Let's go and get him."

They started up the stairs. Braden told Crissy to wait for us, so she hung back while I followed them. Paul fell in step beside me. He said under his breath, "I do feel bad for calling you guys. I just didn't know who else to call. He kept saying Eli couldn't come, and I couldn't call the cops, so it was you guys."

"It's no problem," I reassured him. "For real—"

"Get out, you motherfuckers! Get out!"

Hearing Emerson's roar, I corrected, "And I spoke too soon." Stepping through the second-floor door, Emerson was hunched over with his back to a corner. His nostrils were flaring, and his hands were raised, ready to fight. Braden and Luke were standing in the doorway watching him.

I said, "We're going to need weapons."

Braden asked me over his shoulder, "You used to have a Taser when we were kids. Do you still?"

"You want me to tase him?" I just won the lottery.

He hesitated, "Well, we might need to."

Luke wasn't listening. He walked forward, his hand closing and opening in a fist. He stopped right before Emerson. His shoulders were tense. He was waiting for an attack, but it didn't come. Emerson looked at him like a feral animal. His chest was heaving, and his eyes were fully dilated, almost pure black, but he still didn't move. He was watching, waiting.

Luke glanced back at me, and with a jolt, I realized what he was going to do.

I nodded and started forward. He'd better protect me, or I swear to god...I stopped thinking and let out a ragged breath.

As I drew closer, Emerson straightened. The urge to say, "Here, kitty kitty," was on the tip of my tongue, but I held back. Eyeing my cousin warily, I stopped when Luke held out his hand. Then I waited. I was here. My cousin hated me. He should've lunged by now.

Luke moved so he was standing to the side. He shifted back on his heel, ready for the attack. *Oh fuck it*, I thought. I looked into Emerson's eyes and taunted, "What are you waiting for, Emerson? If you're going to hit me, this is the best ti—"

It happened quickly.

Emerson sprang for me. His arms were outstretched, and his hands were open. He was going for my throat, but—Luke hit him. It was a good solid punch to the side of his face, and Emerson dropped to the floor.

I waited, holding my breath, but he didn't move. Luke had knocked him out. I swung my gaze to his, my knees shaky. "Well, that's one way of handling it…" I trailed off. Luke's eyes darkened before he looked away from me. For a moment, we'd been the old best friends that we used to be. That moment was over, and it was back to him hating me.

I stepped aside, and Luke bent to grab Emerson. Braden, Paul, and two other guys came into the room. All of them carried him down the stairs. I followed behind them, shutting the door. Crissy was wringing her hands together. She darted to the side as the guys took Emerson to the car.

"What happened up there?" she asked me in a rush. Beads of sweat formed on her forehead, and she wiped them off with the back of her hand.

"Uh." What did happen? "Nothing much." And that was the truth. Nothing much happened. Emerson was high. We got him out, and now it was back to life as usual. I hadn't been given a window to my old friendship with Luke. It was a façade. He needed me to act as bait. That was it. Nothing more.

"Oh." Crissy's laugh trembled. "That's good. I was worried."

"Yeah…" I squared my shoulders back. Whatever. I walked away from Luke three years ago. That had been my choice, not his, but even as I tried to make myself believe that, I couldn't. I missed being Luke's friend. Getting that feeling again and then having it taken away, I felt something missing inside me.

They started to put Emerson behind the driver's seat, but Luke shook his head. "No. Do the middle. If he wakes up, we can restrain him better this way."

Hearing those words, Crissy stepped back, bumping into my side. I expected her to move away, but she didn't. She stayed there. Her arm started shaking, and that told me one thing; she wasn't going to help much.

I started for the front seat, but Luke stopped me. "What are you doing?"

"'What are you doing?'" I indicated Emerson. "You need to sit next to him if you're going to be able to restrain him."

"I know." He held his hand out, and Braden gave him the keys. Luke held them out to me. "You drive. Braden and I will both sit in the back."

"Oh, thank god." Crissy darted for my seat.

She closed the door for me, pulling on it so I was forced to step back. Luke laughed slightly. He asked, "Still want to join the band?"

"What do you mean?"

"Not much has changed in three years. Emerson gets high. We carry him home, and we do the best we can. This is how it is."

I already knew how Emerson operated. Was it worth dealing with my cousin, that's what he was warning me about, but the real question I needed to ask myself—was this all worth it, to play with Luke again?

My hand closed around the keys, and I went to start the car, but I already had my answer. Was it worth it?

Hell yes.

CHAPTER
SIX

There wasn't much of a reaction from Luke when I told him. All I got was a nod, and he said, "We're playing Candy Lake's house party tonight. It's a good paying gig. Don't fuck this up."

Don't fuck it up. Sound advice. I smoothed my clammy hands down my pants and nodded. "Sure. I can do that. I mean, I can *not* do that. Not fuck it up, I mean." I was already messing it up.

Emerson rolled his eyes. "Are we sure about this? Chicks bring drama." His lip curled up into a sneer. "Especially this one."

Braden yelled from the van behind us, "One, she's amazing on drums. Two, even though she's my sister and it pains me to say this—it really does—she's hot. We got the girls coming in droves to see us, but guys will come too now. Sorry, Bri. I feel like I'm pimping you out."

I shrugged.

He continued, "And three, she needs to stay busy. We need to keep her away from Turner in her free time."

Emerson grunted right next to him in the seat. "That's my best friend, asshole."

Braden shot back, "You don't agree with keeping her away from him?"

My cousin lowered his head. My brother had him with that one. Luke shook his head. "Why are you making this same argument? I already said she's in." He said to me, "And I mean it, Bri. I know your history with Candy Lake. Be nice. She has two parties every summer and more during the winter. She booked us in the past, and she pays the best. I don't want to lose this gig. We need the money."

Candy Lake? Move over Emerson; she was another admirer of mine. My lips twitched at my own joke. I was lame, and so was Candy Lake. She wasn't as bad as Emerson with her hatred of me. No one was. The last time I saw her, the two of us ended up pulling each other's hair and rolling on the ground. It had been a chick fight gone bad and not one of my glorious moments. I could fight better than that, but she got me on a night when I had been drunk, way too drunk. The party loved it. I had not.

I shrugged. "I won't start anything with her." But if she started something like other girls had in the past, she had another think coming.

"I mean it, Bri. You hated her in high school. Don't start anything tonight." He walked around me and went to the driver's side. As he got in, Braden clapped his hand on the seat. "Come on, Bri. Hop your ass in here so we can go and make some girls' panties wet."

Because that made sense.

I shook my head and got into the van. As Braden slammed the side door shut, I remarked, "We need to have a talk where you remember that I'm your sister."

Braden winked at me. "You are, but come on, you're going to be treated like a dude now."

"For some reason I feel like that's a compliment, but I have no idea why."

Emerson rolled his eyes. "We're treating you like an equal. Stop complaining about it."

"Why don't *you* stop complaining?" I gripped my armrest. "Talk about the pot calling the kettle black."

He was staring at me. "Keep it—"

"Shut up," Luke clipped out, pulling out of the parking lot. "Both of you. Here's the plan. We're going to the party, we'll do the set we practiced with Bri in the basement, and then we'll head back. The two of you don't even need to talk to each other."

"She—"

"Got it?" Luke barked, giving Emerson a pointed look in the rearview mirror.

"Yeah." My cousin lowered his head. "Got it."

"Bri?" Luke addressed me.

"Yeah?"

"No fighting."

I cracked a grin. *We'll see.*

"I mean it."

I nodded. "Yeah. Okay."

The drive wasn't long to get to her house, and from what I remembered about Candy Lake, I wasn't surprised to see the mansion and guest house sitting on the beach, surrounded by trees. Luke drove right up to a stage that was perched in front of the house, facing the ocean. He took off, and the rest of us started to unpack the equipment. No one spoke, which surprised me, but I was grateful at the same time. Emerson still seemed pissed, and Braden kept stopping to check out every girl that walked by us.

Candy Lake was the popular girl in high school. Luke and Braden had been popular, too, but they never cared or worked for it. People just liked them, and lucky for me, they were content to hang out with me. The popular girls and I never mixed well. They talked about things that didn't interest me—fashion, boyfriends, and gossip—and I only wanted to play drums. Growing up as a tomboy, I was the most comfortable hanging out with my brother and his friends.

"Are we ready to go?"

Luke had come back. He hoisted himself onto the stage in one fluid movement. The athleticism shouldn't have been impressive, it was one leap, but it took my breath away. He looked like a damn cat. That had been another thing about Luke. He was gorgeous, dark, mysterious, and athletic. He could've played sports, been worshiped for just that feat, but he only cared about music and...I swallowed tightly...me.

"Bri!" Braden yelled in front of me.

"What?" I jerked back. As I glanced around, they were all looking right at me, and my cheeks instantly reddened. "You guys were talking?"

Emerson cursed and bent back over his guitar, tuning it.

"So, you're ready?" Braden stepped in front of me and took my shoulders in his hands. "I know it's your first time with us in front of a crowd, but you can do it. You're a natural. Our practice set was amazing. We didn't have too many hiccups."

"Emerson hadn't been there."

My brother let go of my shoulders, stepping away. "He plays the same as Gunn, better. Em will be fine. We're good to go." He cursed then. "Maybe you're right. Luke, you think we should do a practice set?"

Luke adjusted the microphone stand, his eyes shifted to me. "Yeah. It wouldn't hurt."

"Good." Braden clapped his hands together and moved to pick up his guitar. "Let's do this shit. We're going to be awesome."

Emerson grunted, rolling his eyes. "Are you on something? If you are, not fair. Share it, cousin." He opened his lips, showing his teeth for a second. "Anything would help to get us through this."

He wasn't talking about the gig. He was referencing me. I got the insult immediately. My eyes narrowed to slits, and without realizing what I was doing, I surged for him. Enough was enough, but Luke stepped right in front of me. He caught me and held me back, throwing over his shoulder to Emerson, "Could you stop? It's getting old, and I'm likely to kick you to the curb instead." One of his hands rested on my hip, and I went still at the touch, feeling burned from the slightest pressure.

I wasn't paying attention to what Emerson replied. I sucked in my breath and closed my eyes. I never thought he would touch me again, not even a hug, not how he used to throw his arm around my shoulders, or not how he would play with my hands when we were bored.

Then his hand dropped, and he turned, glancing down at me. "You okay with that?"

Hearing the gruffness in his voice, my eyes rose to his. I could only nod in response. He went back to the microphone, keeping his back to me, but it was there. I had felt it again. It stung me. The old connection was still between us. Knowing it was there and feeling it for a moment, had my body wired.

I climbed to my seat and picked up my sticks. I was ready to go.

SUSTAIN

The sticks twirled on my palm, and I held them like that, letting them spin in the air. The song had paused. They were waiting for me, but I still let those sticks go. This was my time to shine. Forget Emerson. This was about music—our music. I was the best, and he was going to be reminded of it. No matter what shit he said about me, he'd keep his mouth shut about this. Drumming was what I did best, and this felt so right. I let the anticipation build. The crowd was waiting. Everyone was waiting. My body was writhing with the tempo. The beat poured through my blood, but I savored it, still holding off, and then, it was time. Everything clicked. The song was perfect now, and I flicked the right stick up with my finger, caught it with my thumb, and slammed it down at the same time.

I didn't hear the crowd.

I knew their mouths were open. Their arms were flailing, but it wasn't about them. They were nothing to me. It was about the music. My leg tapped on the bass, and I glanced up, knowing Braden would mold his chord with my beat. He sensed me and instinctually turned. His head bent further down as his fingers played over the strings. He was doing it. There was no contact between us except the music.

Then Emerson joined, and he held his note. My beat continued, pulsating out. It infected everyone. No one was immune, and we raised the climax all the way up.

This was what we did.

This was how we played.

We were a team.

Braden added to the drama, his guitar hitting the higher notes, and Emerson helped build up the tension. We were waiting, all three of us now. We needed one more to join—voice.

Luke was at the front of the stage. His back was turned. His head was bent, and he held the microphone. He was feeling everything, letting the song continue and build. When we were at the right spot, the perfect moment, his head bobbed, and he started to sing.

His voice was clear and smooth. He started with that first note, and the crowd's energy spiked. I still couldn't hear them. I closed my eyes and gave over to the music.

I bled into the beat.

We never stopped because I wouldn't let them. There was a moment's pause—a brief moment—and at the signal, the next song was launched. We ran the entire set. One perfect unit. I rolled the beat through, matching the adrenaline in my body. It was going to be like this every night now. Knowing that, I relished the feeling, anticipating this ride from now on.

As Luke belted out the words and Emerson switched the bass, Braden hit that haunting note.

This was when the crowd felt us. If they hadn't by then, it was this moment when a renewed fever spread through them. My blood was buzzing, knowing we held them by the balls. We decided how they felt. We had control like gods. My arms crashed down with more force, and I gritted my teeth, going with the roller coaster inside me.

More than once, Luke found me and took me on a different ride. He felt it, too. All the bullshit was gone. We were a band. Emerson might've hated me, but he didn't when we played together. A connection ran through all of us when we performed. No one went against us, or we'd all fail.

I had missed this. Playing with Braden. Luke. Setting the rhythm.

I never got off the roller coaster, not even at the end of our set. I craved being up there, setting the beat, yielding that power. After an intense set, I retreated to a back corner and recuperated there. The waves crashed over me, and I gulped for air, feeling that buzz in my blood. I wanted to keep it going, so I started for the bar, wanting a drink. Then a hand touched my hip. *Luke*, I thought. My body instantly molded toward his, and my pulse spiked. Then reality crashed back into place. It was Elijah.

I shoved his hand off. "What are you doing?"

He rolled his eyes, but grabbed my hand and started forward. Eli moved lithely through the crowd. Most knew who he was and moved away so he could pass, but the rest moved on instinct anyway. As we moved inside the guest house Candy said we could use for the night, I started to move around him, but bumped into him and felt something hard inside his jacket. His gaze locked with mine. I caught the warning in his eyes and narrowed mine. "What are you doing here?"

"You weren't supposed to feel that."

"What?"

He jerked his head forward. "You should go."

"We just got done playing our set." What was in his jacket?

"You should go."

A message flashed in his eyes. Then it clicked. Something was going to happen. My lips parted again, and feeling a sense of urgency, I grabbed his arm this time. "What is happening? What's in your jacket?"

"Bri." Another warning flared over his face. "I mean it, go. I grabbed you and brought you over here for a reason." His eyes trailed past my shoulder, and I turned.

I didn't have to look far.

Luke was sitting in a lawn chair.

Eli pushed me forward, a soft touch on the small of my back. He said into my ear, "Go to him and go home. Get Emerson out of here, too."

My ex and cousin should've taken priority in my mind, but to be honest, I was having a hard time remembering what Eli said to do as I watched Luke. A group had congregated around him. Some were sitting in their own chairs. Others were standing and drinking, but most of them were watching him, just like I was. Candy Lake was hovering over him. Her very skimpy, very see-through shirt stuck to her skin, displaying a perfect view of her waistline.

She was bending over and whispering into his ear. Her hand grazed over his chest, testing him, and when he didn't brush it away, her hand grew bolder. It trailed down to the waistband of his jeans and rested on his stomach. Her lips formed a seductive smile. I could imagine her soothing sounds, crooning to him, and then she shifted on her feet. Her hand was still touching his shoulder.

My hands were clenched to the sides of my pants, as if to hold myself back from walking over there and slapping her. Bitch. Bitch. Bitch.

She straddled him.

My eyes were going to pop out. A burning sensation tunneled inside my chest.

He didn't touch her, but he didn't ask her to move either. She leaned forward and pressed her chest against his. Her head tilted, and she nuzzled him under his chin and then trailed her lips to his ear. I couldn't handle it. *He's mine.* I started forward—she leaned back, arching so her breasts were right in front of his face. The bitch wasn't wearing a bra. I was going to lose it. Luke was staring right at me when my foot came down hard.

Our eyes caught and held, and a smirk appeared on his face. I flushed. He'd known the whole time I was watching. Fucker.

I started for them—BANG! BANG! I froze, staring at Luke, who froze, too.

Eli.

Then everything connected in my head. It was a gun inside his jacket. That's why he wanted me to go.

There was silence for one second before chaos ensued. Some people screamed in terror. Some sprinted to their cars or the house, trying to get somewhere safe. When a guy knocked into me, Luke shoved Candy off him and started for me. I couldn't move as I watched him push through the crowd, his eyes fierce and his jaw set. When he got to me, I said, "That's Eli. He brought a gun here."

He grabbed my hand. It was like someone had hit my *Pause* button. His contact hit the *Play* button, and I was ready to go. We turned and ran together. When a group of girls ran the other way between us, Luke let go of me. I swerved to one side, and he went the other. More people streamed past us, but we kept going. Everyone was running away from the gunshots. We were running toward them. Luke kept glancing at me, making sure I was still with him. I did the same. We were moving as one unit again. The feeling of being in tune with him sent a new wave of adrenaline through me. It pushed me faster, and when the crowd began to thin, I started looking around.

Braden. Emerson. Elijah. I needed to find any or all of them. But Braden was my priority.

"Bri!" Luke shouted and pointed to the side. I caught a glimpse of Emerson disappearing around a corner and veered that way. Luke said, "Stay here. I'll get him."

"I'll look for Braden," I said, but he was already gone.

As I moved in the opposite direction, I saw a clump of trees. Braden might've gone back there. Maybe with a girl? I rounded the opening by the trees. No Braden. He wasn't anywhere. No one else was around. They'd all disappeared. I could hear car doors in the distance and saw the flash of headlights as people drove away.

My heart was pounding in my chest from the frenzy. I needed to listen for Braden, if I could hear his voice somewhere, but I couldn't make out anything, so I started forward through the trees. They led away from the beach. The light from Candy's guesthouse was in the west, and I headed that way. As I continued through the woods, I saw the van parked in a clearing and walked toward it. I was about to step into the clearing when a hand wrapped around my elbow and pulled me back. I was pressed against a chest and reared back to scream.

A hand clamped over me, and Elijah said into my ear, "Shut up."

My knees sagged in relief, but I tried to hit his chest. "You scared the crap out of me."

He rolled his eyes. "You were about to get shot."

My eyes widened.

"And before you even start, that gunshot wasn't me."

"Then who was it?"

His hood was pulled over his baseball cap. He'd been standing in the shadows, hidden by his black clothing and a tree. At my question, he pulled me further into the shadows with him and shook his head.

"Elijah."

His mouth went into a flat line.

"Elijah!"

He hissed, "I can't tell you shit, okay? You can't know about this stuff." He cursed, regret flashing in his eyes for a moment. "You shouldn't even be here with me. What are you doing? You and pretty boy should be long gone by now. I told you to go."

"We're looking for Braden and Emerson."

Elijah narrowed his eyes. "They're gone."

"What do you mean?"

"They took off. I saw them running for the cars a minute ago."

"They're safe?"

"Yeah. Emerson texted; he said he'd wait at Rowdy's with the band."

Sudden tears threatened to spill. They came hard and fast. My brother was safe. Emerson was safe. I closed my eyes. Luke. Where had Luke gone?

Elijah watched me. "What's wrong?"

"Luke went looking for them."

His eyes darkened in anger. "Why aren't you people normal? Run for safety next time instead of running toward the danger."

"Are you in trouble?"

"Not the time to hash this out." He tried to shield me with his body, moving me closer to him so I was against the tree. As we both heard twigs breaking behind us, he put his finger to his mouth. I nodded, and we waited. My heart started racing. More branches broke. Someone was coming toward us. A tree branch was shoved out of the way. They were near, just on the other side of the tree. Then they stepped right beside us. Elijah's hand tightened on my arm as his other hand moved to the inside of his sweatshirt. I knew what he was grabbing, and I held my breath.

Please no. Please no. Please go away, repeated in my head. I didn't dare look at who was right next to us, but from the corner of my eye, I saw the shape of a very large man. He was so close. If he turned even an inch, he would see us. Elijah's hand tightened on the gun, and he began to turn it in his sweatshirt so it was pointed at whoever was there.

The man scoffed to himself and spoke into his phone, "Yeah. No sign of Turner. Let's go to his house. He must've gotten out earlier than we thought—"

Someone moved into the trees next to him. They yelled, "He's right next to you! Watch out—"

Elijah shot at him and then shoved me away from him and lunged for the guy next to him. The second guy, the one Elijah had tried to shoot, cursed but hadn't been hit. He grabbed for Elijah, but Luke came out of nowhere. He wrapped a hand around the guy's neck, kicked at his knee so he fell down, and then grabbed onto his arm. He squeezed until the guy went unconscious, and then Luke let him go, stepping back.

He looked at me, an unspoken question in his gaze. I shook my head, letting him know I was all right. Then he turned toward Elijah, but he didn't need help. The guy who had spoken on the phone was unconscious, too. Both Luke and Elijah were too calm. It sent an eerie shiver down my back.

Luke broke the silence. "His buddies are on their way."

"I know." Elijah jerked a hand to me. "Get her out of here."

I said, "Emerson and Braden are heading home. Elijah saw them leave."

Luke nodded. "I know. I came looking for you." His tone was accusing. "I told you to stay put."

"Over here!" someone shouted, followed by sounds of people running through the woods.

Elijah started to say, "Take he—" but Luke had already grabbed me. His arm wrapped around my waist, and he held me in the air, carrying me toward the van. Luke threw me inside and jumped in after me. A guy I didn't know was behind the wheel, and as soon as the doors shut, he took off. I turned, expecting Elijah to be with us, but he wasn't.

"Where'd he go?"

Luke whipped his head to mine, narrowing his eyes. "He took off."

"What? Why? He'd be safer with us."

"No."

I stopped, hearing the authority in his tone and couldn't look away from him. His eyes flashed in anger. He had made a decision. "Elijah is dangerous. The farther we are from him, the better. He'll be fine. He can take care of himself."

That was true. I sat back and leaned my head against the seat while the adrenaline pumped in my veins. Feeling Luke watching me, I asked, "What?"

"No argument?" He was ready for one. I could see it in his eyes.

I shook my head. "No. No argument. I know he's dangerous."

I sensed the surprise from him, but he didn't say anything. He leaned back in his seat, and we were silent the entire way home. I didn't want to think about what Eli had gotten himself into. He wasn't my problem anymore.

CHAPTER
SEVEN

"I need your guitar." I shoved open Luke's bedroom door. I had sprinted from my house and into his. His dad wasn't there. His dad was never there, but I knew Luke was. His music was blaring. I heard it from my house earlier. It got louder the second the door opened, but I saw a girl on his bed. She was bent over. Her shirt was raised, and her legs were positioned out, ready for him.

The girl gasped, glanced over, but didn't move. She had black hair that hung down, covering her face, and she tucked some of it behind her ear. She narrowed her eyes at me. "Who are you?"

I wasn't even shocked. I glanced around. No Luke. "Where is he?"

She shrugged. "He told me to get ready. I'm ready."

I turned around, but a hand came to my side and gripped me. I jumped, not from fear, but at how close he stood behind me. "Hey!"

His grey eyes held mine for a second before the corner of his mouth curved up into a cocky smirk. With high cheekbones, dark hair that he had recently gotten cut so it gave him an edgier look, and a ripped body, Luke had grown up with his fair share of women willing to bend over, ass naked, and waiting for him. His fingers curved into my side, and he asked, "What'd you say before?"

"I need your guitar." I removed his hand from my side and pushed past him, back to the hallway.

"Why?"

"Because."

"Because? I'm not letting you touch it until you tell me why."

"Luke," the girl called from inside. The sound of her seductive whine grated on my nerves. I gritted my teeth and gave him a pointed look, jerking a thumb to his bedroom.

He rolled his eyes, but reached inside and shut his door. It closed with a thud. We heard a 'Hey!' from inside. His eyes narrowed again. "What's going on?"

I groaned, but stifled the sound. There was no way I wanted to explain my mother's last conversation in the kitchen. "I just need it, okay?"

"Why?"

"Luke."

"Bri."

"Come on," I snapped out. Frustration was building in me.

"Spill and then I'll let you."

A litany of curses spilled from me instead, but I surrendered. "I'm going to play in front of some rich prick's store. We need money."

"My dad loaned Carla money last week."

"Which she used already." For food. For Braden and him when they both ate dinner at the house. "Besides, your dad asked for half of it back." I bit my lip to keep from spilling the rest.

The air changed. He didn't react, but I sensed Luke's anger. Every part of me went on alert. "Come on, Luke. I'll use your guitar for the afternoon, get some money, and I'll put it back. You won't even miss it."

"Luke!"

I gestured to his bedroom. "Looks like you're going to be busy, anyway."

He rolled his eyes, but I knew he was still pissed. Raking a hand over his head, he growled. "I should go with you if you're going to be standing on some street corner."

"It's not like that. It's a good area."

"The good areas have the biggest dicks."

"Whatever. Come with if you want, but Carla's got a payment due tomorrow. We need to raise a few hundred by tonight."

He groaned, his eyes flashing from irritation. "Then we're going to be hitting a few stores." He started for his door, then stopped. "Are you still on good terms with that one manager? When you did this before?"

"Yeah, yeah." I shoved him forward. "Let's go. I'll wait in your car."

As he opened the door, I heard the girl say, "Who was that girl?"

"Get out."

"What?"

"Yeah. Come on. Get out. I have something else to do."

"You're going to sleep with that girl instead?"

I hurried down the stairs to the basement where Luke kept his guitar. It was one of his most prized possessions since it was a gift from his mom. He let Braden use it once, but I was the only one he allowed to borrow it more than once.

"Bri!" he called down the stairs.

"Coming." I grabbed it and headed up.

He was waiting outside the door, lighting a cigarette. The girl was stalking down the sidewalk. She turned around and gave him the middle finger. "Fuck you, Luke Skeet!"

He flicked her the bird back and finished lighting his cigarette.

"You too!" she yelled at me. I rolled my eyes and ignored her, then grabbed the cigarette and put it out on the ground.

"Hey," he growled, glaring at me.

"No. I have to deal with that from Elijah, not you, too."

At the mention of my boyfriend, he swallowed his retort. His grey eyes grew black instead, and he muttered, "I don't know why you stay with that fuckhead. He's a drug dealer."

"No, he's not." I started for his car. "And we're not having that conversation again."

"Whatever." He got into the driver's seat and waited as I put his guitar in the back. When it was safe and secure and I was in the passenger seat, he started the car. "I hate this idea. Why does your mom need this so bad?"

I shook my head and kept quiet. He didn't need to know that when his dad asked for his money back, he didn't take only the money he loaned. He took everything my mom had saved to pay our rent. Now it was really late, and if it didn't get paid within the next week, we'd lose the house.

"Bri." A hand woke me up, rocking my arm back and forth. Luke was hovering over me, and unlike the last time I'd been awakened by someone, I welcomed his intrusion. My hand slid around the back of his neck. This was my best friend. I wanted to hug him. No, I wanted more. My body grew warm. I took hold of some of his hair and pulled him down—

The door to the van opened. A blast of cold air hit us both.

Luke's eyes widened, realizing what was about to happen. I saw the flash of recognition. He felt it, too. My heart started pounding, harder and harder against my ribs. He sat up and got out of the van. Shoving past the guy, his back was tense, and his shoulders were rigid.

I sat up, my insides all jumbled at the turn of events, and stayed there, staring at the guy. He stared back, a knowing smirk on his face. He slid a hand into one of his pockets and cocked his head to the side. "You and Skeet hooking up again?"

Again? My eyes narrowed. "Who are you?"

"Dustin Glass."

I wanted to groan immediately. One of Candy's friends. "Didn't you go to Yale and get expelled because of partying too much?"

He flashed a smile. "Harvard."

"Oh god." Even worse. I pushed him out of the way. "Thanks for driving us, but go back and find your yuppie preppy friends. You're out of your league with us here. We're trailer park compared to what you're used to."

He didn't listen to me. Instead of staying at the van, he shut the door and started behind me. Following at a slower stroll, he rolled his shoulders back and kept smiling at me. "I may be rich and dumb enough to get kicked out of school, but I know a sure thing when I see it. Your band is awesome. You guys are going to make it big."

I growled, opening the back door of Rowdy's. Some music could be heard through the door, but as soon as I opened it, it tripled in volume. The smell of smoke, booze, and sweat overtook me for a moment, and I faltered in my step. Dustin reached out from behind me, caught the door and held it open. It was after closing time, so I headed for the main floor where all the music was coming from.

Dustin was right behind me. I could feel his breath on the back of my neck as he asked, "When did you join up with them again? Why'd you quit in the first place? You haven't been around the last couple years. How come?"

Ignoring him, I went through the second door. The music was even louder, but the bar had emptied. A light was on, hanging over the pool table, along with a light in the kitchen. Emerson was at the pool table, a stick in hand, studying for his next shot. A girl was waiting behind him with a pitcher of beer on the table next to her hand. There was a second guy and girl, too, but no one I recognized. Dustin did, though.

He held up a hand, shouted, "Hey, Samuel!" and headed over to them.

Hearing the sound of dishes clanging together and muffled conversation, I walked toward the kitchen. Before I slipped around the bar, right next to the kitchen entrance, I heard a feminine voice ask, "Why would your sister have dated someone like that?"

Recognizing Kelly's voice, I held back.

My brother replied stiffly, "Who cares. She's with the band now."

"The band and my bar."

"Yeah, and about that, have I mentioned how I love that this is our hangout? Play a little downstairs and go upstairs to get a chick for the night."

"That's not what I meant," Kelly shot back.

I could hear Braden's teasing, "Still. I'm happy with the arrangement. Thanks to Luke."

Some of my tension left, and I started forward, then I heard Luke say, "I'm right here, dickhead. You can stop talking about me as if I'm not."

Braden snorted. "I would, but lately you have this habit of acting like you're not even in the room. Makes conversations a little tricky, you know. You have to address a person in order to talk to them."

My hand retracted back to my side, and I held my breath and listened.

"What's that supposed to mean?"

"It means that since my sister started coming back around, you've been checked out. Enough's enough, Luke. Stop treating her like she's a stranger. That's cold, man."

"Stop, Braden." Luke's tone went soft, but the warning was evident. "You're talking about things you don't know."

"I know. Oh, I know," my brother tossed right back, his voice was growing louder with each word. "Stop acting like you don't give a damn. Tonight proves you still do. I wouldn't have left her, but you said you'd take care of her."

"What's your point?"

"It's hurting her. She's already hurting because of Turner. I don't know why you're hurting her even more."

"Stop!"

I shrank back from the force behind Luke's voice. It was deep, feral, and primal all at the same time. He added, "I mean it, Braden. I don't get involved in your relationships. You have no idea what happened three years ago. Stay out of it. I mean it."

The next thing I knew, the door flung open, and I jumped out of the way. Luke stormed out, his shoulders were rigid, his eyes glittering from repressed anger, but he stopped short as he saw me there. Raking a hand through his hair, his shirt lifted, and a view of his obliques teased me. I registered that, felt the hunger rise a notch, but my gaze went to his and all thoughts ceased after that. His grey eyes turned black. Sensing desperation from him, my body leaned forward, closing the space between us, but he moved away.

His rejection punched me in the chest.

He clipped out, "I told you to stay away from Turner or get out of the band. It's the same deal with your cousin. Turner doesn't come around us. That's the bottom line. If he keeps showing up because of you, you're out. This band is my livelihood right now, and I won't allow a drug dealer to fuck that up."

"He wasn't there because of me—" But he wasn't listening. Luke was already gone. The back door slammed shut a moment later.

"Elijah was there tonight?"

Emerson was standing at the bar, holding a pool stick. His eyebrows were bunched forward, and his head was cocked to the side.

"Yeah."

I braced myself for a scathing remark from my cousin, but he only asked, "Are you getting back together with him?"

Why did everyone think that? "No."

"What was he doing there?"

I shook my head. "I have no idea."

"Oh." He paused, his eyebrows still bunched together. "Okay." He nodded and placed the pool stick against one of the bar stools then.

Turning, his hands slid into his pockets. I could see his shoulders hunched forward.

He went to the door, and I asked, "Where are you going?"

"To make sure he's okay," he threw over his shoulder, and the door slammed shut a second time.

My eyebrows arched high. We just got out of danger, and he was going back there?

"Hey."

I turned back around. Braden and Kelly had come from the kitchen, and a welcoming smile was on my brother's face. Finally. Someone wasn't going to snap my head off. He held an arm up, beckoning to me, and I went to him. Melting into his warm shelter, I breathed him in. He was family, and he was safe. "I was worried about you."

His hand patted my arm. "I was worried about you, too."

Kelly moved around us, touching my brother's elbow. "I'll give you guys a minute. I'll be downstairs." Braden nodded at her, and then we heard her call out, "Okay, girls. Show's over. The rock studs are all leaving, so that means you gotta go, too."

"Come on," one girl grumbled.

"Nope. Come on."

They protested again, but Kelly shooed them out, and right before she left herself, she called back over to us, "Lock up on the way out, okay?"

Braden was still hugging me to him. He called over my head, "We will. Be down in a bit."

The door shut again, for the third time. Then he looked down at me, moving a step back to lean against the kitchen door. "You okay?"

"Was that true? What you said before?"

He frowned.

I added, "That Luke came back for me?" I was trying to tell myself that it didn't matter, but hope had taken root in me. It was deep, deeper than I wanted to admit.

"Oh." He continued to frown and then nodded. "Yeah. I was coming back for you when our paths crossed. He said he was looking for me and that you had run off. I told him where Emerson was waiting for us and I was going to get you. He told me no, that he'd get you himself, and I needed to take Emerson and get a ride back here."

Luke had come back for me. "Really?"

"Really." His eyes were narrowed, trained on my face, and I knew my brother was reading every emotion inside me. "What the hell happened between you two? You started dating Elijah, and I knew the two of you drifted apart, but I assumed it was because of Elijah. Now that Turner's not back on the scene, I thought everything would go back to normal, but it's not."

I sucked in a breath. Luke had been right. Braden had no idea what had happened three years ago. "I can't, Bray. I just..." It was too hard to think about. "I can't."

He held a hand up. "I'm not asking for details. I don't want to know, but make it right. Whatever happened, correct it, Bri. The band needs you, and we have a real shot at going somewhere."

"I—"

"Fix it with Luke. I mean it. Fix it." Then he walked past me. Right before he got to the back door, he called back to me, "The door's locked, so just shut it behind you. Go tonight, Bri. Go and fix it with him. Please."

Then the door shut again, and I breathed in and out, one long shuddering breath. Braden was right. I needed to say something to smooth things over. I wasn't sure what I was going to say, but Luke was pissed. I missed my friend. *You miss more than that*, a voice whispered in my head. I told it to shut up, went out the door, and headed for Luke's house.

CHAPTER
EIGHT

I was tense.

My nerves were stretched thin, and I couldn't go downstairs. I needed a moment. We had never talked about that night. Stepping inside, I glanced at the kitchen. It was immediately to my right, and I could see it all over. It was like I was there again—three years ago when everything changed. Luke was on his stomach on the floor. His shirt had been ripped, so his entire back was exposed. A huge tear was opened over his back, and there were marks all over him. Lashings. Imprints of fists. Half his back was a deep red, and there were other parts that were already black. Fresh blood seeped out over dried blood.

He'd been beaten. The entire side of his face was swollen. The eye turned toward me was swollen shut with blood streaming from it.

At first, I thought he was dead, and my heart stopped. A moan left him, and my knees almost gave out. I wanted to push all the blood back into him, for all the bruises, broken bones, cuts, and marks to go away and for him to be fine.

I wanted all of it to go away.

Braden was the one who called 911. He heard me screaming…I still didn't remember that part.

Luke hit a jarring note on his guitar, drawing me from the past and back to reality. Seriously. I'd been ready to take on two thugs beside a dumpster for my stupid-ass cousin, but this had ice filling my veins.

I rolled my eyes upward. What was wrong with me?

The melody was addictive. I felt it reach deep inside me and take root. My breathing wavered as he kept playing. He moved down a chord, and the sound of it seeped into me, smoothing out the haunted memories. Then he began singing. His voice was soft and low, but I could hear it as if I were in the room with him. He was weaving a spell. It was like he threw a spear that had a rope attached to it at me from a hundred yards away, and it embedded deep into my stomach. Then he began pulling on it. I couldn't fight because it would yank out my insides, but damn, I didn't want to go with it. This whole thing with Luke was both painful and exhilarating at the same time. I had two urges going through me at once. One was to crap my pants, and the other was to start doing cartwheels.

I was just messed up, which is why I started down the stairs. I still had no clue what to say, but I had to do something.

He was hunched over the guitar in his lap with a beer at his feet. His eyes were closed. As he hit another chord, his thumb beat out the bass. Since he was only wearing jeans, I saw some of the scars on his back. I wanted to go to him, run my hands over those scars, and make them disappear. I couldn't, though. We weren't close anymore.

So many ghosts within you
So many haunts to pull you away
You look, I reach out and there's nothing to do
They take you from me again, far away
I can't, I can't, I can't take your hand

He kept singing, and my heart felt like it was splitting in two, but then he faltered. His eyes opened, and he looked up. He didn't stop playing, but he stopped singing.

I felt like he was strumming me. I couldn't look away from his gaze. His thumb stopped hitting the bass, and his fingers slowed on the guitar. "What are you doing here?"

A fever took over my blood, heating me up. "I," my tongue wet my lips, "um, I'm here to talk about you and me."

His gaze clouded over, and his eyelids lowered. He bent his head back over his guitar, but he didn't start strumming again. "There is no you and me. You're in the band. That's it."

I swallowed the lump in my throat. "Luke," I started.

"No." He stood up abruptly, setting his guitar to the side. As he advanced toward me, his eyes were smoldering.

When my back hit the wall, I realized I had nowhere to go and could only watch as he closed in on me. A part of me wanted him to keep getting closer; the other part of me was still thinking about crapping my pants.

He leaned a hand against the wall beside my head, keeping a few inches between us. His eyes were hard as he said, "There is no you and me. That died long ago, remember?"

"Luke."

"No, I don't want to hear it. You left me in the hospital, and I found out three weeks later that you were dating Turner. That's how you ended our friendship."

There was more to it, so much more, but I couldn't tell him. I'd been quiet all these years, terrified of what he would do if he knew the whole truth. My hands wrung together. "I didn't want to end it like that. I didn't."

"But you did."

No, I hadn't. I started to shake my head. I wanted to deny it, but I had let him think that. "I was there. I wanted to go to the hospital. I... just... couldn't, but that didn't mean I was thinking about..." I wasn't making it better.

"I woke up, and you were with Turner." He leaned in close, his breath coating my skin, caressing and taunting me at the same time. "But you had been with me the night before. You told me you loved me. You didn't, though. You lied to me." He pulled back, and I felt his cold stare. "What are you doing here, Bri? The past is done. There's no going back."

I wet my lips again. They were so dry. So was my throat. "Braden told me to smooth things over with you. The tension between us is going to affect the band."

"Because of your brother. The band. That's why you're here." He didn't move, but I felt him withdrawing. "He's right. Having a hot chick in the band will get us more attention. I've already gotten gig offers for next week, more than normal, so you're part of that reason, and the other reason I'm allowing you to play with us—is because I owe your brother. He's been there for me." Unlike me. That was his insinuation. "He wants you with us because he's scared that if you're not around me, you'll go back to Turner." The corner of his mouth curved up in a mocking smirk, making him look lethal. "Little does your brother know that I don't matter. Whatever friendship we had means nothing now. The only thing you want from me…" He paused as his eyes skimmed down my body, taking in my shallow breaths, my full breasts, my nipples pressing through my shirt. If he touched me, I would've trembled. He took all this in, and the mocking smirk turned into a knowing leer.

He stepped close to me again. The edges of his jeans grazed against my waist, but he still held himself back, raking me up and down, then scanning my face. With his lips close to mine, holding just out of reach, he murmured, "The only thing you want from me is this." His hand touched my waist, and I gasped, surging upright, feeling burned from the sensation. He leaned down so his lips lightly rested above mine.

He was torturing me. It felt like he was taking a hot poker to me, singeing me with each poke, and he was enjoying it.

His breath was searing on me as he stared me down. I couldn't move. I couldn't look away. The longer he held me, the more I wanted him against me. I started to lean against him, but he took my hands and raised them above my head before I could touch him. I was trapped. He had them pinned. His eyes never left me—he hardly even blinked— heat simmered just below the surface. He was keeping it masked from me, but I still saw it. I licked my lips, needing to unleash it. I needed to feel it, taste it.

"Luke." I knew what he was doing. He was trying to break me, and it was working.

"Is that what you want?" He bent so his eyes bore straight into mine. One inch. That was all that separated us. "You want this? Then what? Maybe the tension will leave? Everything will be fine?"

My body grew heated, and my heart began pounding. Fuck it. I needed him.

He saw the surrender in me. Triumph flared in his gaze, but instead of closing the distance, he moved away. As he put more distance between us, I groaned in protest. No. It wasn't going to happen. As he let go of my hand, I snaked it behind his neck, grabbed a fistful of his hair, and pulled his head to mine. Our lips pressed together. Then his arms wrapped around me, and my legs wound around his waist. Feeling his mouth, hot and hungry on mine, I let him do whatever he wanted. I wanted him to do more. Holding me and kissing me wasn't enough.

I grinded against him, feeling the pleasure building. Shit. An ache was building in every part of my body.

Then he ripped his mouth from mine and dropped me. I felt his fury directed at me, and he shook his head, slowly, staring down at me. My body trembled, wrecked through and through, and I couldn't speak.

The torture was there, looking back at me. "Bri." His hands went to my hips, and he crowded me against the wall once more. I closed my eyes, feeling the touch of his hands on me. My jeans had ridden low while my shirt had moved up. He was touching my bare skin. A soft caress, and I swallowed, feeling a burn where they touched. My skin was shivering. It was begging for more of him, but those fingers remained firm. They didn't move.

He said, "I have been there for you, all your life."

Hearing a note of finality, my gaze found his and hung there.

He added, sounding sad, "I have crawled into your bed more times than I can remember. I have held your hand. I have hugged you, carried you at times, and watched as you walked away from me. One touch." His palm pressed against my chest. He flattened it, but it didn't move. It stayed there, as if literally cupping my heart. It pounded like it wanted to go to him, straining toward his hold. He shook his head. "This is what happens. I can own you." His breath coated my face again. He was so close. "I can own your body, make you do anything I want..."

He hated me. I was almost panting for him.

I was pathetic.

He added, "You and me, we'll never be what we were." He grinded against me, and I bit down on my lip. A groan escaped me. I wanted what he was promising me. He laughed against my face, and I felt it graze my cheeks. Then he said, "Unless it's this, because this is all I'll give you. Nothing else. Not again."

My heart was pounding. I couldn't look away.

His chest was heaving. "I don't know why you came here. I won't give you anything else except…" He waved a hand at me.

My arousal was evident to both of us, but so was his. Lidded eyes looked back at me, darkened in desire, but there was steel determination, too. He wouldn't give in, no matter what. A deeper part of me ached for him. I missed our friendship.

"I'm sorry." I wasn't sure what I was apologizing for. All of it? Only what he knew, not what he didn't know? I wasn't sure anymore. My mind was muddled.

"I thought it'd be fine, having you with the band, but it's not. You've avoided me for three years, and *this* is what happens between us. How long until my dick is deep inside you?"

His hunger was raw. "Luke," I whispered.

"Go, Brielle. I'll act normal. You will, too. If we can keep up our game faces, everything will be fine. I'll be nicer, and maybe Braden won't worry about it then." He moved back another step, putting more distance between us. The farther he went, the clearer my mind became.

I nodded to myself. He was right. About everything. It was either sex or nothing. We were no longer friends. My fingers curled, holding onto the sides of my jeans. I ached to be in his arms again.

"Go."

I started for the stairs.

"Wait."

I stopped, my pulse was pounding.

"Just so we're clear." His eyes were stormy, but cold again. "I'm allowing you to play because you draw more attention to the band. If you want out, say the word. I'll ask Gunn to join then." He went back to pick up his guitar.

"Okay." I raked a hand through my hair, my chest still heaving. I felt drunk from him. My pulse was still throbbing. I had to get out of there. Making my way back up the stairs, I ignored the kitchen, even though I felt the memory still there, lingering in the back of my mind. I stepped off the porch and headed for the sidewalk when I heard a movement and glanced over.

Elijah was standing on the sidewalk, just a few feet from me. His hands were in his sweatshirt, with the hood up, and he smirked at me. "When are you going to grow some balls and tell him what happened?"

"Shut up." Now was *so* not the time. "I only told you because I was drunk one night."

"It wasn't your fault what happened to him."

Yes, it was. "Go away, Elijah."

He nodded and turned around. Before he left, he glanced back. "I came to make sure you were okay, you know."

"Just go." We were done. We were over. He needed to leave. "Focus on whatever you do nowadays. Selling drugs, expanding your fucked-up empire, whatever it is. I'm not a part of it anymore."

He bit out a laugh and started to move forward. "You never were, Bri. I always kept you pure."

I snorted at the thought. Pure. I was the furthest thing from that.

A soft laugh came from him as he walked down the sidewalk. The sound faded as he disappeared around the block. It sent a chill through me, but I ignored it and crossed the street back to my apartment building. Not that I expected to get any sleep.

CHAPTER
NINE

"So, the band's name is Braille, right?"

I stopped filling a bowl with chips as Dustin grabbed a handful of them, filled his mouth, and grabbed for a second handful. He had become an almost permanent fixture next to me when he showed up earlier. After dinner with our mom, Braden made me come to a party at Luke's house. I hadn't wanted to go, but he told me the band would play at some point during the night, so I didn't feel like I could turn it down. I was in the band. I had to be there. And because I sucked at being social, sign me up for chip duty.

"Dustin, why are you here again?"

"Because you guys are awesome." He licked his fingers and reached for another handful. I knocked his arm aside and filled a separate bowl. His eyes lit up, but before he could reach for it, I gave him the entire first bowl. He added, "And because of future pussy. I know there's going to be mountains and mountains of vagina buffets. I already told you earlier that I'm not dumb. You guys are going to be dripping—" He stopped at my glare. "Well, not you, because you know," he gestured to my chest, "you have a mighty fine rack yourself."

"Dustin!"

"I'm just stating the obvious. You're a chick. You're not going to get those juices, well, unless you bat for the other team. I'd be all for that." He winked at me.

"I'm going to neuter you."

"Oh. Kay. Back to the first question." He continued to beam at me, his cheeks plump and moving around as he ate his chips. Around a mouthful, he asked again, "So, the band's name is Braille, right?"

I groaned, but went back to the cupboards for more chips. "Yes. Why do you keep asking?"

Keeping his bowl of chips close to his chest, he followed behind me. "The band's name was kinda named after you, right? Brielle. Braille. I get that part."

"Yes," I clipped out, walking around a group of girls chugging their beer. "Brielle and Braden. The guys thought it was funny. Why?"

"I remember when you guys first started the band, but you left it, right?"

I was gritting my teeth. For some reason, this guy was getting on my last nerve. "Dustin," I warned.

He leaned over my shoulder, too close for comfort. "Yeah?"

"Get to the point and then back the fuck off me."

"Oh." He moved his body back, but continued to lean forward so his head was right next to my ear. "That better?"

"No." I grabbed the rest of the chips and wound back through the crowd. Instead of filling the bowls, I just dumped the bags onto the tables. People could do with them what they pleased. Then I went in search for Braden.

Dustin went with me. "So yeah," he kept going with his question, "you quit the band, and they kept the name, but now you're back with them?"

"Yes. So what?"

He stuffed another handful of chips into his mouth and shrugged, cocking his head to the side. "I guess nothing. I'm just trying to get all the history down in my head."

Spying Braden in a corner with Luke, I veered toward them. They were surrounded by a group of girls. No surprise there.

"For what?" I asked Dustin.

"I'll make a great head roadie. Putting that out there."

As I got next to my brother's side, I rotated my head toward Dustin, taking in his over six-foot frame. He appeared to be a mix of all-American-boy and preppy-douchebag-frat-boy. His blue eyes, blond wavy hair, and square jaw made him look like an innocent, nice guy.

"Dustin," I said.

"Hmm?" He flicked at his earlobe. "All ears here." He chuckled to himself, putting another chip into his mouth.

"You were a popular jock in school with us."

He bobbed his head up and down. "I'm with you. I was."

"Your parents are rich."

A second bob, followed with another wink. "Still are, I believe."

"You got kicked out of Harvard, right?"

"Oh, yeah. Too much booze and chicks." His head was continuously moving up and down, going along with each question I asked. "Living the carefree life, I might add."

"And you're kissing my ass because you're hoping for a future spot as the head roadie with the band?"

"Yep. If you guys will have me."

"Why?" I was dumbfounded. "You should be interning at your dad's company, whatever it is that made *Forbes* magazine."

He snapped his fingers and pointed at me. "See. That's why. I don't want that responsibility, not yet anyway. Here I am. Living a hobo-lifestyle." He patted the bowl. "Got my chips." He gestured to Braden and Luke. "Got some future rock star friends." Then he sent a charming wink at the group of girls who had been talking to Braden and Luke. "And hopefully some future ass, too."

Some of the girls laughed, while another gasped. One girl gave him the middle finger. A second rolled her eyes, but none of them left.

"I said hopefully, ladies. Hopefully." He pointed to Luke, Braden, and me. "These are good people, my future people." Lifting his hand, he crossed his fingers. "Here's to hoping, anyway."

Braden and Luke were grinning. At the sight of the relaxed amusement on Luke's face, I was startled for a moment. My body warmed at the sight, and the corners of my own mouth curved up in response. Because he smiled, I wanted to smile. Then he glanced to me, and the smile faded. So did mine. I was zapped by the abrupt change.

He leaned forward, murmured something to Braden, and left.

I watched him go and felt the kick of rejection against me. It had been like this for a month now. Since talking to him, things had gotten better. A tiny bit. We performed, and once we were on stage, everyone clicked. It shouldn't have been like that, but that was the one place all four of us didn't hate each other. It was like all the bullshit had vanished, and we were back in the beginning. Emerson was easygoing.

Braden was...still Braden. Luke was my best friend again, and I loved everybody. As soon as we were done, though, the same tension immediately returned. Awkward silence was the norm now, as we set up before our gigs and as we tore down afterward. There was no gig planned for this weekend, and a part of me had looked forward to a weekend of working at Rowdy's and not feeling chewed up inside and out, just by being around Emerson and Luke.

I hadn't known about the party until Braden mentioned it earlier. And watching Luke walk away, for what felt like the hundredth time this month, I had enough. I stormed after him without thinking.

I bumped into two of the girls at the same time, pushing them back.

"Hey," one girl cried out.

The other hissed under her breath, "Bitch."

I skewered both of them with a look.

They wanted Luke. There were so many girls, always the same, always wanting to end up in bed with him. I wanted to obliterate them, all the time, all at the same time, and it was becoming a different hunger all on its own inside me. I did my best to ignore the feeling as I followed Luke across the road to Rowdy's. He went inside through the back door and down the basement stairs.

It was raining, but I didn't feel it.

The bar was louder than normal. Cheers, hollering, and music crashed against my eardrums, along with the smell of smoke and sweat. I gritted my teeth. Good. I wanted to yell, and the basement was a perfect place to get it out.

When I pushed open the last door, after going down the stairs, I didn't hold back. I didn't think I was able to anymore. "You can't keep leaving."

Luke was behind the bar. He straightened, a bottle of whiskey in one hand. "What?"

"You can't keep leaving. This is ridiculous."

"What are you talking about?"

I flung my hand out in the direction of his house. Pointing at the air in a savage motion, I added, "Before. Just now. I came up to the group, and you left." I missed my friend. "I'm sick of it. I'm sick of you. I'm sick of *this*. It's been a month of this. If you won't let me in, then…" my chest was heaving, and I spat out, "let me go!"

Aw, shit. I didn't mean that. Dread quickly lined the bottom of my stomach. He was going to kick me out, once and for all. It was going to be the end, and *I would never get him back.* I was startled at the vehemence behind that thought.

My eyebrows bunched together. It had just hit me. I hadn't joined the band to be in the band. It wasn't about staying away from Elijah. It wasn't about making Braden happy. It wasn't even about me playing the drums again, although now that I got back to it, I didn't think I could quit again. No. This was all about Luke. Ever since he picked me up. It had taken root in me then, and the yearning for him had dug deep, burrowing so much inside me that I had forgotten he was even there.

I wanted *us* back. It wasn't just about sex.

A dark storm was brewing in Luke's eyes. His knuckles were white as he gripped the neck of the whiskey bottle. "Are you fucking with me?"

"No." With a deep breath, I raised my chin. "But I want to."

His eyes widened, and he jerked back from the bar. Then his chest went up and held. "What did you say?"

Screw it. The decision fell into place. Everything lined up perfectly, and I wet my lips. This was the real reason I followed him. I wanted him, any way I could get him. "You heard me. Sex or nothing. I can't do nothing." Not anymore.

His chest abruptly fell and rose back up again in a gaping breath. His jaw was clenched, and his eyes were dark with the same hunger that was gnawing inside me, but he wasn't moving. Why wasn't he moving?

He couldn't move, a voice whispered in the back of my head to me.

I had left him three years ago. It was my turn to go to him, so I said a small prayer in my mind and started forward. My foot moved out in an unsteady motion. He turned, watching me, as I made the slow progress to him. One step at a time. My knees shook, my palms were sweaty, and my vision blurred as I focused on his face. I took that last step around the bar and stood inches away from him.

Now or never.

Please, don't reject me, I silently prayed. I wasn't sure how many rejections a girl could take.

"Luke." I raised a hand.

His chest was moving up and down at a rapid pace now, and his eyes never left mine. The hunger was there, but he was holding back. My arm began trembling. I forced my fingers to spread out so my palm touched his chest. I felt his strength pulsating underneath my hand. Moving my hand lower, I could feel his heart under my palm, and I closed my eyes.

Please, Luke, I whispered in my head. *Please, touch me back.*

My forehead rested against his chest. I stood there, feeling him. One touch. I ached for it, and then his hands went to my hips. It was a light touch at first. I felt him take a deep breath at the same time, and then in a nanosecond, everything switched. His hands grasped me hard, lifting me in the air as he crushed me to his chest. I was placed onto the counter, and he was between my legs. Strong. Commanding. Hot. All those sensations blasted me at the same time. His touch was demanding as he gripped me to him.

"Bri." His tone was hoarse.

I opened my eyes, seeing his burning brightly down into mine. Then I gasped softly. There was something else there, more than just desire. Recognizing it, my pulse raced, but I couldn't let myself admit what it was. If I did, and if I was wrong, he would shatter me.

Slowly, so agonizingly slowly, his forehead came down to rest on top of mine as his eyes kept boring into me. One of his hands held a firm grip on my hip as the other touched my cheek tenderly. He traced his fingers over my cheek, down to my lips. His thumb held the underside of my jaw, and he tilted my head back. I felt like I was pleading for him to touch his lips to mine.

He tucked some of my hair behind my ear. "Are you sure it's over with him?"

My throat had swollen, so I couldn't talk. I nodded instead.

His hand trailed down my arm, taking hold of both of my hips again, and he tugged me to the edge of the counter. My legs fell open, wrapping around his waist. Every inch of us was pressing into the other, but I wanted to get closer. I had to. Too damn long we'd been apart. His touch was like oxygen to me. I began to move against him, rubbing up and down. My lips opened, and his gaze darted down, lingering there now.

He asked again, "You're not going back to him?"

There was no way I could do it now, not after…I knew where this was going. His hand left the counter and slid underneath my legs. He tipped me backwards, slowly lowering me until I was on the counter. Under heavy eyelids, I watched him, feeling exposed as I waited for his continued touch. We had made out and slept in the same bed, but we had never *been* together. His hands held my hips, anchoring me, but he didn't close the distance.

I couldn't taste him yet, and the need was escalating. I was beginning not to care what happened later. I needed this night.

"Bri," he murmured, his breath caressing me again. I couldn't talk, so I sat back up. His fingers caught my shirt and pulled at the corner while his knuckles grazed my side. "What is this?" he asked, his voice gruff. "Just sex?"

I didn't care. I didn't respond, but I would take anything at that moment. If that made me pathetic or weak, so be it. I just needed *him*. Sliding my hands under his shirt, I pushed it up until he took it off. It was tossed to the floor, his eyes glancing up once to catch mine before falling back to my lips. Then I leaned forward, just a tiny bit until my lips pressed harder against his. I waited, my heart pounding all the way in my eardrums. The hunger was so deep, and then Luke let out a breath, and I knew it was time. His lips opened over mine, claiming me, and I arched forward to meet him.

Everything went up a notch. His hands lifted me from the counter, and I wrapped my legs tighter around his waist. Wherever he was going, it didn't matter. As his tongue swept inside, a part of me sighed from contentment. This was it. This was enough. The taste of him was everything I had missed, and I couldn't get enough. As he lowered me to a bed, I ran my hands over him, anchoring him to me this time.

He gasped against my lips, but then reared back and ripped off my shirt. He tore the straps on my bra so it fell away. As my fingers went to his jeans, his went to mine, but it wasn't enough. He held me in the air and pulled off my pants. My underwear was torn away like my bra, and then he stopped, his chest heaving for air, and I lay back, panting the same. My pulse was pounding all over. I hadn't realized how strong until that one touch from him.

It was blinding.

With eyes that were almost black, he watched me. Holding his gaze, I pushed his jeans down. His boxers went next, and he sprang forward. As my hand went to him, he bent at the same time to lift me further up the bed, coming with me as he reached for a condom at the same time. Holding himself up with one hand, he gazed at me, never leaving me as I began to caress him. He was hard. His heartbeat matched mine. I could feel it from him, and I licked my lips. One taste wasn't enough. As he bent down and touched his lips to mine, I knew it wasn't ever going to be enough.

As he pushed inside me and began thrusting, I clung to him. My head fell back against the pillow, but I moved with him. Our hips were joined. Every inch of us touched the other. We were fused together. This was what I had been missing for so long. This was our first time together, but it had been missing from my life.

He rose above me, over and over through the night, and I knew without a doubt that I was addicted to him. There was no going back.

CHAPTER
TEN

Luke trailed kisses up my throat, poised over me, and I tilted my head up, enjoying the feel of his lips. Hearing my own groan, I laughed and peeked open one eye. He smirked down at me. He asked, "Enjoying yourself?"

Running my hands up his back, I applied pressure under my nails, letting them lightly scratch his back. He always loved this, and when his eyes closed again, I knew he was enjoying it again. He was distracted, so I scooted down in the bed, wound my legs around his waist, above his hip bones, and pushed myself up as I used my legs to pull him down at the same time. Our positions were reversed with me on top.

Luke's eyes opened, and he ran a hand underneath my shirt. "That was nice and smooth."

Straddling him, I sank down on him, rubbing myself over the front of his jeans. We had come home from school earlier. We were supposed to be writing songs for the band, but that turned into flirting, and eventually all pretenses were given up. We headed upstairs to Luke's bedroom, and for the last hour we had been sharing kisses and much more. My hand fell down to his jeans. They'd been unbuttoned earlier, but that was the farthest we had gone.

"Bri." Luke sucked in his breath, stilling under my hand.

Feeling brave, braver than normal, I bit down on my lip, and my hand slipped inside his jeans. His hands fell to my hips, and he gripped them hard. Feeling the power my touch had over him, I wanted to do more.

The sides of his mouth were strained, but he jerked it up into a smile, remaining still under my hand. One of his hands left my hip and cupped the side of my face. His thumb traced over my cheek softly, as he asked, "What are you doing?"

"I want to." I looked down at where my hand was between us. I didn't say anything more, and before Luke could question me again—he was always making sure I was okay—I shifted down on his lap. Feeling him through his boxers, my hand went inside. He was already hard, but at the touch of my finger, he sprang upward.

"Bri," he whispered.

I looked up and saw his eyes were clouded. He was enjoying the touch of my hand, so I rubbed my finger up and down. His eyes closed. Slowly, he lay back down, and I wrapped my whole hand around him, just holding him for a while.

I was enjoying this power over him.

"Luke," I started to say. I wanted to do even more.

"Bri?"

I shook my head. I was going to do this for him. Other girls had done this for their boyfriends. Luke wasn't my boyfriend. We never gave ourselves a title, but he was mine. We were best friends. Everyone knew about our connection. I wanted to feel him in my mouth, but I was nervous. If I did this—and my mouth watered just thinking about it—maybe I could finally call him my boyfriend. He never asked me to be his. Neither did I. We just were, but I wanted to know. I wanted to call him my boyfriend and not just 'my Luke,' even though everyone already knew he was mine.

I slowly lowered my head closer to him. "Hey, hey." Luke sat up, pulling away from me.

I looked up, confused. "What's wrong?" The rejection hit me immediately. He didn't want me to do that for him. He didn't want me, repeated in my mind. Luke didn't want me after all.

"Stop," he said, lifting my head so I was looking him directly in the eye. It hurt. There was pity in his. I tried to look away, swallowing back the bile burning in my throat. I didn't want him to feel sorry for me when he turned me down.

"Hey," he said again. He caught my face and held me firmly.

I couldn't look away, but I wanted to. His rejection hurt.

"This is not what you think." He shook his head. His other hand went to my waist, and he lifted me off him. Holding me in the air for a moment, he scooted back and then placed me back on his lap. He was sitting upright, his back against the wall. When I tried to move away, he caught both sides of my face and turned me so we were nose to nose. He was looking into me now. I felt like he was stripping me bare, exposing how much I loved him, and deciding I wasn't enough for him.

"Stop."

I had yet to talk. The burning was too much. I shook my head instead.

"I love you."

What? My eyes widened, and I stopped fighting. Had I heard that right?

The lines around his mouth softened, and he traced his fingers through my hair, smoothing my tendrils back and tucking them behind my ears. His fingers continued to rub down my jaw, falling to linger on my lips. He rubbed his thumb over them, and a rakish smirk appeared on his face. He said again, "Did you hear that? I know what you were going to do, and I want that. Holy shit, do I want that, but I wanted to tell you those words first."

He loved me. Relief and joy pushed all the other emotions aside. I couldn't talk again, though. The feelings were overwhelming.

"Do you?"

I laughed, my voice was raspy, and I nodded. Some tears fell from my eyes. Luke wiped them aside. "You do?"

"Yes," I whispered.

He nodded, his gaze falling back to my lips. "My dad's going to be home soon. I don't want..." He trailed off as he indicated the bed.

He didn't want it to be here, not when we could be interrupted.

I nodded in a jerking motion. "Okay."

We heard the door open at that moment, followed by loud footsteps. The wood protested and creaked from under his father's weight. Then his deep voice boomed a second later, "Luke?! You here?"

Luke shook his head. His hands fell to wrap around me, pulling me against his chest. His forehead lowered to rest on my shoulder, and I felt his lips brush against my neck as he said, "See? Perfect timing, huh?"

I didn't care. His dad was an ass, but I didn't give a damn right then. My hand cradled the back of his head, and my fingers tangled in his hair. "We can go to my place."

"Yeah," he continued to whisper.

"Luke?" His dad's voice was louder and clearer. He was at the bottom of the stairs. "You up there? Answer me."

"He's going to come up here."

We had to go. I nodded and slipped off his lap, going to his window.

I awoke to those same kisses being trailed up my throat, and it took only a slight second for everything to register. This was present day. That had been the past, before everything went wrong, and Luke was back. Luke was with me. I felt him push inside me, and my body reacted, instantly curving to move with him, my hips adjusting so he could go deeper.

Raising my hand, he pressed it to the headboard above me. He smirked down at me. "Morning," he said as he moved out, then back in. Harder. Deeper.

My throat choked on a gasp. My lips opened, and I managed to get out, "Morning to you, too."

He slid out, and then paused at my opening.

My eyes widened. "Wha—"

He shoved inside again, and the corner of his mouth lifted. His other hand held my hip prisoner as he slid out and slammed back inside. He kept going, in and out, in and out, all the while holding my gaze. Wave after wave of pleasure filled me. I stretched out, savoring the feel of him. He was all over me, claiming me. As he kept going, my hips moved with him. Rolling my head to the side, still holding his gaze, I gave him a side-grin, and he chuckled. He caught my chin, making me look him square in the eye again.

I didn't know what was going on, if he wanted to dominate me, but I loved it. Feeling his thumb enter my mouth, my tongue flicked up to meet him, and he pulled it back out. He trailed his thumb down my neck, between my breasts, and all the way over my stomach. His hand lingered at the tip of me, rubbing slightly there.

I gasped, the sensations mingled with the pleasure of him inside me. They wound together, and I couldn't think or talk. My hand held onto his shoulders, just grasping there, as he kept moving inside me at the same time as his finger was rubbing over me.

The tremors were building in me. I felt them coming. I didn't want it to end. I wanted to be woken up like this every morning, but as he began thrusting faster and harder, going so damned deep, my climax was rising. Building. It was going to crash through and then—I surged up, pressing against him—it filled all of me.

I went over the edge. As the aftershocks were still clambering in me, making my body physically shake, Luke caught me against him.

He held me in place, pausing in his thrusts. He hadn't come, so I knew he would start again so he could finish, but he was waiting until I was done. As soon as my trembling slowed and a deep satiation filled my bones, he began moving in me again.

This was for him.

I lay back down and held onto his shoulders. His hands rested on either side of me, and he began to thrust harder again. As he did, his head bent. He was riding me hard. One of his hands went back to gripping my thigh and then, without warning, he pulled out and flipped me over. I had a second to grab hold of the bed before he slammed back in from behind me. Taking hold of my hair, the other hand resting on my back, he was pumping harder and harder, his hips going strong against mine with each thrust. Then, with a guttural groan, I felt him come, and he collapsed on top of me.

One of his arms wound underneath us, and he hugged me to him.

I felt his heart start to slow, felt his body began to cool off, as mine did as well. We lay there like that for another moment. Then it started to trickle back to me.

I had come to him.

I had begged him.

I had stripped myself open to him.

I bit down on my lip. What next? Would he leave? I wanted to grab the blanket and cover myself, but then Luke did that. He covered both of us after tossing the condom into the trash, and he moved beside me. "You want coffee?"

Coffee.

He asked about coffee.

I blinked rapidly. "That'd be nice."

"Okay." Slipping out from the covers, he tucked them back in place behind me, and I could hear him pulling on his jeans. I was lying on my side, so I didn't turn over to watch what else he was doing, but he crossed to my side of the room where the thermostat was.

"What are you doing?"

He didn't look back at me, but his shoulder muscles shifted under his skin. His thumb touched something on the thermostat. He glanced over his shoulder to me. "It's cold in here. I'm turning the heat up."

"Oh."

"Are you cold?"

I heard his question, but I was distracted by his tattoos. I'd gotten a peek at them earlier, and I saw them last night, but I hadn't really looked. Sitting up, wrapping the blanket better around me, I inspected them now. They were birds. I counted three of them, and they ascended up his bicep and over his shoulder. It looked like they were flying off him. On the inside of his side, under his arm, a large tribal tattoo was there.

I pointed at them. "What do they mean?"

He'd been waiting for my response, but a frown graced his features. The atmosphere in the room shifted. It'd been light, intimate, but it was tense and distant now. Not knowing why, I held my tongue. My instincts were warning me to tread lightly here, then I heard Luke answer in a quiet voice, "Each bird stands for someone who has left me." He came over and sat next to me. Lifting his arm, he pointed at each bird. "My mom. My dad." His eyes fell to my lips as he pointed at the last one. "You."

My stomach flipped over on itself. Why would he want to remember who had left him?

"They're reminders that no matter who leaves you, you keep going. You persevere. No matter what, but." He shook his head as a laugh left him, sounding regretful. He raked a hand over his head. "Anyway, that's too heavy for now. How about coffee? Did you still want some?"

"Yes." My throat was dry. He had a tattoo for when I left him. I… hated that.

"Okay. I'll get some from upstairs quick."

"Wait." He started to stand. My hand caught his and tugged him back down. "We're at Rowdy's."

He nodded. The sight of his smile transformed his entire face. Luke had a mesmerizing beauty to him, and as he smiled, it had the same effect that I witnessed the night before. It kicked up his charisma. It's what pulled people in.

He sighed, shaking his head as he stood. "No one will be around. I've stayed the night here before."

With other women. Reality crashed back down on me. Luke wasn't mine. He hadn't been in so long. He'd been with others, and I knew there would be so many more.

I moved back. "Right. What was I thinking?"

He moved to the door. "You were thinking we'd be caught, but no one's here this time of day. Kelly always locks up around three in the morning. She won't be back in until eleven, ten at the earliest."

"Yes, you're right."

He paused before slipping out the door. "You okay?"

"Of course."

He stared at me, his eyes squinting, and he raked a hand through his hair. His head tilted at an angle. "Listen," he hesitated. His hand grabbed a fistful of his hair. "Things are weird with us. Getting that phone call pissed me off. The one you made from the police station."

What? I sat up, readjusting the sheet so I was still covered. That'd been a while ago. "Why?" I could almost feel my heart pausing. Luke kept so much from me. We had sex, but I knew there was a cement wall around his heart. I'd once been lucky to be allowed past that wall.

Was he going to let me back in?

His hand grabbed the doorframe above his head. Leaning there, that pose accentuated how lean he was. He was the image of a panther stretching. "I know it's dumb, but Turner got you in trouble. You *finally* called for help. I know you were calling your brother, but I was here, and he wasn't. I was happy, but I was damn mad at you. Mad at him, too, for putting you in that position. A lot of the shit inside me from the past few years came out, and I've been a dick since then. I kept waiting for you to go back to him, but you didn't, and I don't know." He let go, and his arm dropped back to his side. He was lost in thought, and his hand raked through his hair again. "I'm sorry. For everything. I should've shut down Emerson more than I did. I should've done a lot of things."

My hands curled into the blanket, pulling it tighter around me. I wasn't sure what to say to that. It was…my heart was right there, pressed against my chest. My throat swelled up, and I managed out, "Thank you."

He let his arm drop a second time. "Yeah. I know I said a while back it was sex or nothing, and you've been nice, really nice, actually."

"What are you saying?" I sat further upright. The blanket was wrapped so tightly around me now, but I pulled even harder on it. A red mark was going to stretch across my chest soon.

"Nothing really." He gave me a half-grin. "It doesn't have to be just sex or nothing. I don't know if that's why you followed me here last night. I don't want you to feel...I have no idea what I'm saying. I just wanted to apologize for being an asshole since you came back around."

Now I was really confused. "Luke." I shook my head. "We just had sex."

"I know."

"A lot of sex."

The other corner of his mouth twitched up. "I'm aware."

"I didn't fuck you so you'd be nice to me."

His eyebrows shot up. "I know. I know. I'm not saying—Bri. I'm not saying that."

"Good." My hand let go of the blanket, just a bit. The material loosened around me, but I was still clutching onto it. "I didn't know where you were going with that."

He grunted, and his hand rested on the back of his neck. "Neither did I. This whole thing, you and me, I have no clue what's going on. You've got me spinning. Then again, you always did that to me before. I'd be wound so tightly, I didn't know if I was up or down some of the time."

"So?" My lips were suddenly dry. My tongue darted out to wet them, and I gestured to the bed. "What does this mean?"

He straightened from the doorway and took a step closer to me. His hand hooked on his jeans, hanging there. "That's what I'm saying. I've got no clue, but I won't be a dick anymore."

"Oh." I was confused. "Well...thank you?"

He gestured to the ceiling. "Listen, let me get some coffee. I'll come back down, and we can figure our shit out."

That sounded wonderful. I closed my eyes, relishing the sound of Luke heading upstairs. He was going to get something for me. He was coming back. We were going to talk about 'us.' My hand curled into the sheet. Us. I hadn't thought...I blinked back a sudden onslaught of tears. I hadn't thought this would ever happen. An emotion was filling me, but I didn't want to figure it out. I'd let it simmer there. I didn't want to deal with whatever the emotion was, because if I did, and if it didn't work out with Luke, I couldn't handle it. I needed to stop myself from jumping too far ahead.

There was an 'us.' That was enough.

For now.

CHAPTER
ELEVEN

KNOCK! KNOCK!

"Hey!"

Someone knocked again.

"Bri? Luke? Let me in!" A voice yelled through the back door as they kept pounding on it.

I had tensed at first and went to the basement doorway, but I held back. Recognizing Braden's voice, I relaxed, but when Luke walked across the floor for the door, my muscles tightened once again. He wasn't—I thought he'd call through the door, but not let him in. Nope. It was in slow motion, like watching an accident happening, but I couldn't stop it. His hand unlocked the door and wrapped around the doorknob. It twisted to the right, and yes, I sucked in my breath. He opened the door.

But nope.

His foot acted as a doorstopper. With only his head and shoulders in the doorway, Luke still blocked Braden from coming downstairs. I scurried from the doorway and grabbed my clothes. I could hear the murmur of conversation, but it was only a matter of moments before Braden pushed his way through, or Luke would let him inside. Either way, I knew my brother was going to see me in my post-coital glow. As I ran my hands through my hair, trying to smooth it out, I tried to tell myself this wasn't a walk-of-shame. I had nothing to be ashamed of, and I wasn't walking anywhere. Still. It was embarrassing.

"Yeah?" Braden's voice was clearer now.

The door opened.

He stepped inside, and Luke moved back, allowing him to enter. I double-checked my appearance in the mirror. I thought I looked okay. Rolling my eyes, I knew this was ridiculous. Like Braden wouldn't know what we had done?

The steps creaked under their weight. They were both coming downstairs.

"…we have to go. It'd be good for the band."

Luke replied, "She crashed here tonight. You can ask her."

"Hey!" Braden saw me.

I looked up. Moving from the bathroom, I smoothed out my shirt. My reflection showed that I looked presentable, but the mirror was more smudged than clean, so the real test would be my brother's reaction. He did nothing. He only threw his arm around my shoulder and jostled me. "My favorite twin sister."

"What do you want?"

He laughed, giving me a loving squeeze. "Nothing…that you shouldn't want."

My eyes narrowed. "Spill it, brother. I have a shift to get ready for in a couple of hours."

"Okay." He released me, but held up a finger. "One, you need to get out of that shift. Two, go home and shower. You reek of sex. That's like spoon-feeding Emerson. You know how he is."

Luke and I shared a look. Yep. He had noticed. I'd been an idiot to hope he hadn't. Crossing my arms over my chest, I tuned in as Braden continued with his list. He had four fingers in the air, saying, "…it's for the band. We can't not go, you know?" He waved those fingers at Luke. "Right? You're with me."

"I am."

"You are?" I cocked my head to the side. What was going on?

"Of course, he is." Braden was shaking his head, his eyes filling with disbelief. "You don't agree?"

"What is happening?"

The four fingers dropped back to his side, and my brother looked at me like I had grown an extra head. I checked both sides, and nope, there wasn't a second growth there. I murmured, "Say it again, Bray. I missed the third finger." I cringed. "And I didn't mean that how it came out."

The disbelief slid away, and my brother's eyes sparkled. The corners of his mouth pinched inwards as he tried not to laugh.

"Come on." I groaned. "Tell me what the third point was. I didn't hear it."

"Okay." Two short laughs slipped from him. "The Feast is tonight. You know, where all the bands get together and take turns jamming on the stage. No outsiders are allowed. Only everyone who matters—"

His chest puffed up. He was going to launch into a spiel about The Feast, but I held up a hand, stopping him. "We know what The Feast is. We're in the same band."

"I know." His mouth turned down. "Last year all those college students came. Not cool. I know it was Mel from D's Boobs that let everyone know. No outsiders allowed—"

Luke interjected, "Unless they're invited." His arms were crossed over his chest, and I tried not to stare at him. Ogling Luke in front of my brother, especially after the night we had, wasn't needed, but still…my eyes lingered on a bird tattooed over his bicep.

"One or two," Braden snapped. "Not thirty."

"I know." Luke's arms unfolded, and his hands slid inside his pockets. His jeans slipped an inch lower, exposing how his obliques cut into a V, heading downward. It was like a big arrow pointing where to go. My hand twitched, and my mouth watered. Goodness gracious. Ripping my eyes away, I knew my cheeks were flushed. I had to get ahold of myself, but I'd just been with him moments ago. The feel of his body on mine as his arms held me was addicting.

I wanted another taste.

"So, how about it?"

Braden's voice grated against my eardrums. He was waiting for my reply. Again. "Uh, sure."

"Really?" His eyes lit up.

What had I agreed to? My stomach tightened, and I looked at Luke. He was shaking his head with the corner of his mouth curled up.

"Good. Okay." Braden clapped his hands together. His fingers started tapping against each other. "Here's the plan. Brielle, you give your shift away, then go and shower. Luke," his nose wrinkled, "you shower, too. I have to check on Mom. She wasn't feeling good earlier, and then we can go." His hands separated and pointed in opposite directions. "Just don't shower together because I'm here, and that's gross. When you're done showering, come to the house. I'll call Emerson and have him meet us there. He doesn't need to ride with us. Band bonding is good, but the extra car ride might be too much bonding."

Band bonding? My mouth dropped. "What?"

"Okay." My brother ignored me and clapped his hands together once more. "We have a plan. I feel good about this. Be ready in thirty minutes. I'll grab the coffee and donuts." He didn't stick around. He dashed up the stairs. As the door closed behind him, I turned heated eyes to Luke. "What the hell did I just agree to? The Feast is tonight. It's always late at night and in the park."

He was shaking his head, but his shoulders were lifting slightly. "Paul Montrose—"

"From Shifter?"

"Yeah. He's hosting a pre-Feast shindig today."

"That's not bad. A car ride to his house…"

Luke moved back a step, scratching underneath his jaw.

"What?" This wasn't going to be good. I knew it…I waited.

"It's not at his house. It's at the river."

The river was an hour away. I squeaked out, "All day? That's how long this will go?"

His head moved up and down. "I'm sorry. I thought you heard your brother."

"Oh my god." I pressed my hands to my temples. They were throbbing already. "A whole day with Emerson?"

"I'll be there." His hand fell away and slid back inside his jean's pocket. "I should've stopped your brother from coming down. If it's any consolation, I think your brother just wants to go because Avi is going to be there."

I rolled my eyes. That made it worse. "So, my brother is subjecting me to an entire day of torture with Emerson so he can get in some hot singer's pants?"

The corner of his mouth twitched. "Apparently her vocals are supposed to be off the charts."

"Grammy winning off the charts?"

Both corners of his mouth were stretched. He was trying not to laugh. "I guess. Does that make it better?"

I groaned. "It's done. Avi's vagina had better be the best he's ever felt because a whole day with Emerson…" I shook my head. "Someone's going to end up in the hospital."

***

It was nuts when we got there.

"Took you long enough, my future band masters." The first person we saw was Dustin. Barefoot and wearing only black swimming trunks and a yellow inner tube around his waist, he lifted his beer in a salute. When we got closer, we could see a small rubber ducky was duct taped onto the inner tube. A six-pack of beer dangled from his waist, hanging from a cord that had been looped around the inner tube.

"What the…" Braden stopped beside me, holding a cooler of beer on his shoulder. "I thought this shindig was insiders only."

Dustin's hand went to his chest. "That hurts, my future best friend. Insiders only? I'm a Grant West purebred." His hand went to the rubber ducky. "Is no one going to mention my buddy here?"

I didn't care.

Braden scratched the back of his neck.

Luke's eyebrows bunched forward.

"That hurts." Dustin squeezed the duck so it squeaked. "His name is Hitchcock. He's a rebel."

"How'd all these people get invited?" Braden asked, scowling.

"Okay." Dustin indicated behind him, his hand sweeping out like he was on *The Price is Right*. "Yes, I'll admit I might've overextended my privileges of being your future head roadie, but these fine folk heard the words 'river,' 'drinking,' and 'bands.' I couldn't fight them off with a bat. They were salivating over the idea of hanging out with some local bands, especially one that's going to be famous." His hand moved back in front of him, and he pointed at us with a finger. "That's you guys."

The river was a specific spot where people were able to camp, barbeque, swim, and fish. It wasn't known to a lot of people, but a few guys from another band found the spot five years ago. It was spread by word of mouth, and eventually anyone who was in a band, knew a band, followed a band, or were friends with a band knew about the place. There was no parking lot, only a large patch of grass, and the beach was a sand bar. As Dustin was speaking, a group of girls ran past us in their bikinis, wearing straw hats and cowboy boots. One of the girls paused long enough for me to read Grant West University on the back of her bikini bottom.

It wasn't a local secret anymore.

I skimmed the line of cars. "I'm betting there are twenty cars here."

Braden scowled, tightening his grip on the cooler. "No outsiders allowed."

"Paul's coming." Luke pointed ahead of us where a guy had broken apart from the crowd. He was walking toward us, moving in a quick gait.

Like the last time we saw him, he was gripping a beer in his hand and waved with his other. "Hey, guys. I'm glad you could come." He pointed over his shoulder. "This was all last minute. A bunch of us thought an all-day party was the way to go today." He put two fingers to his mouth, making a sucking sound. "You know, we didn't want the party to stop, but, yeah. Emerson was there. I gave him the invite. He was supposed to let you guys know. When he didn't show this morning, I figured I should get ahold of one of you guys. You never know with him, do ya?"

Emerson at a party? I muttered under my breath, "What a shocker."

Dustin's duck squeaked.

"Everyone looks drunk." Braden bent down, setting the cooler onto the ground. "There's no way everyone's going to be able to drive to Grant West tonight. The Feast is happening here tonight."

Just then, someone struck up a guitar chord, and a loud 'whoop' filled the air. One of the bands was warming up their instruments. It wasn't long before a crowd had gathered around them, and people started dancing on the sidelines.

"Yeah, we've been calling everyone today, letting them know the change of location." Paul saluted us with his beer. "We'll do it proper next year. It looks like they're starting up a jam session. You guys are welcome to join, as always. In fact, I know they wanted you guys to come. Bri," Paul said to me, "some of the new bands were hoping to talk to you. They're looking for a good drummer, thought you might know of someone."

"She's ours," my brother growled.

"Braden." Luke's eyes flashed a warning. "Chill."

"Sorry," he said to Paul. "Sorry, man. I just don't like the idea of outsiders coming in. I liked our tradition how it was." His eyes skimmed over me, and I understood my brother's concern. If The Feast was overrun with outsiders, it was no longer just ours. It was theirs. It became about performing instead of playing music. Then his head shot to the right, and he asked, "Is that Avi?"

Without waiting for a response, Braden grabbed the cooler and took off, heading for a girl who was swaying back and forth. Her hands were weaving in the air like she was playing an invisible cello, her head was back, and her eyes were closed.

"Braden's got a thing for vocal chords." Dustin was petting the duck as if it were a real pet. "Cool. She's hot."

Paul asked us, "He must not be that upset?"

"He'll get over it." Luke stepped forward and clapped Paul on the shoulder. "Braden cares about music and ass. He'll get both here tonight. It might be fun, doing The Feast like this for the year."

"Hey, Paul!" a shout came from the group. A girl was jumping up and down, pumping her arms back and forth each time she launched herself in the air. "Come on!"

He started heading for her, but threw over his shoulder to us, "I'll see you guys over there. There's lots of food and booze, among other things."

Dustin moved closer to us as Paul jogged back to the group. "Hey…" His tone was suddenly serious, very unlike Dustin.

The hairs on the back of my neck rose.

He added, "I gotta warn you two. I overheard some conversations from some of the people." His hand slapped against his chest. "Not my people, other people. Like, people I didn't invite, but aren't in all your 'inner musician' circle, if you know what I mean."

"Yeah, yeah." My unease spiked. "What'd you overhear?"

"There are dudes here who don't like your ex." Dustin's eyes darted to Luke's and held there for a moment before swinging back to mine. His hand had a death grip on Hitchcock's neck. The air was pushing all the way up into the head and was straining at the ends. His duck was going to explode. "Paul doesn't know any of it, but there's a group who wanted Elijah called, but they're acting shady about it. They're hoping he comes with Emerson for some reason. He's got competitors, right?"

I heard the cop again, asking me, *"Someone else runs Grant East. Are they the ones moving in?"* Braden's voice overlapped hers, saying, *"Paul said some other guys were at the party— guys he didn't know. He asked Emerson about them, but Em was adamant that he needed to leave them alone."* An image of Paul flashed in my mind, as he walked around the side of his house, *"I wanted to call Elijah, but Emerson kept saying in the bedroom we couldn't call him…"*

I grabbed for Luke's arm. "Elijah can't come here." The words were out of me before I realized I had thought them, but I was right. These guys, whomever they were, were Eli's competitors. "It's too dangerous for him to come here."

I held still, knowing how that sounded. I was the ex, speaking up for Elijah, but it was the truth. "I'm sorry, Luke. We have to stop Elijah and Emerson."

"Too late."

Those words came from behind us, and we saw Elijah and Emerson, both standing there. My cousin was already scowling, but when wasn't he? He was decked out in sandals, swim trunks, and a tank top that had a large fist on the front of it. With sunglasses covering his eyes and a red cooler of beer, he looked ready for a day in the sun. Elijah, on the other hand, was the opposite. He was decked out in his usual wardrobe—a black sweatshirt and jeans over sneakers. However, his hood wasn't pulled up. He tilted his head to the side, and his hand scratched the bottom of his chin. He asked, "'Too late' for what, Bri? What are you hoping to stop us from?"

Luke and I shared a look. What did we do?

Luke decided for me. He gestured to the crowd behind us. "We think your competitors are here. Are you vying for new clients? Is that why you're here?"

"What?" Elijah narrowed his eyes.

Emerson stepped to the side. We were no longer two facing two, but more of a circle now. As he did, he glanced behind me and checked out the group, too, before turning so his back was slightly toward them. He lowered his voice. "Those are Brute's guys. You can't go over there, Eli. They'll think you're here on their territory."

Elijah was looking past our shoulders, his gaze firmly trained on the group. I had no doubt who he was looking at. The longer he studied them, the more my alarm rose. This wasn't Easygoing Elijah; this was Dangerous Elijah. I almost snorted. Of course. This side came out when it dealt with his business.

His eyes slid to mine. "You got a problem?"

"What are you going to do?" I jerked a thumb over my shoulder. "Fight 'em? Paul lives in Grant East—"

"What do you know about Grant East?"

"I know what the cops told me, you know, when they raided your house, and I got my ass hauled to the station. They said Brute runs Grant East. What are you doing here, Elijah?"

"My best friend asked me to come here. I came to hang out."

Emerson let out a deep groan, his hands shoving into his pockets. "This is going to suck. They've got four guys. Four to one. Those aren't good odds."

Elijah's top lip curled up into a sneer. "Thanks for having my back, Em. Really appreciate it."

"What?" Emerson held a hand out toward Luke. "My band's here. I'm not fucking that up. I'm not asking Braden or Luke to step in for me either. Look." His hand gripped the back of his neck. "Let's just go. We can party somewhere else."

All of us regarded Emerson. There was a moment of silence.

I burst out laughing. "Who are you, and where is my usual-hating cousin?"

Both of his lips curled up, and he was seething at me. "Don't start, Bri."

"You don't start," I shot back. "What the hell, Emerson? You're always up for a fight. You're always up for partying. And there are girls here, who, I'm sure, are only too eager to hook up with a musician. It's like shooting ducks in a barrel here, and you want to leave? Out of the goodness of your heart?"

"I'm looking out for my best friend." He stepped closer to me, his neck craning forward as a vein stood out. "Something you wouldn't know about." He gave both Elijah and Luke a meaningful look.

Now my blood was boiling. Crossing my arms over my chest, my chin lowered, setting in place. I was just getting started. "Fuck that. I was being nice just now. I was leaving out the big one, the one that seems to be your only priority. You know what else is here? Your favorite. Dru—"

"Okay." Luke clamped a hand over my mouth and pulled me into this chest. He kept his hand there, lifting his arm over my head so he could lead me away from Emerson. His other hand urged me forward, pressing against my hip. "Let's not do this. We're going to go. This probably isn't the best place for any of us to be, considering the circumstances."

I pulled his hand from my mouth. "My brother."

"I'll get him," Elijah said too quickly. He was walking toward the group before any of us could stop him.

"Oh, fuck." Emerson released a resigned breath of air. "This isn't going to end well."

"I'll stop him." Luke moved around me, and he was off, hurrying after my ex before I could blink an eye.

"What just happened here?" I grabbed my hair and held on. An anchor dropped to the bottom of my feet, and I couldn't move.

"Shit."

For once, my cousin wasn't spewing his hatred at me. He was focused solely on the impending clash that was going to happen as Elijah was already to the group. Luke was right behind him. As we watched like spectators, four guys I didn't recognize moved forward to meet Elijah. Three were shirtless and wearing swimming trunks. One wore jeans, but was still shirtless. He was tall, too tan, and looked like a bodybuilder. Two of the others had similar physiques, while the fourth was tall and lanky. All four of them were covered in tattoos, up and down their arms, over their chests, and around the necks.

As we waited, I felt my pulse starting to beat harder and harder.

Luke got to Elijah, and he pulled him to the side. Braden noticed them and stood. Avi slid off his lap, and he hurried over to them. All three stood in a small circle, having a conversation. Elijah looked over at his competitors. The one in jeans made a show of cracking his knuckles, and he smirked.

Luke moved so he was blocking Elijah's view, and he gestured to Emerson and me. Elijah wasn't concerned with us. He stepped around Luke, raising his chin at Jean Guy. The small gesture was enough of a challenge. Jean Guy started toward them, but then Paul stepped in the middle. He was strumming a guitar and inclined his head forward. He said something to Jean Guy, who was still watching Elijah. As if sensing the impending fight, a group of girls started dancing between the two groups. One girl, I recognized her as Avi, touched Paul on the shoulder and started belting out a song. She began swaying to the music again, and soon the crowd had moved over to completely block Elijah, Luke, and Braden from Jean Guy and his three friends. It was then that I let out an exaggerated burst of air.

Elijah, Luke, and Braden were heading back to us.

"What are you so goddamn worried about?" Emerson was glaring at me.

"You might not want to start with me."

"Oh, really?"

"Really."

He folded his arms over his chest, turning the same loathsome focus back on me. "Why do you say that?"

"Because I'm fairly certain those guys are your drug dealers, and Elijah won't like finding that out since you're his best friend."

"He won't sell to me."

My body had stiffened again. I expected another snarl from my cousin, but that was all he said. Then the guys were to us, and without saying a word, Elijah went past us, heading for his car. Emerson hightailed it behind him, leaving Braden and Luke with me.

All three of us waited and watched them go.

I had a feeling that we had escaped a disaster waiting to happen.

CHAPTER
TWELVE

After driving back, Braden wanted to go to Rowdy's to see Kelly, but first he headed home to check on our mom. She was still sick. When he got to the bar, he reported that she was sleeping, but it was my turn to check on her before bed. He was looking at Kelly as he said that and added, "And you have to sleep there."

I didn't ask where he was going to be. The answer was obvious. When I tried to help Kelly behind the bar, she waved me off so Luke and I played pool, drank beer, and hung out like we were best friends again. While watching my brother at the bar as he flirted with Kelly, I gripped my pool stick tightly for a moment.

I was happy.

I didn't want anything to take this moment away.

"You okay?"

Luke was waiting for me to take my shot. I replied, meaning it, "Yeah, I'm good."

"Good. Now don't sink the eight ball."

"Smart ass." I winked at him, then bent down, and hit the white ball. The eight ball was the only one left to sink, but I missed it. As Luke took his shot, I put my stick away. I didn't need to look to know he had won the game.

"What? You're calling it quits?"

Pointing at the clock, I said, "It's almost closing time, and Braden said it was my turn to check on our mom."

"I'll go with you."

My heart slammed against my chest. The day had been fine. There'd been people around us most of the day so that meant no 'talk' time, but hearing his voice as it dipped low, a tingle ran through me. I felt light-headed. Pressing a hand to my forehead, I felt myself nodding. My voice said, "Sure. That'd be great." The reply sounded like it came from a distance, like someone else had answered for me. But no, it was me.

Luke's hand touched the inside of my arm and slid down until his palm fitted into mine. He wasn't looking at me as he did it, and the whole motion was intimate. My mouth went dry. Feeling my stomach doing somersaults, I followed behind Luke as he led the way out of Rowdy's and across the street to my mom's house.

When we walked into the house, everything was dark. Braden had said she had gone to bed, so Luke waited as I cracked open her door. The room was dark. She was in the bed with the blankets pulled over her. She seemed fine, and I started to step back into the hallway, but a sixth sense pulled me to her bed. I didn't question it.

Flipping on the light, she still seemed fine... until I saw the blood seeping through her blanket.

I stopped, my hand instinctually pressing to my own stomach. Something was wrong. Then my body switched to automatic pilot, and I watched myself moving forward, reaching for the blanket, and pulling it back. There was blood between her legs. So much blood. Her pajamas were coated in it, and she was pale. I might've gasped, but I wasn't sure. Then Luke was behind me. His hands wrapped around my shoulders, and he moved me behind him.

I couldn't move. I couldn't look away from all that blood, and instead of seeing my mother's body, I was seeing his again.

I started trembling as the memories invaded me.

Luke's body was on the ground with blood everywhere. He was on his stomach, and his head was twisted to the side. His eye was already swollen shut, and his cheek looked broken. I stumbled into the kitchen and fell to my knees, but I was so scared to touch him. I couldn't speak. I couldn't breathe. My heart was pounding so loudly, I couldn't hear anything.

"Luke." I sobbed, pressing the back of my hand to my mouth. "Luke."

"Shit!"

Dazed, I looked up to see Braden standing in the doorway. His eyes were wide and scared. "What the fuck happened?"

The sobs were choking me, but I managed to whisper out, "I'm scared to touch him."

"Bri." Braden darted over Luke's feet and around me. I heard him in the distance on the phone. "I have an emergency..."

Help was coming. Help would fix Luke. My hand went to his shoulder. There was so much blood everywhere. Where was the wound? I needed to put pressure on it to make it stop bleeding, didn't I? Stop it somewhere? I wanted to do something. My hands fell to the bottom of my shirt, and I started to lift it off.

"What are you doing?" Braden had come back to kneel beside me.

"I don't know. Something." I peeled it off the rest of the way, leaving me in the tank top I'd been wearing underneath. Balling it up in my fist, I started to press down on one of the larger wounds. I wanted it to soak up some of the blood, but it wasn't enough. Braden realized what I was doing and disappeared for a moment. He returned with a pile of towels, and both of us started to absorb the blood, being gentle as we did so nothing could get infected. When the paramedics got there, they stopped in shock. Two piles of bloodied towels were on either side of us, and we were covered in it, too.

One asked, "Are you two hurt, too?"

I shook my head and gestured to Luke, choking out in a hoarse whisper, "Him. Help him."

Only him. Always him.

We were pushed backwards so they could work on Luke, and it seemed like ages before they loaded him into the ambulance. As they did, one said to Braden, "We have room for one person. Whoever it is, decide now."

Braden turned to me, but I waved him ahead. I said, "You go."

Instant confusion crossed his face. "What?"

"Go! I mean it."

The paramedic climbed inside and reached out to close the door. He yelled out, "Decide now, buddy!"

"Go!" I yelled again.

Braden shook his head, but leaped inside the ambulance. The door slammed shut right behind him, and my body jerked from the force of the door. As they took off, I felt my heart break.

Luke's voice brought me back to the present. With his shoulder lifted to help cradle the phone pressed to his ear, he said, "Lots of blood loss. She's pale. Uh, her pulse seems okay, but I couldn't find it that well." He paused. "Yeah, she's breathing." He looked at me. "Bri, an ambulance is coming. Can you give them information?" He held the phone to me, but I was still seeing his body, not hers. "Bri!"

No. It was my mom. My mom's body was in the bed, not Luke's. It wasn't him. I grabbed the phone, shoving the haunted memories away. "Yes." The phone operator asked me more questions, and I answered what I could, but as I did, I was aware of Luke's gaze. He had gone back to my mom's side, feeling for her pulse, but his eyes weren't missing a beat from me either. He knew something was wrong with me, but I couldn't let him know. Shame hung over me in a dark cloud, and I turned away, clutching the phone as I focused on whatever the operator was asking me.

Help my mom. That was my main focus right now. Help her, like I hadn't been able to help Luke.

"Bri—Bri!" Luke snapped his fingers in front of me.

"What?"

He pointed to the hallway. "Grab some towels. I'm going to go and make sure they find the right house—"

I grabbed his arm, stopping him. "No." I couldn't be here. "I'll go. You stay here with her. I need to call Braden."

"Okay. Yeah." Luke nodded in a rushed motion. "That's fine. Go."

After grabbing some towels for him, I hurried outside. The street was eerily calm. It was in the middle of the night, and only the one streetlight lit up the block. I flipped on our outside lights and dialed Braden's number, as I went to the end of our block.

A girl answered, but his voice came on a second later.

"Braden!"

"Whad?" He was slurring.

I asked, "You're drunk?"

"Why?"

"Is that girl drunk, too? What happened to Kelly?"

"Come on. Don't start on me."

"Where are you?" The phone was sliding out of my hands. They were so sweaty. "Are you at the bar?"

"What? No. I left an hour ago. Where ar—"

"It's Mom."

He stopped. I heard movement from his end, and his voice was suddenly clearer, "What?"

"It's Mom. We checked on her, and she was bleeding. She's uncon—"

"What?!"

"Luke called 911. They're coming to the house now."

"Shit! I'm on my way."

Flickers of red and white lights started to appear around the corner, and they grew brighter and brighter until the ambulance slowed enough to turn down our street. I gripped the phone tighter and hurried out. "Don't. They're here. Go to the hospital. If you're drunk and the girl's drunk, call a cab."

"Bri, do I—"

I hung up and waved both of my arms in the air. "Over here! Here!"

Everything went fast after that. They pulled into the driveway, and not much was said between the paramedics and me. One had already gone inside to assess Mom. She radioed within seconds for the gurney, and the rest of the paramedics went inside with it. A younger male followed behind them with a bag and clipboard.

I stayed outside and bent my head down, my hands braced on my knees. Then I breathed. I just breathed.

"Hey." I looked up to see Luke headed toward me.

The paramedics bypassed us with the stretcher my mom was strapped to. When she was loaded into the ambulance, one of the paramedics asked, "Anyone riding with us?"

Luke waved him off. "Go ahead. We'll be right behind you guys." He faced me and asked, "You ready to go?"

I nodded, raking a hand over my face. "Uh, yeah." I looked at the front door.

Luke said, "I already locked up." He had my keys in his hand, and he pointed to my car. "I'll drive. You're too scatterbrained right now. Did you call Braden?"

Luke got behind the steering wheel. I got into the passenger side. "He's going to meet us at the hospital."

"He was sober?"

I shrugged. I didn't care. "He'll get there." Braden always pulled through. *Unlike yourself*, my own inner thought laughed at me, remembering Braden's words.

Luke wasn't my mom.

This wasn't my fault.

My jaw firmed, and I shoved the memories back down, once and for all. I had to be there for her, not paralyzed with fear. *This wasn't my fault*, I reminded myself again.

"Bri? You okay?"

"What?"

"You're acting weird. You checked out before. What's going on with you?"

His eyes were warm with concern, and there was no judgment. Pain sliced through my chest. Of all people, he was the only one who had the right to judge me. Feeling more tears, I swallowed over a damn lump in my throat and moved my head up and down. "I'm fine. It's just…" Did I tell him? Was now the time?

"It's your mom. I get it." Luke gave me a crooked grin, the streetlights flashing over his face.

Yeah. My mom.

This wasn't the time.

"Bri?"

"Sorry." My mom. "Yes, it's my mom."

He reached over and took my hand in his. "She'll be fine." Our fingers interlaced, and he squeezed my hand. "The paramedics didn't seem too worked up. I'm sure she'll be fine. Your mom is a badass. She's tough as nails."

I clasped onto his hand with both of mine and just held onto him. When we got there and found her room, the doctor met us at the door. He held us back, shooing us to the side as my mom was wheeled right back into the hallway.

I pointed at her bed. "That's my mom. Where's she going?"

The doctor nodded once. "Surgery. We need to go in there and find out what's wrong. It will be a few hours." I wanted to ask him questions, but it wouldn't have mattered. He wasn't listening. The doctor hurried after them, and they all disappeared behind another set of doors.

"Bri!"

Braden was hurrying for us, a girl in tow behind him. His hair was disheveled. He had one hand twisted in it, and his other hand was dragging the girl behind him, but she didn't seem to mind. They were both barely dressed. My brother looked like he had just pulled on his shirt. It was sticking to the top of his chest, and his jeans were sagging low on his hips, still unbuttoned at the top. The girl looked slightly better. Her skinny jeans were glued to her. She only had one of her sandals on her feet. She was gripping the other in her free hand, and her shirt, a large flowing top, slipped off one of her shoulders. She tugged it back up, but it fell right off again. Her hair, like my brother's, was a mess. Bleached blonde and sticking in the air. She was trying to calm it down, but with her shoe in her hand, it was becoming more of a mess.

They both reeked of alcohol and smoke. I didn't want to ask who drove. They were there; that's all I cared about.

"Mom?" Braden pressed, his eyes wide and urgent.

Luke answered for me, still holding my hand. "She's in surgery. The doctor told Bri it'd be a few hours."

"A few hours?" Braden looked in pain. He cursed. "I need coffee. Now."

"There's a coffee machine in the cafeteria," a nurse mentioned as she breezed past us.

"Okay. Well, we'll go down there. Bri," Braden said, "you want coffee?"

I nodded. "Yes, please."

He tugged the girl with him, heading down the hallway. "We'll be back. Hopefully more sober." As they started forward, the girl glanced back over her shoulder and gave Luke a tiny smile.

I almost went after her. The sight of her smile had me gritting my teeth and wanting to use her sandal against her head.

"Easy," Luke murmured, holding me back.

I rolled my eyes. "I know. I know, but seriously, she's with him. They just screwed, and she's giving you the look?" I sneered at her even though she wasn't looking at him anymore. "Girls like her make the whole Girl Power thing go up in smoke."

Luke laughed. "You usually handle those girls better. You stressed about your mom?"

Among other things, I thought. "Yeah."

"She'll be okay. I'm sure of it."

"I hope so."

"Come on, let's find out what room she'll be admitted to when she gets out of surgery."

"Yeah. Okay."

We were showed to the room Mom would be brought back to, and coffee was delivered to us. It was an hour later, with Luke sitting in the chair beside me humming a new song and playing with my fingers, when we got our first visitor.

I sat upright, pulling my hand from Luke's. "What are you doing here?"

It was Elijah.

Luke sat up with me, but threw me a frown. I flushed. I don't know why I had acted like I was doing something wrong. Then I asked again, "Eli, what are you doing here?"

"Uh." His gaze was trained on Luke. "I'm here for Skeet."

"Me?"

"Luke?" I asked.

"Yeah. Uh…" Elijah glanced around the empty hospital room. "I heard you were here. Can I talk to you outside?" He stepped out right away, and Luke followed, sending me another confused look.

It wasn't long before he poked his head back in. "I have to go do something. Stay put. I'll be back."

"Wha…wait!"

But it was too late. Again. They both hurried down the hallway. I darted for the doorway and watched them disappear around a corner, turning down the hallway that led to the hospital's main entrance.

My alarm went off. Wherever they were going, it wasn't good.

CHAPTER
THIRTEEN

"I forgot your coffee, so I went back." Braden came inside the room with a proud smile on his face. "Here you go."

He looked more sober. His hair wasn't messed up anymore. It looked like he had wet it so it wasn't sticking up, and his clothes had been righted. His shirt was even tucked inside his jeans. I looked past him, but didn't see the girl that had been with him. As I took the coffee from his hand, I asked, "You ditched the girl?"

He grimaced. "All she wanted to talk about was Luke. The girls have it bad for him. Seriously." Then he realized whom he was talking to. "Were you two holding hands earlier?"

Change of subject. Now. I coughed. "The doctor hasn't come in yet, but a nurse just did. She said the surgery's done. He should be here soon."

"Oh, good." He slid a distracted hand through his hair, upending it again as he glanced around the room. His hand dropped back to his side. "Where's Luke?" He winked at me. "Or are you going to change the subject from that question, too?"

I clutched my coffee tighter. "Elijah came and got him."

"Elijah?"

"Yeah." I cringed. "I have no clue where they went. Neither shared. They took off right away."

"Shit." Braden grunted, hopping onto the bed and dangling his feet off the end. He pulled out his phone, texting as he said, "I'll figure it out. They'll tell me." After a few minutes, he shrugged and placed his phone beside him. "Maybe not. Sorry." His phone lit up. "Huh?"

"Who is it?"

"Kelly from the bar." He answered the phone, "Hello?" After another moment of silence, he asked, "For real?" Then hung up the phone and shook his head.

"What is it?"

"Something's going down with Emerson. Elijah was in there asking for him."

"Isn't the bar closed? It's almost four."

"Yeah. That's the thing." He shook his head. "She said he was in earlier, and just now, she was heading home when she saw Elijah's truck run a red. She was at the stoplight, and she thought she saw Luke in there with him."

My mind was made up. I stood and grabbed the keys. "Which way were they headed?"

"What are you doing? What about Mom?"

"You stay. You're good at that. I'm not." I started for the door. "Which way, Braden?"

He hesitated.

I barked out, "I'm going anyway. It would help if you gave me a general direction."

He let out a sigh. "South on Broadway. She was at the 117th stoplight."

That was all I needed. I hurried for the lobby, but braked as I saw the doctor heading past me. Grabbing his arm, I asked, "My mom?"

He stared at me for a moment before recognition sparked in his eyes. "Oh. Your mom is stable. She had a miscarriage, and some of the fetus was still attached to her uterus. She passed out because she's anemic. She's sleeping now, but they're taking her to her room. We want to watch her for a day, at least, maybe two to make sure everything's passed this time."

She'd be fine. That was all I needed. "My brother's in there. Can you tell him this same news?" I didn't wait for a response; I was already jogging back to the lobby. It didn't take me long to get to the parking lot and into my car. Then I headed for Broadway. Zooming past the 117th stoplight, I kept going straight. I didn't know what I was looking for, but if Emerson was involved, a party or a fight was my best guess.

It was Kelly's car that I saw first. Pulling up behind it, I got out, pocketed my phone and keys, and walked up to her driver's seat. She was still inside; her hands clutched the wheel as she leaned forward.

Her eyes were big, almost bulging out, and she was biting down hard on her lip.

I tapped her window.

She let out a scream, jumping back in the seat. When she saw me, she immediately swallowed her cries. Rolling down her window, she cursed at me. "You gave me the biggest heart attack, I swear." Then she noticed the dried blood still on my clothes. "What are you doing here?"

"What are you doing here?"

Her eyebrows shot up. "*Hello*. Eli and Luke together. That's not normal. How could I not follow them?"

She had a point. "Where are they?"

She grew wary and pointed ahead. There was a long line of cars parked on the street before her, but all of them led to a run-down house that was brightly lit. Loud music poured from it, and there was a large group of people standing on its front lawn, all of them holding beverages. Some were drinking from big cups and beer cans, while others were drinking from bottles still encased in brown paper bags. I glanced around the neighborhood, taking note of the rest of the houses with doors and windows broken. Some windows even had iron bars on them. This wasn't a good neighborhood, which made the knots in my stomach tighten even more.

"I don't know what they're doing here. I haven't worked up the courage to go in there," Kelly said.

I heard the fear in her tone, and I understood.

"And it's Eli and Luke. I thought I was seeing things, so I followed them, but it was them. They were running inside when I drove past. By the time I circled back to park here, I..." She faltered. "You can understand."

I did. I wiped my hands over my jeans. "I'm going in."

"What?" She grabbed my hand through the window. "Don't. Think, Bri. Be smart."

I was thinking. I wasn't sure about being smart. I loosened her hold on my arm and patted her hand twice. "I dated a drug dealer for three years. I didn't know he was a drug dealer, but still. We went to parties like this. I might even know people in there besides them. I'm sure it'll be fine."

Oh, hell no, it wasn't going to be fine. As I started forward, my entire body tensed. This was foreign territory. I lied to Kelly. Yes, Eli took me to parties, but they were never this bad. The closer I got, the more I wished I had a steel bat with me instead of my phone and keys.

Nice weapons, Bri. They'll do a lot of damage.

"Oh, you fucker!" one guy laughed, stumbling backwards until he was right in front of me. "Well, hey there, gorgeous."

I moved around him. "Excuse me."

"Come on." He shifted and wrapped an arm around my waist.

The alcohol on his breath was overwhelming. I was close to gagging, but I didn't panic. Not yet. "Do you know Elijah Turner?"

The guy released me and stepped back. His entire demeanor changed. Instead of the drunken flirt, he was cold. Raising his head, he asked, "You're a customer?"

"Maybe."

Disgust flared in his eyes. "You don't need Turner. This is Brute's house. He can get you whatever you need that Turner can, but better quality. Turner sells shit for quality."

It was his competitor's place. That realization settled in at the same time we heard shouts from the backyard, "Get 'em!"

I turned and took off at a full sprint, but I wasn't running away. I was going for the backyard with the leech, along with his buddies from the front yard, hot on my trail. As we circled the house, the sight stopped me dead in my tracks. Elijah and Luke were pinned against the back fence. Both were sweating and bloodied. Elijah's normal sweatshirt was off, and his undershirt had been ripped. Luke's shirt was barely on as well. He had blood streaks spread down his chest, and both were sucking in mouthfuls of air.

If I hadn't been so panicked at the crowd forming around them, I would've appreciated the sight. They looked gorgeous, sweaty, and deadly in that moment, but I didn't stop to salivate. I pulled out my phone and called Kelly. She sounded terrified when I told her the plan, but she had to do it. I glanced back up; they were running out of time. The crowd had tripled, and a lone guy stepped forward. He was enormous. Big shoulders. Big hands. Big everything. He was bald, like Emerson, with a snake tattoo that slithered up the back of his neck and headed to the top of his head, resting above his forehead. He was gripping a bat in one hand, and he pointed to the sidelines with his other. He yelled out, "You come here, Turner? To start shit with me?"

I glanced to the sidelines. Emerson stood there, gripping a beer can. Moving through the crowd, I got closer and could tell my cousin was on something. He kept blinking like something was in his eye and shaking his head back and forth. He was teetering back and forth on his feet, too.

Then I got it—why Elijah had come for Luke at the hospital. He needed back up from someone else who cared about Emerson.

"You show up at my house, at my party, and you try to take one of my clients from me?" Brute pointed to Emerson with his bat and swung back around, tapping it against his palm in an intimidating gesture.

Elijah snorted, rolling his eyes. "He's not your client."

"He is, actually. You don't sell to him, so where do you think he's going to go?"

"Yeah." Eli moved forward a step, his hands in fists. He glared at his competition. "I said what I said. He's my best friend. He's not a client anymore."

Brute gestured around him. He laughed. The sound was cocky and eerie. "Look around. These are my friends. They're here to back me up, not you. Not your pretty boy. Do your 'best friend' a favor and let him stay. He's here to party. Let him have a good time."

Elijah was still staring at Brute, but Luke was looking through the crowd, and I knew the instant he saw me. He didn't move. He gave no indication, but a murderous look started as he continued to look at me.

He wanted me to leave.

I wasn't going anywhere. I raised my chin. Whatever they were down for, I was joining them. I didn't give a shit if I was a girl. I could fight just like they could. We had all grown up in our neighborhood. It wasn't that great of one, so we'd all been in our fair share of brawls. I wasn't a stranger to this scene.

He clipped his head to the side, a slight inch. He wanted me to leave.

I ignored him and scanned my surroundings. I needed a weapon, something to give us enough time before we could get through the back. There was a frontage road behind the backyard, and I knew Kelly was pulling her car up. It was just on the other side of the fence. We needed a distraction, and then everyone could climb the fence and get into the car. She could take off, she was our getaway car, but judging by Eli's heated glare, I knew he wasn't ready to go. He wanted to fight.

Eli lurked forward another step, closer to Emerson this time. "He's coming home with me, and you're going to stop selling to him."

"You're an idiot, Turner." Brute pointed to the crowd with his bat. "It's thirty to two—"

Eli cut him off, growling, "I have people, too. You don't think I could've come here with them? I didn't. I did this as a friend. I doubt you'd want me selling to your sister."

Brute stiffened. He dropped his bat to his side, but gripped it harder around the handle. His voice sounded low and menacing, "You better leave Rose alone or—"

"Or what?" Elijah threw his head back; his eyes looked abnormally dilated, making him look crazy.

I had witnessed Elijah fight many times. I hadn't known the real reason behind half of those fights, and maybe they were like this—over drugs and drug territory— but it didn't matter. Elijah was a fighter. He was easygoing, full of crude jokes, but when the switch was flipped, he was dangerous. Tall and lanky, a lot of people underestimated him, but Elijah's reputation was solid. He wasn't one to be messed with. If he fought, he usually won. In the back of his mind, I knew he was willing to go down swinging, even against thirty people. He would take as many of them out as possible, and all while Emerson was high as a fucking kite on the sidelines. I glanced back to my cousin. He wasn't even watching the fight. He had wandered to a tree and was trying to catch the leaves off the branches.

I snorted. What a piece of shit.

Then I realized my mistake.

People turned around and started to notice me. As more and more saw me, they began to back away so a small circle had formed around me.

Well. I took a breath. Oops.

Then Brute walked to me and nodded behind me. He asked the leech, "Yours?"

"No way." The leech was spineless now. He held up his hands and stepped back, away from me in an exaggerated motion. "She came here looking for Turner, said she was a customer."

Brute swung back to Elijah. "Yours?"

Repressed frustration flared in Eli's eyes, but he glanced to Luke who moved forward. Luke said in a quiet growl, "She's mine."

A girl piped up from the crowd, "She's Turner's ex."

There was complete silence for a full minute as everyone digested that information. When it had, Brute skirted between Luke to Elijah. Then he smiled. "Well, if this isn't awkward…for you guys."

Luke started for me, but I shook my head. He stopped as Elijah shifted, holding a hand out to stop him.

Then I saw the headlights behind the fence. Kelly was there. She was supposed to open the door and keep the car running. I waited another minute, but then Emerson moved to the back of the fence. The light from her car had attracted his attention. This couldn't get any better.

I looked at Luke and motioned to the fence. He turned, seeing Emerson. He frowned slightly, but lifted a shoulder. I wasn't sure what that meant, but I hoped he would follow my lead. Then I looked up at Brute, standing right in front of me. He reached out to grab my arm.

My first instinct was to evade, but I didn't. I squashed that sensation and gritted my teeth as his meaty hand wrapped around my arm. He dragged me forward and shoved me ahead of him.

"Who does this bitch belong to?"

Well, that pissed me off.

Elijah started laughing, but he pointed to Luke. "Not sure how she's going to handle being called that, but she belongs to Pretty Boy here."

Luke threw him a dark look, moving forward so he was standing slightly in front of Elijah. "She belongs to me."

Brute dragged me to face him again. He breathed on me, his face too close now. "Is that true? You're a pretty thing." His free hand touched my cheek.

I held still, ignoring the growing need to kick this guy in the nuts. It was clawing inside me, crawling to the surface, and I started to concentrate on keeping my calm. I could feel Luke's anger mounting at the same time. Glancing at him through the corner of my eyes, he was like a statue. His hands were loose at his sides, but his head was lowered like he was getting ready to charge. Luke didn't have the explosive burst of energy like Elijah did, but he was just as dangerous. Luke thought out his moves. Each punch he threw was precise and delivered to weaken his opponent. If he had a knife, I would've started to worry. He would've gone for Brute's jugular, and that would be a whole other set of problems. As it was, I finally spied a knife. There was a girl right behind Brute who held one. It was dangling from her fingers, right next to her leg, and judging from the alarm in her eyes, I didn't think she knew how to use it.

Luke said from behind me, "Let her go." His voice was calm and low, but a shiver went down my spine. He was close to making his move. I looked back at him. Elijah had moved to stand next to him and watched him carefully, too. When Brute heard the new threat, his head went back up.

He narrowed his eyes, and his hand dropped from my face. "Or what, Pretty Boy? I don't know you, but you'd look more comfortable being in some fancy magazine than here with the big boys."

Then I heard something click at the back of the fence. I turned my head, narrowly missing clocking Brute square in the face. There was a door to the yard and Kelly stuck a hand through it, waving at me. That was her signal. I hadn't asked for her to find a door, but I had hoped there would be one. She just saved us a lot of time. And Emerson was right there.

It was time.

Brute was breathing down on me, still gripping my arm firmly. He lifted me, making me stretch to stand on my tiptoes. I looked right at Luke, then Elijah. Both saw the change in me and narrowed their eyes. They shared a questioning look, but I didn't care. I hoped they would follow my lead. I closed my eyes, remembering the times I fought with Braden.

"You have such a hard head!" he had shouted one time after I head-butted him. He'd been right. I did. Not much could hurt my skull. I had laughed then, sticking my tongue out at him.

"And I'll do it every time you wrestle me. Get ready for headaches, Braden!"

He had yelled back, but ran off, yelling for our mom.

"Here's one for my brother." I reared back and brought my forehead back as hard as possible into Brute's face.

Crying out, he dropped me instantly as he bent forward and cupped his head with both of his hands. No one moved for a second. They were all shocked, but I wasn't. I darted forward, plucked the knife from the girl's fingers and immediately started backing up. I was in front of Luke before anyone thought to run after us, but I kept backing into him.

I yelled to Elijah, "Grab Emerson. There's a car for us back there!"

Then everything happened at once. Everyone realized what had happened. Luke's hands gripped my sides, but he switched our positions immediately. He took the knife from me and blocked me instead, moving backwards. Then we both darted for the fence.

Elijah had grabbed Emerson. He had a firm hold on his arm, and he dragged him to the fence, but Emerson was still dazed. He didn't know what was going on, so Luke went to him and grabbed the other side. Both of them hoisted Emerson in the air. They half-dragged and half-carried him the entire way. I held open the fence door. As soon as they were through, I slammed it shut, but I couldn't lock it.

"Fuck!" I screamed.

"We don't have time!" Luke yelled at me as he and Eli threw Emerson into the back of the car. They both climbed inside, and Kelly yelled from her window, pounding the steering wheel, "Come on, Bri!"

Spying a chair, I wedged it underneath the handle. As soon as I did, they were there. I heard shouts from the other side and then someone ordered, "Go around the back. Block their car in!"

"Let's go!"

I sprinted and dove for the seat.

Kelly pressed her foot down on the accelerator, flooring it before I even shut my door.

We got out of the alley just as they were running for their cars.

CHAPTER FOURTEEN

Kelly was a badass driver. She ducked down side streets, through alleys, and took us on a drive down streets I didn't know existed in Grant West, but no one had followed us. When we finally relaxed, Emerson farted.

"Seriously." I groaned, covering my nose.

Kelly was hunched forward, her knuckles almost white as she held the steering wheel with a death grip. A laugh fell out of her, and she whispered, almost to herself, "You guys are nuts."

"Yes, nuts." Elijah was waving his hand in the air. "That's apparently what Em ate last. Shit, man. Seriously."

Emerson laughed, still sounding high as a kite. "Sorry, guys. There were peanuts everywhere. They were talking to me."

"I'm sure," Luke griped. "Move over, come on. Kelly, you need a bigger car. Three guys in the backseat is not comfortable."

She glanced up in the rearview mirror. "No offense, but I don't usually buy my vehicles based on how many guys I can fit in the backseat, although, maybe I should." Then she shrugged, turning onto the main highway that ran through Grant West. "This night's been lovely, so enjoyable, but, uh, where am I supposed to be driving to? I'm running low on gas."

Luke met my gaze in the mirror, too, but he asked Elijah, "Do we need to worry about retaliation?"

"No."

Elijah's answer was too short.

I turned around in my seat. "Hey. Retaliation. Give us the truth this time."

He looked up, searing me with the anger still suppressed there and said, "I said no. I meant no. You won't be touched. I promise."

My eyes narrowed. "I don't like how you're saying that." My

fingers curled into the seat, and I swallowed over a knot forming in my throat. "Are you going back to finish things?"

"You can't do that."

Elijah whipped his head to Luke's, silencing whatever else he was going to add. Then Eli murmured, way too softly, "This is my business. I know how to handle things."

"You didn't back there," I argued.

He snorted. "A mistake I won't be making again."

I remembered his words. That he could've taken his crew there in the first place. "You really thought you could go in and get Emerson, and there wouldn't be a fight?"

"I had hoped." He turned to look out the window, raising his hand to idly tap against it. "I know better now. Trust me, Bri, I won't be involving you or Pretty Boy in any more situations. I guarantee that."

Luke spoke up for him, telling me, "Emerson was personal, not business. That's why he got me."

"I know." But I was still worried about Elijah. I looked back at my ex. "Just don't get yourself killed."

"What?" Elijah snapped. "You mean like my old man? My brother? Nah, no way, Brielle. They both got shanked in prison. No, no worries. I won't get myself killed, not like them anyway."

"Elijah—" I started.

Emerson quieted me. "Shut up, Bri. I'm seeing fucking rainbows, and even I can tell you're fighting a losing battle. If the moron wants to throw down, let him throw down. It's what he does. He's stayed alive this long. He must know how to do something right."

I growled back, "Go back to fucking a rainbow, Em. All of this happened because of you."

"Whatever. Worse shit has happened because of you."

The car got deathly silent.

Let it go, Bri. Let it go. My blood was starting to boil. *Think cold showers.*

I waited, but nothing. My blood was still boiling. It kept going higher and higher, until I couldn't contain it anymore. It exploded out of me. I looked back and locked eyes with Luke. He saw what was going to happen and started to throw up a hand, but dropped it right back down. A slow smile started to spread across my face. It was probably an ugly looking one, but I didn't give a crap. I wanted Emerson's balls. He was going to keep riding my ass if I didn't do something about it, and today was that day.

I lunged for Emerson.

Throwing my body toward the backseat, I ended up sprawled between the seats. Without pausing, I rained punch after punch on him, using my fists. I didn't use my hands—not dainty-like little slaps. I wasn't going for his hair. I wasn't going to scratch his face. I used as much of my body behind my blows as possible. Like I said before, I wasn't a stranger to a fight.

Then everything turned into chaos.

Elijah and Luke did nothing. They didn't hold me back or anything. Emerson was dazed after the first punch, so I continued, and Kelly screamed. The car veered toward the middle of the road, but she righted it before slamming on the brakes. At the abrupt stop, I fell backwards. Luke grabbed my arm, holding me still so I didn't go through the windshield, but he wasn't going to stop me. I wasn't done with Emerson.

Then Kelly threw open her door, and so did Elijah and Luke. Emerson was still in the middle, covering himself with his arms now. He hurried out the side, and I tried to climb after him, dropping all the way into the backseat and following behind him, and he tried to shut the door in my face. Curses were spewing from him now. Seeing the door coming for my face, I blocked it. Flipping around in the seat, I kicked it open and was on my feet instantly.

I charged for him once again, but Luke wrapped an arm around my waist. He hoisted me up in the air, holding me like I was a doll. He said over my head to Elijah, who was somewhat blocking Emerson, "Are we going to let this happen?"

"Fuck you, Brielle! You whore!"

Elijah shrugged, ignoring Emerson. "I'm game. He deserves an ass kicking anyway. Bri can hold her own."

I struggled against Luke's hold, but his arm wasn't going anywhere.

He only lifted me higher, and his arm dug across my hipbones. I yelled back, wiping the back of my hand over my mouth, "Fuck you back, Emerson! You piece of shit. I'm tired of your mouth. I've never done a goddamn thing to you."

Kelly whimpered from behind us, "You guys are nuts."

Luke glanced at her, turning me around with him, and we saw she was sitting on the ground. Her face was ashen, and she was rocking back and forth, shaking her head at the same time.

Luke dropped me back to the ground, but kept his hands at my sides. "You okay?"

No. "Yes." I pried myself from him to put some space between us. "I'm good. I just lost my momentum."

"You sure?"

I turned my back to him. I didn't want to see the concern and care in his eyes. I didn't deserve to see that. Elijah's gaze was hooded, and when he glanced at Luke, the speculation was deep in those greens of his, then he shook his head.

"What a cu—"

I saw that word forming on my cousin's mouth, and I was in his face before he could finish it. No one would call me that name. My fist hit the side of his face just as he almost said it. All the anger that had left me rushed back in full force. Fuck it. I was taking him down, family or not.

Emerson fell back. I had used my entire body's weight behind my hit, so there was some force there, but it was only enough to stun him. He was muscular, and I wasn't an idiot. I couldn't fight him that way, so I launched myself at him, wrapped my legs around his waist and flipped myself backwards. He came with me, and I was able to throw his body to the ground. Before he could get back up, I brought my knee down to his groin. A primal scream ripped from his throat, but he flung his hands up and shoved me off. I hit the ground, banging my elbows, and I knew my skin had been ripped on my arm somewhere. I felt the burn, but I didn't care.

Emerson struggled to his feet and bent over, cupping himself. He looked up with pained eyes, so I waited. His features started to tighten. I saw the snarl returning and braced myself, waiting for his next insult.

"You fucking whor—"

One more time. I launched at him, wrapped my legs around his torso, and did the same thing. I hit the ground with my shoulder, jarring it, but I kicked at him once again. Another guttural scream came from him, and this time, when I stood up, he stayed in the fetal position, whimpering.

I wiped some blood off my face—not sure how that had happened—and flicked it to the ground. "Stop calling me names. Stop fucking with me. Just stop, Emerson! Stop!"

He looked up, and I stopped talking. There was so much hate in his eyes. I felt punched in the gut. Pressing my hands to my stomach, I moved back and shook my head. His hatred was never going to end. I considered him family, but he considered me an enemy.

I choked out. "What did I ever do to you?"

"To me?" He laughed, a bitter, ugly sound. He was still bent over, struggling to stand up. His face was pinched in pain. "It's not me, you bitch. It's what you did to these guys. He's my best friend." He pointed at Elijah, and then swung his hand to Luke. "And he's like a brother, and you, you fucked them both over."

My eyes got big. "That's why you hate me? Because of my love life?"

He shook his head, spitting out some blood. "I was there, Bri. You were upset, and I was coming to check on you, but I saw you. I know who you were with and what he had you do." He kept shaking his head, regret forming as he looked at Luke. "You've never told him what happened. His dad almost killed him, and you've never once told him why. You just left and went straight to Elijah. You left him bleeding there and went to my best friend. You fucked them both in that one move, and you've not once had the balls to tell Luke the truth."

"Emerson," Elijah murmured.

"Stop." Emerson rounded on him. "You know it's true. Now it's happening all over again. She's fucking both of you again, except this time she's just going back to him. I'm tired of it. I'm tired of seeing two people I care about in pain all because of this bitch."

"That's enough," Luke ground out, but I saw the question in his eyes.

I had to tell him. The time had come. If this was why my cousin hated me so much, it was way past due.

"No! You don't even know, Luke. I'm sticking up for you. For *you*, man." He jerked a hand to Elijah. "And my best friend, too." He looked to me. "Bri, it's gone on long enough. Tell him and drop out of the fucking band, too." He spat at my feet. "You don't deserve to play with us."

"Emerson."

The rebuke didn't come from Elijah or Luke. Both had fallen silent. This time it came from Kelly. She was back on her feet, darting to the middle of us. Crossing her arms, she stood at my side and glared at my cousin. "That's enough," she hissed. "I don't care what Bri has done that you've decided to appoint yourself her judge and jury. You have no right to speak to her the way you do, and if you keep doing it, you're banned from the bar. For life. Every time you step foot in there, I'll have you tossed in jail."

"What? We practice there."

"Trust me." She raised her chin, challenging him. "Rowdy will back me on this one."

"Whatever, you're a bit—"

"Shut up!" Luke and Elijah yelled at the same time, and Luke added, "You need to play there, asshole. Shut your hole, for once."

Elijah added, "Besides, you're all pissed at her, but I knew."

"What?" Emerson dropped his mouth. "You knew?"

"The whole time." Elijah winked at him. "She told me, dipshit, and you can stop with the name-calling at least." He took a drag and gestured to Luke with his cigarette. "Besides, you don't want to screw up your future. That guy, that band, it's where you need to go to get away from Brute." As he said that last name, the easygoing Elijah was gone again. Back was Drug Dealer Elijah with danger simmering beneath the surface as he added, "And you and I are going to have a chat about that one. I'm tired of getting calls that my own best friend is baked out of his head."

"You sell drugs. Who are you to judge?"

A harsh laugh ripped from me, hearing that coming from my cousin. "Who are *you* to judge?"

He whipped back to me, his hands forming fists, but Luke stood in the middle of us and held out his hands. "Stop. Just stop, you guys. She kicked your ass, literally. You're still half-baked, and you're going to start another round with her?"

"I can get a few good hits in." There were other dark promises lurking in the depths of my cousin's eyes as he continued to glare at me.

I flung my hands out. "I'll kick your ass again."

And I started forward, right into Luke's hand, he pushed me back and turned to glare at Emerson. I heard the quiet venom there as he said, "If you don't turn off your attitude to her, I will kick your ass myself. I'm fed up with it."

"But Luke—"

"I don't give a shit!" he roared back at him. His shoulders and arms were rigid, and his jaw was clenched tight.

He was gorgeous.

"Change your attitude, or you're out of the band. I mean it. Gunn can fill in for you any day of the week," he clipped out, and then snapped his fingers and pointed to the car. "Get inside and keep your fucking mouth shut."

Emerson let out a disgruntled sound, but Elijah grabbed him and started pushing him to the backseat. "Come on. Don't rock the boat, Em. Trust me on that." As he continued to herd him into the car, I heard Emerson grumble, "Where the hell did she learn those moves? From you? Did you teach her that?"

Elijah laughed, getting in behind him. "I wish. That would've been a whole other level of fun."

Then Luke grinned at me. "You remembered." Pride shone from him as he ran a hand over his jaw. "I about shit a brick when I saw you throw him down."

"Yeah, I remembered."

Kelly grunted beside me. "I stand by what I said. You guys are just nuts." She let out another deep breath. "But fun at the same time."

Luke laughed, following me to the car with his hand at the small of my back. "We usually have Braden with us, too."

She let out a deep laugh. "I can't imagine the stories you guys have, especially with him."

Then we parted. Luke's hand dropped, and he went to the other side of Emerson. I went to the passenger side, and Kelly got behind the wheel again. No one spoke on the way to the hospital.

When we got there, I went to check on my mom and Braden. Elijah took off. No one asked him where he was going. Luke went with Emerson to the emergency room to see if he needed stitches; the place under his chin where I had kicked him hadn't stopped bleeding.

It was a surreal ending to the entire night, but in some way, it was fitting. We all went our own ways.

CHAPTER
FIFTEEN

"You never told me you broke up with Eli."

"Huh?" I was curled up next to my mom in her bed. She wanted to watch a movie, but I hadn't been paying attention. Thoughts of Brute, Luke, and the things Emerson had said were plaguing me. It had been a week since that night and there'd been no retaliation from Brute. I didn't know what Elijah had done to deal with him, but I guessed that he had somehow. I focused on my mom again and saw she was waiting for me to answer her question. "Oh. Uh. That was a while ago."

"I know." She folded her hands underneath her head. Her blue eyes were trained solely on me. The movie, whatever she had picked, was completely forgotten. "I asked your brother why Luke was with you and not Elijah. He told me about the break up. Why didn't you tell me?"

"Why didn't you tell me you were pregnant?"

She stiffened, biting down on her lip. "Oh, Brielle." Her tiny shoulders lifted up and down as she sucked in some air. "That baby...I didn't know about it, and before you start, the guy was a one-time deal. I was lonely. I was stupid, and I won't be making that mistake again."

"You were lonely?"

"Bri." She patted my arm. "I'm almost forty-five, single, and I work too much. Being lonely is a side effect of not knowing how to pick the right guy. You, I don't know, sometimes I think you have the same problem as me, but Luke was with you. Are you two..."

"Oh! Um." I picked at the blanket. "I...I don't know. No. We became friends again because of the band."

"With joining the band again?"

I nodded. "Yeah." I flattened my hands over the blanket, forcing myself to stop picking at it. "You know that night dad left us? When he tore the whole house up and you locked us in the bathroom."

"I do." Her voice softened. "I didn't know you remembered it."

My throat swelled up. "How could I not?" A rueful laugh slipped from me, but it ended on a soft sigh. "I was so scared that night."

"Oh, Bri." Her hand rested over mine and she squeezed it. "I had no idea. I'm so sorry. You and your brother." She chuckled to herself. "I had babies when I was a baby myself. You and your brother raised each other. I've always felt so bad about that. I wasn't there for you two like I should've been."

"Mom, no." I covered her hand with my free one. "You were working. And dad—"

Her free hand covered mine now. Her eyes roamed over my face. "You're so beautiful. Your father was a mistake, but I got you and your brother from him so I can't complain too much. He wasn't well."

No, no he wasn't, but there was more. I couldn't tell her what he made me do. I wanted to, but she would've blamed herself about that, too. "He wasn't a good man, was he?"

"No. No, he wasn't." She pulled her hand free to tuck a strand of my hair behind my ear. Lingering there, she patted my cheek. "You and Braden both got his stubbornness and his love of music. He used to manage a band, did you know that?"

I shook my head. "I didn't."

"He did. With Luke's dad. They were best friends."

The next question should've been what happened next. A normal child would've had more questions about the father who abandoned her, but not me. I knew what happened next. I was a part of it, and Emerson was right. I had to tell Luke. He had to know. It was time. With the decision made, I headed for Rowdy's later that evening. I felt like puking the whole night, but it needed to be done.

After our gig, Braden cornered me when I was coming out of the bathroom and informed me that Luke wanted to talk after we played.

I couldn't stall anymore, but when I went back to find him, Luke was talking to a woman. She was tall, over six feet with blonde hair styled to cascade down her back. Her hair must've cost a couple hundred to get that sultry and sophisticated look perfect. With a small pout on her lips, she tilted her head to the side and gestured outside. Her hand rested on Luke's arm, and I expected him to brush her off.

He didn't.

Instead, a man came through the crowd and joined them. He looked like the Ken to her Barbie. Seconds later, all three of them went outside together.

"Look at that," Emerson murmured into my ear, coming from behind me.

I gritted my teeth, letting my war-mask slip into place. "What do you want, Emerson?"

He was looking at where they had gone. "Don't take it personal. He was bound to move on from you. It was only a matter of time, and that woman," he wolf whistled, "is an upgrade. I'd do her, too."

"She had a date."

"Bri. Come on." He wiggled his eyebrows. "Can we say swinger?"

"Get out of here. Luke's not a swinger."

He laughed, but there was a bite to it. "I'm kidding. I bet that guy was her brother. Didn't you see how they looked alike? Don't you have Twin Radar?"

"Now, you're pissing me off." I started to edge around him. Kelly was waving for help behind the bar. "I don't have Twin Radar, but I do have Bullshit Radar. Whatever you're doing, just stop. It makes you look like the bad guy."

He followed right behind me. A soft, taunting laugh teased in my ear. "Now, you really need to wake up. I am the bad guy. I'm always the bad guy."

A large group planted themselves in front of the bar. I went around them and looked back over my shoulder. Emerson was disappearing out the door. Maybe he was right, and that couple was twins.

"Bri!" Kelly was waving again.

Either way, I couldn't go and find out. I shoved through the last of the group and slipped behind the bar. I tried to keep an eye out for him, but the crowd was too large. We were busy all the way until closing and even an hour afterward. When I entered Luke's house, I saw him sitting on the couch in the living room, hunched over his guitar. A half-empty bottle of bourbon was on the floor next to his feet, and he had sheet music spread all over the coffee table. Shirtless, his guitar in his lap, and his hair sticking up like he'd been running his hand through it the entire night, I almost forgot why I was there. A vision of myself straddling him flashed in my mind.

I pulled at my shirt. The room got hot all of a sudden.

His words stopped everything. "Did you come down here to tell me what Emerson was talking about?"

Ice went through my veins. "I want to."

"That's not an answer."

"Who was that woman you left the bar with earlier?"

A corner of his mouth lifted. "That's not an answer either."

"How about…" I took the guitar from him and placed it onto the floor. He leaned back in his chair, his hands coming to rest on my hips. I felt them grasp my sides and closed my eyes, feeling his fingers graze my skin. Bending forward to rest my forehead to his, I murmured, "We enjoy tonight."

One night. Then the truth. I needed him.

"Tonight." His hand skimmed down my leg. His pulled me onto his lap, and my legs parted, already knowing I would feel him soon. My arms around him felt heavy, like I had melted, and I shivered, feeling my body come alive as he traced a finger up my spine. His hands snaked inside my jeans after he undid the button, pulling me closer.

I gasped, but pressed down. No more thoughts. Just the feel of us.

He was right there. I rocked against him, feeling him harden and grow under me. Shit. I couldn't get enough of him. He leaned forward and pressed his lips to my chest. My heart skipped a beat. I was nervous and giddy at the same time, my stomach fluttering. I was addicted. His touch enthralled me. I kissed the side of his face, moving in a slow line closer and closer to his lips. I felt his heart race as I lingered at the corner of his mouth. I was enjoying the power I had over him. I licked his bottom lip—just a dab. He tugged me tighter to him, and a low growl formed in the base of his throat.

Luke stood, carrying me with him as his lips fused with mine. I sighed at the feel of them. Home. I didn't register that we were in the bedroom until I felt the covers beneath me. I gasped as his tongue slipped inside. He tasted me while his demanding fingers ran the length of my back and lifted my shirt in the next instant. I was heated, needing more of his touch. As soon as my shirt was gone, my breasts were crushed against his chest. His jeans were a rough barrier between my legs, and I shoved at them. I wanted him inside me.

When my fingers went to my zipper, he caught my hands. My gaze followed the small grin teasing his lips. While holding himself arched above me, he pinned my hands above my head, and then pulled my jeans off with his other hand. I kicked out, helping him. When they were gone, he came back and began grinding against me, building the tempo. I growled, wanting more, but he held me captive.

He kept moving so damn slow while I shivered. Using my legs, I pulled him onto me.

I felt him throbbing for me, too.

Fuck it. I didn't care who had better control.

I was drunk from his touch. His hands released mine, and one combed through my hair before it cupped the side of my face. His lips touched mine, a small graze before they opened over mine, fusing together once more. My tongue brushed against his, and I was feverish from the feel of him. It was intoxicating, and then, he was right there at my opening. I began to beg. A small whimper came from me as he stayed there, teasing me.

I didn't know the next time I would have him. I wanted him forever.

Then he slid inside me.

He was home. I was home.

While he slid in and out of me, I began writhing underneath him, wanting him to go faster and deeper. I needed more.

"Luke," I gasped.

He nuzzled my neck before looking up. "What?"

We were both out of breath, our gazes lidded. I shook my head. The words couldn't form. I couldn't talk. I'd tell him later. Later…

He kept thrusting in me, claiming me. I was right there.

The edge was close when he placed a hand on my hip and moved even faster and deeper. With his head in the crook of my neck, his breath coated my skin. He plunged inside one last time, and we both went over the edge. He trembled on top of me as I did the same beneath. Smoothing a hand down my arm, he kissed my neck softly, and we both waited for the sensations to slow.

I loved him.

I was going to tell him. I had to, but I knew he would leave me.

"Bri?" He slid out of me, and I almost grabbed onto him, not wanting him to leave. He rested on his elbow, gazing down at me. "What is it?"

I couldn't. I could still feel him inside me. That was how it was supposed to be. He and I. But he was going to leave. I already knew it.

His voice dipped low. "Tell me what's wrong."

My eyes opened. A mask had slid over his face, and he stood from the bed. His jeans were refastened, and he stood there, shirtless and barefooted, staring down at me. His hair was messed up from me; my fingers had raked through it as he thrust inside me. The memory of what we'd just done sent renewed pain and regret through me. They sliced into me like a thousand little knives. I swallowed painfully and gathered what was left of my pride.

He moved farther away from me and leaned against the bedroom wall. His eyebrows furrowed together, and his jaw clenched as he waited. "You're going to tell me what's wrong. Now."

"We've talked about that day, when your dad did what he did." That was my opening statement?

Luke fell silent. He didn't move.

I looked down at my lap. The words didn't want to come, but it was time. Elijah was right. I had to tell him and hope he'd come back to me. So I started, "What your dad did was my fault."

He said one word.

"Explain."

That was it.

I took a breath and started, "I was coming home from school. I remember being so jealous. Candy and her friends had been talking to you. She was flirting with you, and I thought you were flirting back. In hindsight, you were just talking to her, but it still hurt, so I left without waiting for you or Braden that day. But anyway, he was there when I walked past the street before our block, waiting in his car." My fingers curled inward, latching onto the others. "I should've run or screamed or something, but he told me to get into the car, and I did." My eyes squeezed shut as I remembered the sound of his deep baritone voice and how commanding he spoke. I obeyed him without question. I felt the chill of the leather seats, and the cold air blowing across my face again. "It was my dad, Luke."

He stiffened, becoming a statue.

"I need you to do something for me," had been the first words he'd said to me.

"Earlier in the day, he had driven to your house to see your dad, but he hadn't been there," I said.

"Fucking Garrett owes me money. He's not here. He's playing cards at Oiley's right now, so this is what you're going to do for me." He pointed at the house. *"You're going to go in there. And don't tell me you don't know how to sneak in. I know you do. You and that kid are always sneaking into each other's rooms, been doing it since you were tiny. So, you're going to break in and go to Garrett's office."* He stopped talking and leaned closer. His eyes grew even more determined, and an ugly gleam appeared—one that drenched me in a cold sweat. He said, *"In the office closet is a back wall. You can slide it to the side, but you gotta press it in. When you feel it move, slide it to the left. That's where he keeps all his money."*

"H...h...how much?"

"Huh?" he snapped out.

"How much do you want me to take?"

"All of it. Duh." He gestured to the house again. *"Get going, before your little boyfriend comes home looking for you."*

I couldn't move. It felt like a hand had been plunged into my chest and took hold of my heart in an ironclad grip.

"Bri!"

I jumped in my seat.

"Go. Get this done."

My hands were shaking, but I moved on autopilot. Climbing out of the car, I shut the door and then leaned against it for a moment. I closed my eyes.

My hands were behind me, gripping the door handle. I wanted to go back in, but I couldn't.

"Bri." He pounded on the door, yelling from inside the car. "Get!"

I jerked away as memories of those fists hurting my mother played in the forefront of my mind. I bolted toward the house as if he had hit me right then and there. The closer I got, the more I felt myself leave my body.

"It was easy, actually. I snuck in through your window, and everything was how he said." My mouth was so dry. "I was the one who robbed your dad. I took the money—"

"He blamed me." Luke's voice was painful. It was hoarse and so quiet. "He beat me when I kept denying it. I was in the hospital for a week, Brielle."

I never went to the hospital. I couldn't see him that way. "It was my fault."

"That's why you went to Elijah?"

My head moved up and down, but it didn't feel attached to my body. "I'm sorry, Luke. I'm so sorry."

The room was so tense, and I was afraid to look at him. I was afraid to do anything. He was going to leave. I knew it. I'd be kicked out of the band, and I'd never be with him again. I was going to lose Luke, but it had been right to tell him. Finally.

He stood up; I still didn't dare look at him, but I heard him pacing. When he spoke, there was an anguished tone to his voice. "I wanted to talk to you tonight because the two people you saw me with are from a record label. Peter and Priscilla Montley. They're twins, too. They came to hear us play. They'd like to manage us, and if we sign with them, they've promised us a record deal. We've all discussed it, and the guys are in. You've been so busy I haven't had the chance to tell you about it until now."

My hands were shaking.

He added, "You lied to me, Bri. Three years. I can't—he had beaten me before, but this—you lied to me. I can't...we're going to Los Angeles tomorrow." He paused a split second, and then rasped out, "But not you. I don't want you to have any part of this. I—"

He left.

SUSTAIN

I waited for him to slam the door shut, but it didn't come. The door was left hanging open as he walked away.

It was over.

CHAPTER
SIXTEEN

They left the next morning. Braden had been the only one to say goodbye. My mom asked later if I had said my goodbyes earlier because I wasn't outside when they picked up Braden. I couldn't answer her. I didn't want to see the judgment in her eyes.

CHAPTER
SEVENTEEN

Four months later, I was trying to shove my way through a crowd of girls to grab a drink from the kitchen. When I got there, I heard a girl squeal, "Hubba hubba! Luke Skeet is going to help me birth my babies."

I whipped around. The crowd of girls were surrounding something. Moving to get a better look, I saw an iPad with a YouTube clip playing. I couldn't see what was on the clip, but hearing the excited squeals, the bottom of my stomach fell out. They were watching my band.

Her friends laughed, and another said, "Shut up. He's my future husband."

"I heard they're from Grant West."

"No way?! Are you serious? Isn't that clip in Nebraska?"

The first girl spoke, nodding like she was close to the band, "It is. My cousin used to watch them play at some bar there."

"Grant West, as in two towns over?"

I couldn't move. I knew they'd been writing music, and Braden mentioned an impromptu tour last week, but this time I was hearing strangers talking about them. I couldn't tear my eyes away from the group of girls huddled in the corner, clutching their phones, staring at their screens with rapt attention. I was riveted by their reactions. These girls spoke as if Luke and the band were gods.

"Can you move?"

That last question was directed at me. I glanced back, saw a line had formed behind me, and moved to the side.

"Bri?" Wes said my name. He was tall and angelic-looking with blond hair, blue eyes, and overall dreamy. I could almost see the halo attached to his head. He was one of those guys that was too-nice-of-a-guy. He was the lead singer of my new band. Or, correction, I had joined his band, Callen. He smiled at me and placed a hand on my shoulder. "You okay?"

"Yeah." I gave him a small smile, but rolled my shoulder a bit so he'd release me. As he did, an apology flashed in his eyes, and he moved back a step. I saw his lips move and knew he was going to say another 'nice guy' comment—one that would make me feel like a bitch— so before he could speak, I said, "This is a good gig."

"What?" He leaned closer and then nodded after I repeated myself. "Oh, yeah. Yeah, it is. The guy who lives here said there'd be a big crowd. There's a bunch of other bands here, too. I don't know if they're all playing, but he booked two others." He signaled to a group of people standing, clustered in a small circle. One guy was bobbing his head in rhythm to the music, and another guy was beating out a fast pace with his fingers in the air. Wes said, "That's Jersey over there." I caught a small twinge of jealousy in his gaze when he mentioned the band. "They have Avi. You heard about her, right?"

I nodded. I knew Avi. Her voice was raved about by others, but that wasn't how I knew her. I wondered if she still kept in touch with my brother, and thinking about him, I glanced back at the girls who were still gushing over their phones, watching videos of the band that I should be with.

Wes followed my gaze and made a sound. "I see."

I looked at him. "What?"

"Sustain." His eyebrows shot up, and he ducked his head, looking dejected. "I get it."

"Sustain?"

"Your old band."

I continued to frown at him. "What are you talking about?"

"Sustain." He stared at me. "They used to be your band."

"My band's name is Braille."

He sighed, his mouth moving in a grimace. "I thought Callen was...never mind." Then he moved closer again and leaned toward my ear. Resting a hand on my shoulder as he pointed to the squealing girls, he spoke clearly, "They're talking about your old band. They changed their name since you're not with them. They aren't Braille anymore. It's Sustain now."

I moved his hand off me. "Is this a joke?" Why hadn't Braden told me this? But I knew, even as I thought that, I knew why he didn't. It was because it would be more final. They were a different band. They were moving on without me. New name. New member. New direction. I was out. Four months later, it still hurt.

"No joke. They're getting big, Bri. You must be proud. I mean, that's your brother, your cousin, your b...your friend."

"How big? What do you mean by that?"

"It's like they exploded this week. I mean, they were big already, but now they're signed, and they're traveling. It was kind of genius. I heard their label wanted them to do a mini-tour, test out some of their new material before doing a big launch. They've got fans all over now. They were picked up to headline for another band, too. That's huge, but," he was studying me intently, "you must know all about this."

My lips pressed in a flat line. "Yeah, Braden calls home all the time. I must've forgotten about a lot of this."

A renewed squeal came from the girls' corner again, and they began waving their phones around. I could hear their voices over the noise in the room, but the music paused in that slight second, and I heard Luke's voice fill the air. It was slight, but they had programmed all their phones to play at the same instant, so Luke's voice rose in volume.

"Hello, Phoenix!" Luke called out.

Phoenix. They said Nebraska before.

I needed a beer. "When do we play again?"

Wes had been watching me the whole time. "You didn't know any of this, did you?"

I couldn't answer. I didn't want to.

He took a deep breath. "I'm sorry, Bri. I thought you knew. Hell, I thought you would've been proud. They have a website for their band, too. There's not much on there, just their future shows and pictures, but there are lots of comments. A lot of girls go on there. They're nuts for Luke and Braden."

"When do we go on again?" *Please, shut up.*

"Um," he hesitated.

"Wes," I snapped, glaring at him. "I'm going to go outside and drink. I need to know when to come back in."

"I can come get you. We don't have a set time, probably a half hour or so."

"You'll come get me?"

"You'll be okay to play?"

I rolled my eyes and shoved through the crowd again. Snagging a case of beer, I went out the back door and inhaled. I needed the crisp air since the air inside was stifling. My lungs had started to constrict. Veering to a few vacant seats I had spotted at the edge of the yard, I passed a large group of people hanging out on the patio. Grateful for the trees surrounding me and blocking me from view, I plopped down, set the case beside me, and opened my first beer of the night.

I hadn't made it a habit of playing while I was drunk, but I knew I could do it. I could handle Callen; they weren't as good as my old band—I stopped thinking and downed the beer.

"Don't do that."

My hand clenched around the beer can, and I gritted my teeth. Of course, he would be here. Twisting around, I glimpsed Elijah emerging from the trees surrounding me. He dropped to the chair beside me. Pointing his lit cigarette to the beer, he said, "Give me one."

I did, but scowled. "'Don't do' what?"

He leaned back, finished his cigarette, and opened his beer. "You look ready to drown your sorrows or whatever cliché shit that is."

"What are you doing here?"

He laughed and shoved his free hand into his sweatshirt, then took a long pull from his beer. "I'm at a party. What do you think?"

"You're selling."

He shrugged. "Who cares if I am? Pretty Boy's gone. From my viewpoint, it looks like you need a friend. So," he angled his chin up with a wicked gleam in his eyes, "do you need a friend, Bria?"

"It's still not Bria."

"But you need a friend, don't you?"

"Not you."

He scoffed, finishing his beer. He held out his hand, and I put another beer in it. Then he shrugged again, slumping down in his chair and getting even more comfortable. "Get the stick out of your ass. Pretty Boy isn't here anymore. I am and you need someone around you that you trust. I know you don't trust that new band you joined. They look like a bunch of pussies."

"I don't trust yo—"

"Yes, you do," he cut me off, and it was true. I did trust Elijah. I didn't approve of some of the things he did, but I trusted him. He asked, "Are you okay? No bullshit. Are you okay?"

I shrugged.

He laughed, the sound bitter and short. "Stop moping. It's not the end of the world."

"Shut up."

"You shut up," he shot back. "What's your problem? Your boy's on tour. Who cares? He'll be back."

I finished my beer and threw the empty can at him. He deflected it, and I rolled my eyes. "You just asked if I was okay, and now you're telling me I'm okay. Make up your mind."

"I did. I changed my mind. You're back here getting drunk, waiting for your band to play, and sulking because you're not with Pretty Boy. Get over yourself, Bria." He had first been amused, but all humor slid away. He was frustrated now. I saw it simmering in the depths of his eyes. "You don't have problems, Bria. You told your guy the truth, and he left, but he'll be back. He'll always come back to you. Your life isn't over. Me," his eyes fell flat as he finished, "I have problems. Things you don't want to hear about."

I glared at him, but there wasn't much heat to it. He didn't know. He didn't know Luke like I—

"Your boy came to see me." He finished his second beer and pulled out his cigarettes to light another one. As he touched the cigarette to his lip, breathing in and taking a drag, I waited until he let it back out. Smoke filled the air, covering the space between us before he added, "The morning before they left."

After we had made love.

Elijah added, "I'm supposed to watch over you. I'm supposed to stay away from you, but watch over you at the same time. If you can figure that out."

I had to laugh at that. "You're asking me to believe that Luke would ask you to watch over me?"

He shrugged, letting out more smoke. "I'm supposed to keep my distance from you, except, you know," he waved his cigarette around, "in case I find you like this or in some other jam." The somber mask faded, and the corner of his lip formed a crooked grin. "So, are you?"

"Am I what?"

"Are you okay?"

I growled, exasperated by this conversation. "You're giving me whiplash. Stop it. Am I okay? I'm okay. I don't have any problems, and now you're asking me *again* if I'm okay?"

He laughed, finishing his second cigarette and then his beer. The finished cigarette was dropped into his empty can. He handed it over. "You're not thinking 'poor me' shit anymore, are you?"

I had opened my mouth to retort, but it clamped shut again. He was right. All the pain from before was gone. I sighed. "You're right. I'm just annoyed now."

"No, you aren't." He took my beer, finished it, and grabbed my hand. Pulling me up with him, he slapped my ass as soon as I was on my feet. "You got that fighting spirit back. That's what I did for you."

He was right. I shoved him away, though. "Whatever. You just like to mess with my mind."

"Yeah, you know that's what I do best." He tugged me after him and we started back for the house. When it was time to go back on stage, I took my seat and looked out over the crowd. Luke and my brother had the same view, but it was bigger. They were making a name for themselves.

Well, fuck them.

I grabbed my drumstick and twirled it in my hand before slamming it down. I'd make my own name, with or without them.

LUKE GUNN

SUSTAIN

EMERSON BRADEN

CHAPTER
EIGHTEEN

LUKE

We were flying back.

My gut was in knots, and I hated it. The year had been amazing. The label sent us on a mini-tour, wanting to test out some of our new music. The response had been great, so great that we were pulled back to finish the album and sent out again on a world tour. Everything happened so quickly. Our songs went to the top of the charts. We were asked for interviews. Girls tried to sneak into our rooms and onto our tour buses. Other musicians, bands, and celebrities reached out in congratulations.

It was a whirlwind. It was amazing. It was our dream come true, but the craziness was starting to die down a little bit, and we were on our way home for our first break.

I didn't want a break. I wanted to keep going. I wanted to keep recording, keep playing, and keep being relevant. I didn't want to go away and become forgotten. Our managers wanted us to write more music. I had more music. I had music coming out of my asshole, but our managers said this was needed. The band had to relax and replenish, whatever the fuck that meant. I just knew that I wasn't happy to go back home. The guys were, though. Braden was ecstatic. Gunn dropped a bombshell and said he had a girl waiting for him back home, and then there was Emerson. He was a different type of bomb waiting to go off. He'd been a chore to deal with the whole time.

Emerson spent most of his time getting high. At first, concerts had to be rescheduled because he was sent to do a quick detox. He'd finish and come back in time to play. When this started happening too often and when he couldn't play, they hired a guy to play as his replacement. His nickname was Em2.

Priscilla and Peter thought going home would solve Emerson's problem, but it was the opposite. I had no doubt it'd only get worse. Hell. We all had our own problems there. Mine came in the shape of a heart-shaped face with long black eyelashes, lips that made my dick stand up in a salute, and long legs that could wrap around me in a fucking pretzel.

We hadn't talked since I left. I thought she would've come out to visit. Braden flew out their mom multiple times, but Brielle never came with her. I didn't know how to deal with her. Going back and seeing her made me feel like I was signing up to ride a tsunami as a carnival ride. Fun in theory, but dangerous from the get-go.

She gutted me. Three years. She had lied to me for that long.

"Yo, man." Emerson plopped into the seat next to me. He leaned over, looking out the window of our jet. "Still nothing, huh?"

"We don't land for another hour. There won't be anything until we start to descend."

I watched him closely. He was sweaty, and his speech was jerky. He was jonesing for a fix. "So, what's the plan?" he asked, bouncing his knees and wringing his hands together. When he noticed I was watching them, he stuffed them inside his pockets. His leg picked up its speed. "We have that radio interview, right? Then what?"

Then he was going to get high. "Then we go home for a vacation."

Priscilla came up the aisle and paused at our seats. She and her twin brother, Peter, had been managing us since we left Grant West. We weren't their first band, but we were the first to hit it big. She'd been so giddy back then, but now there were worry lines around her eyes, and she pursed her lips together for a moment. Her gaze lingered on Emerson, and I knew what she was thinking. I was thinking the same thing. How long until the next disaster? "You guys need to take a month off and then head back into the studio. We can't wait too long before your next album goes out. Time is money."

He shot her a dark look. "Thanks for the reminder."

"No problem." She patted my seat twice. Her voice was high, and her smile was forced. "That's why you guys have me." Then she glanced at me. "We'll be arriving in an hour, and a car will be there to pick you up. They'll take you guys straight to the interview."

Braden popped up from the seat in front of us. "Then home? After that, we go home, right?"

"Of course." The forced smile looked etched in plastic. "You're eager to see your family?"

He remarked, "No, I'm eager to get laid in my hometown."

"You guys are so funny."

As she moved forward and disappeared into the front section where her brother had set up their office, Emerson extended his middle finger in the air and muttered, "I hate that bitch. When can we fire them?"

Braden got up and took the seat across from us. "We can't. We're under contract."

Emerson groaned, slumping further down in his seat. His hands covered his bald head. "I can't handle another album with them."

"Album and tour," I corrected. The anger had been simmering in me. They weren't the only ones tired of the 'Peter and Priscilla Show.' They agreed to anything for a buck, whether or not we wanted to. "My lawyer's looking into the contract. They'll get us out."

"Maybe Bri can be our manager then?"

I stiffened, but made sure not to show any emotion. Feeling Braden's gaze on me, studying me, I relented, "Yeah, maybe."

Emerson grunted. "Fuck that. My cousin's a bitch. No offense, Bray."

"Fuck you."

Emerson ignored him. "Bri's not exactly the friendly type, you know. Her personality sucks. My mom says she's never at home; she's probably whoring around." As he said the last line, he was watching me, and when I didn't react, a smug smirk appeared on his face. "You know how Bri can be."

"Really?" Braden shot back at him. "'Cause from what I hear from my own sister is that she's working two jobs, ass-wipe. She won't let me help her out. She's still helping at Rowdy's and drumming for Callen."

Emerson shrugged. "I'm just telling you how I hear it. Elijah's my brother. He and Bri are still tight."

Narrowing my eyes, I threw at him, "But not dating tight?"

"What?"

"They're not dating again?"

His jaw clenched, and he rolled his eyes. "Who cares? My cousin's a slut. We're all thinking it. Why can't we just say it? Luke, you bought that old bar. Come on, you can't tell me you bought it for any other reason than to get away from her? The place is a dump. I've seen the pictures. Be real. You got the place because you don't want to go back and live so close to her again. Am I right?"

It was a spur-of-the-moment purchase and part of the reason I'd bought it had been to get away from Bri, but that was after our first big paycheck. When I was still angry with her. Hearing it now, having it thrown in my face—I started to get up from my seat. Emerson had overstepped one too many times, but Braden stopped me as he said, "Because we're not all thinking it. Only you're thinking it, so shut up." He leaned over and punched his leg. "Would you just shut up, Emerson?"

I lowered myself back down.

Gunn grunted, moving back to his seat, "I can't say a bad word about the girl. She's a kick-ass drummer, and it's because of her that I got to play with you guys."

Emerson's eyebrows furrowed together. A tendon stuck out from his neck, and he waited until Gunn had taken a seat in the back of the jet before muttering, "Our bass guitarist hardly says two words a night, and he's suddenly giving speeches in Bri's defense? What? Did she sleep with him, too?"

There was no warning.

As soon as the words left Emerson's mouth, Braden was on him within a split second. He pinned his cousin to the chair and delivered one, two, three punches. Emerson tried twisting out from underneath him, but Braden had him trapped in a cement grip with nowhere to go.

The outburst was violent, but eerie at the same time. Both had fallen silent, and the only sound was of Braden's fist hitting Emerson's face. A hard smacking sound that was muffled by the plane.

I was the only one witnessing it. Gunn must've tuned out in the back.

After the third punch, Emerson twisted his face and choked out to me, "Help."

"You can be a real bitch, you know," I told him.

Braden hit him again. "You stop talking about my sister like that, you asshole." He delivered a fifth hit.

When I saw blood, I knew it was time to intervene. Grabbing Braden's raised hand, I tipped him backward so he fell into the aisle. Emerson jumped from his seat in a flash. He launched for his cousin, and I had flashbacks when Brielle had done the same thing. I twisted and caught him around the waist. Heaving him back, I threw him into his seat. "You stay."

"So, he can hit me all he wants, but I can't get a few hits in?" Emerson spat at me, wiping some of the blood from his mouth. "Are you kidding me?"

Braden had shot back to his feet. Gunn was coming back up the aisle, and at the sight of the big guy, Emerson let out a disgusted sound. "This isn't fair! He attacked me. I should get one hit, at least."

"Stop talking shit about my sister!" Braden yelled and started for him again.

Gunn moved forward. He grabbed Braden's upper arm and said, "Hey, hey. None of that. You got him. It's done."

Braden stopped again, but twisted his arm free. No one argued when Gunn talked. He was six-three and was a solid two fifty of muscle. He wasn't security, but he could've been.

Emerson snarled. "I can't believe this. Luke, of all people, you should've let me get a few hits in."

"You did."

He stopped short, registered the joke, and grew heated. His face got red. The color spread up, all over the top of his bald head, and he sat back up. "I was just looking out for you, and that's how you treat me? Don't tell me you're going to go back to her?"

I stiffened.

The joke was gone, and my anger came back, hitting me full force. I warned him, pressing him down even harder, "I wouldn't talk shit about something you know nothing about. You got that?"

He quieted, held my gaze, and sighed as he shoved my hand off him. "Whatever. I'm so sick of this crap."

Braden laughed at that. "You're sick of this? Sick of being in a band? Sick of touring, doing what we love to do, being rich? Yeah, I'm sure you are. You're sick of having a life. That's what you're sick about."

I closed my eyes. This was going down a different road—one we hadn't been down yet.

I could sense Emerson's fury coming back to him. He had a short fuse, and it never took much to light it, but Braden had just pushed the wrong button for him. He was about to pop off and then he did.

"You shut up! You have no idea what you're talking about—" He shot up.

I shoved him back down. "Oh? You mean like with Bri and me?"

He quieted, but kept his gaze locked on mine. He was still heated, and his chest was heaving up and down with each angry breath.

After another hard poke, I asked, "Why don't you do us a favor and keep your mouth shut for once?"

Braden laughed from behind me. "Unreal."

Emerson continued to glare up at me, but did as I asked. After a moment, he hit my hand away and pushed up from the seat. Braden tensed. We all tensed, but he turned and went to the front of our section, right next to the curtain that separated us from our managers. He threw himself down into one of the seats and grabbed for his bag. When he took out his iPod and put in his earbuds, we all breathed easier.

Braden was shaking his head. "I love him. He's blood, but if they had extended this tour, I would've ended up killing him."

Gunn patted him on the chest. "I think a couple of us would've had shovels at the ready."

Braden paused, frowned at the big guy, and then barked out a laugh. "Em was right about one thing. You're Mr. Chatty tonight."

"Going home to my girl." He winked at Braden. "I'm doing all sorts of somersaults and have soft, pastel-looking butterflies on the inside. That's what my girl does to me. Reduces me to a pile of dribble." With those last words, he turned back to his seat.

Braden laughed to me. "Still surprised about his girl. I had no clue until he mentioned her the other day."

"I didn't either."

"Huh."

Braden cleared his throat, straightened his black shirt, and flicked some imaginary dirt from his black pants. Then he said, "So, about my sister…"

"Yeah?" I closed off. I wasn't ready to talk about her. Hell, I didn't even know how I felt about her myself.

"Is it going to be a problem?"

"What do you mean?"

"You and her. I know things didn't end on a good note with you two."

I fixed him with a dark stare. "Your sister and I are…" I closed my eyes for a brief second. What the hell was I going to say here? "There's nothing there, Braden. Not anymore."

"Oh. Okay…?"

"What do you want from me?" Fuck it. Let's be honest for once. "Look, I know you want her back in the band, but she and I haven't talked since we left."

His eyes darted to his cousin.

I added, "I know you want him out. We all do, but that's a battle for another day. Let's just enjoy that we're getting home soon."

"But Bri's the best drummer we know. I can switch back over—"

"Let's deal with it later. We're almost home, Braden."

"Yeah. Okay."

Leaning back in my seat, I couldn't deny he was right about one thing—Emerson was a loose cannon. He'd have to go, but the real question was when that would happen. Braden was a good drummer, but Brielle was the better drummer, and she knew us. We could trust her, well, my mouth twitched…for the most part.

CHAPTER
NINETEEN

"Hello, hello, hello! This is Jack and Jill from KXJB 92.3 and guess what, folks? However good it might be out there, it's not as good as it is in here. You want to know why? We have the boys from Sustaiiinnnn! That's right, folks. For the next hour, Luke—"

"Hello."

"—Braden—"

"What's up?"

"—Emerson—"

"Yo."

"—And the one they call Gunn—"

"—Here—"

"Jill here, and I know there are a lot of female listeners out there who want to know, *drooling* to know more about you guys. Ladies and gentlemen, if you have a question, call in to our station or tweet us at #kxjbsustain with your questions. For the next hour, we have these rock stars, semi-gods, with us live. Luke! I'm just going to jump in with the first question, get right down to business—"

"Oh, no."

"Jill says she's asking for the listeners, but we all know she's asking for herself."

"Jack! Who's doing this interview?"

"I might have to. You've got some of your own drool there, right on the side, Jill.

"I'm going to ignore my co-host and pretend to be the professional deejay they hired me for—not a word, Jack. So, Luke, here's the first question. I have to know, and thousands of other women want to know, too…are you single?"

"Ha! The right question is which girl is next? Right, buddy?!"

"Yeah, what was it? For a while there, you were beating Braden and me with girls. Nah, man. The Skeet ain't single."

"Thanks, Braden and Emerson. You're really making me look good."

"Anything for you, Luke."

"I'm surprised Gunn didn't jump in there either—"

"You were a man-whore for a while."

"Thanks, Gunn."

"Anything for you."

"Oh, man! So this is Sustain uncensored, huh? Give us more dirt. I'll be honest here. I know Jill's silently panting over there, but I have to admit that I'm interested, too. You guys blew up the charts. Who were you a year and a half ago? You guys are everywhere now, but before—where are you guys from? What were you guys doing? We want to know everything about you guys."

"Uh, first things first, Jack. Girlfriends. I want to know. Who has one, and who doesn't?"

"I'm going to tackle this one. This is Braden speaking, and that question can be directed to only one of us. Right, Gunn?"

"My private life is private, Braden."

"Ha! No doubt. He dropped the bomb on us today that he's got a girl back home waiting for him."

"Do tell, Gunn! And for the ladies at home listening, you should know that the other three members are not answering this question. In fact, they didn't even look at me as I asked it. Come on, Braden, Emerson, Luke. Everyone wants to know. Anyone special back home for you, guys?"

"Yes, I have to add to my co-anchor. They're still not answering Jill's question."

"So, does that mean there is someone special at home?"

"We're single. We just don't want to admit to how many women there've been."

"Speak for yourself, Braden—"

"Watch yourself, Emerson. I don't think any one of us has done some of the dirty shit you've done."

"We are live and uncensored, ladies and gentlemen. What you just heard was a smackdown delivered by the front man and some who have labeled the brains behind the international and platinum-selling band, Sustain. Luke, all jokes aside, let's talk real for a moment."

"Bring it, Jack. What do you have to throw at me?"

——— ——— ———

We waited in the hallway after the interview while Priscilla remained inside. She was still talking with the deejays.

Emerson watched her, leaning against the wall next to me. He grunted. "This is going to take forever. Where's the bathroom? I need to take a dump."

As he went in search of the bathroom, Braden shook his head. "Better here than stinking up our bus."

"Van," Peter added, still focused on his phone.

"What?"

"Van. You guys are taking a van."

"We've always taken a bus. Why a van now?"

"Because." Peter finished his last message and tucked the phone into his pocket. A bored expression that mingled with contempt gazed back at us. "You said you wanted to be inconspicuous. Rolling into town in a big tour bus isn't that. It's the opposite."

Gunn, Braden, and I shared a look. We wouldn't mind the van, but we knew someone who would. As one, all three of us turned to where Emerson had disappeared.

Braden let out a quick laugh. "No way am I breaking that news to him."

"He will just have to deal with it, won't he? Like a good little boy," Peter murmured, typing a new message on his phone.

I smirked. "I don't think Emerson was ever a good little boy."

Gunn nodded beside me.

Braden looked ready to say something new when Peter's phone buzzed, and our manager hit a button, bringing it to his ear. "Hello?" Silence. "Oh, yes. Wonderful. We are ready and waiting."

"The van is here?"

Peter held a finger to Braden and waited as the other person said more. He finished with, "Sounds great. We will be ready for you guys. See you in a few." Putting his phone into his pocket, he knocked on the window and made a motioning gesture to his sister to hurry up.

Priscilla came out and led the way to the back parking lot. A large white van was waiting for us. I asked, "What about all our stuff?"

"Already sent ahead. Everything will be waiting for you at that bar you own." Priscilla opened the door, and we were presented with stiff and awkward-looking seats.

Gunn peered around me into the van. "I should take the middle." He added, "For myself."

Braden laughed, but climbed inside. He headed to the very last row of seats. I slid in beside him, leaving Emerson his own row before us. There was one other row between Emerson and Gunn. I expected Peter and Priscilla to climb inside, but instead, Peter headed to the driver's seat. It wasn't long before Emerson strolled out the doors, hiking up his pants and then tugging them back down as his hand scratched his crotch. Priscilla was waiting beside the front passenger door. As he saw the van, he stopped and began shaking his head. "No, no, no, no. This won't work. What happened to the tour bus?"

She let out an impatient breath. "You guys didn't want a big to-do. Sorry this isn't 'diva' enough for you. This is it and hurry up. I made a couple of calls. You guys have some people waiting for you."

Braden leaned close to me. "And here comes the temper tantrum." Braden began to count backwards. He started from five and got to one when Emerson blew up. There were expletives, threats, demands, something about blackmail and an email was mentioned, and he kept waving his middle finger in the air. Priscilla remained silent the entire time. When he quieted down, enough to take a breath and embark on another tantrum, she said, "Get your ass in here, or I will drop you from the band. I can kick anyone out, and I can bring anyone in."

His head jerked back, and his gaze whipped to mine. I saw the question in his eyes. Could she do that? I didn't think she could, but knowing them and knowing the contract they had us sign, I wouldn't have been surprised if that was a loophole we hadn't realized was there.

"Shit," Braden murmured beside me. He slumped down in his seat. "We have to get that crap looked at."

The threat worked. Emerson climbed inside, and the rest of the ride was in awkward silence. He was ready to explode. The rest of us were waiting for it, but when we got to the outskirts of Grant West, we were relieved. The explosion was postponed as Peter pulled the van into a gas station lot. A light was positioned at the far end of the lot where a line of cars were parked and he headed for them. As we got closer, some people were standing outside their vehicles, waiting for us, but one person drew my eye. There, sitting on the end of the van by herself and looking bored to death, was Brielle.

I was gutted. I'd forgotten how beautiful she was.

Braden saw Bri at the same time and exclaimed, "Hell, yeah!" He darted out of the van and flung his arms out. "Bri!" She had one second to react before he lifted her in his arms and whirled her around. He got to hug her. He got to say he loved her, brother or not, and it pissed me off that I was jealous of him.

Braden set her down when I got out of the van.

She looked up. Her eyes widened as she saw me before looking away. Shoving her hands into her pockets, she looked down and stepped back from her brother.

I stopped before them. My hands itched to lift and touch her, but I kept them at my sides. She had lost weight. Her skin was a little paler than I remembered, and she had let her hair grow even longer. It swept down past the middle of her back.

"Hey," she murmured.

"Hey," I replied.

She flinched at my voice.

Braden cleared his throat. "You came to pick us up? Thank you."

She shook her head up and down in a short, clipping motion. "Yeah." She bit down on her lip. "Uh, not to make you guys hurry, but I have a gig. Mom offered to come and get you, but I wanted to do it. I have enough time. Did you want to come?" She was asking her brother, her eyes focused squarely on him. She darted a sideways look at me, swallowed, and skirted back to focus on her brother.

Braden's head popped up. He stood straighter. "Where's the gig? Of course, I want to come."

The corners of her mouth curved up, and her shoulders dropped, looking more relaxed. "We're at Rowdy's." There was a small amount of pride in her voice.

"Hell, yeah. Going our same route, huh? I can bartend," Braden teased, throwing an arm around his sister's shoulders. "Just like that one time when I covered for your ass."

"You mean that *one* time versus all the times I covered for your ass?"

"Details, Bri. Who can remember that far back?" Braden was joking when a car pulled into the lot. It braked to a spot away from the rest of the vehicles and then took off again, spewing dirt from behind the wheels. It fishtailed in a tight circle until it was facing the road again, then it came to another complete stop.

Emerson thrust a fist into the air. "My ride is here. Catch you later, fools."

"You're not coming to watch the band?" Braden called after him.

Emerson kept going, but turned and jogged backwards. He lifted a hand in a farewell wave and shrugged. "I've seen enough bands play, and I don't give a shit about seeing Bri play anymore."

"Fuck you, too," Bri called after him, giving him the middle finger.

Emerson laughed and turned back around. When he opened the back door, heavy metal music poured out. Someone handed him a joint from the front seat, and Emerson shut the door. It wasn't long before the car peeled out of there.

Braden cursed, "That's a record. Five minutes he's back and that crap happens?"

Bri was still biting her lip.

I skimmed an eye over her and said to her brother, "It doesn't matter. He'll crash, and the Terrible Twins will sweep him back up."

Braden grunted. "True."

"Terrible Twins?"

He answered her, "Our managers. They're twins, too, remember? I told you."

"Oh, yeah." She glanced at Priscilla who was conversing with the city official. "I'd forgotten."

She hadn't. I knew that much, and when she cast me a glance under her eyelashes, I saw the question in them. She wanted to know if I had slept with Priscilla. Well, fuck that. My jaw clenched. It wasn't her business anymore.

CHAPTER
TWENTY

"Luke!"

My eyes snapped open, and I groaned. I didn't need to check my phone to know it was early. Priscilla banged on the bar's door again. "Luke, come on! I see you on that cot. Get up. We have work to do today."

It's too early.

I rolled over and moved to the edge of my cot. When she kept banging, I groaned and cradled my head in my hands. Jeezus, woman.

"Luke!"

"Shut up!" I glared. She could see me through the door. "I'm coming." Stalking to the door and flinging it open, I snarled, "You have to take a dump or something?"

"What?" She tightened her hold on a bunch of folders she held against her chest.

"I was sleeping. Give me a minute to collect myself." I glanced down to make sure there was no morning wood. There was, but I readjusted my jeans. I had slept in them. All the clothes in my bag were dirty, and I'd forgotten I had no clean clothes here.

"Let me in." She shoved past me. Surveying my new home, she scrunched up her nose. "This place reeks."

"It hasn't been aired out for a while."

She started to walk toward the hallway. "Where's the bathro..." She trailed off, her finger tapping against her chin. "You have an apartment back there."

"I do."

She rotated around and pointed to the cot. "But you slept here, in the middle of your bar...on a cot when I can see the corner of a bed in there..."

I rolled my eyes and went behind the bar. I needed coffee, and then I needed to find a painkiller. My head was trying to murder me.

"Luke."

"What?" I shifted through a bunch of stuff until I found the coffee maker. Sweet Lord. Why the hell was it all the way in the back?

"Why are you sleeping on the floor of your bar?"

Because the apartment wasn't home. Because bars had become like home and because I didn't want to go back to my other home. Too many bad memories were there and too much of Bri, just too much. I would've felt her everywhere. I growled at Priscilla, "Because I wanted to. Stop poking your nose into my personal life. This," I indicated the bar, "has nothing to do with you."

She rolled her eyes. "Well, the name of this place is fitting. The Shack. That's what it looks like you're doing, shacking up here. I still don't understand why you got this place, but whatever. You seem touchy today." She gestured to the coffee maker. "As soon you get some of that, I want a cup, too." Then she raised her head and fixed me with a pointed stare. I'd come to recognize that look, and I had enough time to brace myself for whatever she was going to throw at me, but she only said, "Emerson is going to be a problem."

After starting the coffee, I leaned against the counter behind the bar and folded my arms. One of my eyebrows went up. "You say that like I'm going to argue with you." I held up my hands. "No fight here. I agree with you, but he's my problem, not yours. We'll deal with him."

"Okay." She placed both of her palms onto the table. This was when she usually dropped the ditzy attitude and shocked whoever her prey was with razor sharp ruthlessness. I smirked. It wasn't going to work on me, but she could try. She did. "Let me give you some facts—"

I laughed, cutting her off. "Save it. Emerson is ours. We'll take care of him."

She clamped her mouth shut, glaring for a moment, and then switched as she scanned an appreciative gaze up and down me. If she thought I was going to be turned on or become uncomfortable, she was forgetting one thing. I shook my head, smirking at her. "Priss, I'm a rock star. Your cougar preening does nothing for me. All it does is show your age and your claws."

"I have very long claws."

The coffee was done, and I poured a cup. "I'm sure you do. Sharpen them elsewhere. I'm not the pushover I was a year ago."

"So jaded, so early on, aren't you, Luke?" she mocked me, picking up more of her files. "Has this past year really been that bad? We made you famous and wealthy. We couldn't have been that bad of managers, could we?"

I laughed, poured a second cup and then dumped the rest of it down the drain. As she started to protest, I flashed her a smile. The protest died, and she went back to her seat. The chill had gone up in the room. As I started for the apartment, I murmured, "You didn't make us famous, Priss. We did. I did. And when I've finally gotten us out of that damn contract, we'll be even more famous, just for the sake of rubbing it in your face." She stiffened in the chair, and I winked at her before motioning to the door. "Now, get your ass out of here. I have no contractual obligation to allow you on these premises."

Then I strolled to the apartment and shut the door. She'd go. She had done what she needed to do. Even though she hadn't said the words, I got the underlying message from her. Either we dealt with Emerson or she would.

I wasn't sure if I wanted to see what she'd do to him, so it was time. Emerson needed to be dealt with, once and for all.

I owed Bri's ex a visit.

———

A girl with blonde hair and red highlights was on Elijah's patio when I got there. She opened the screen door and banged on the wooden door. "Beth!" The screen door hit her on the backside, but she ignored it and banged again. "Get out here! Beth!"

I paused on the sidewalk. Eli's front door was rarely used. Bri and Emerson always used the back door. I wasn't sure if I should wait behind this chick or go around, but she must've sensed me. She rounded swiftly. Her eyes narrowed, and she huffed at me, turning back to knock once more. Her hand formed into a fist, and she held it in the air. Her body went rigid, and she sucked in her breath, whirling back to me. Then her eyes were wide, and her other hand half covered her mouth. "Holy freaking shit. You're Luke Skeet."

"Hey." I frowned.

"Holy freaking hell. Holy, holy shit. Holy—" She started for me when the door opened. Another girl dashed out, ramming into her friend and barreling down the stairs. She darted into a red car and slammed the passenger door shut.

The blonde hadn't moved. Her eyes were still wide open and glued to me. She barely reacted as her friend pushed her into the doorframe. "Holy moly cabana…shit. I cannot believe…oh my god."

Catching movement from the doorway, I looked up and saw Elijah there, holding a coffee cup. He was shirtless, his jeans hung low on his hips, and his hair was sticking up. His gaze trailed over the girl to me. A cocky smirk appeared.

"Turner." I wanted to punch him. Every time I saw him, no matter where, when, or why, I wanted to hit him.

"Pretty Boy." He yawned the word, idly scratching at his chest at the same time. Then he rubbed the corners of his eyes and gestured to the blonde with his coffee. "You better get going, Hannah. Your cousin is in rare form this morning."

"You know Luke Skeet?" she asked him the question, but was staring at me. "How does a lowlife like you know a rock star super god?"

Elijah whistled through his teeth. "'Lowlife'? What has your cousin been saying about me?"

She rolled her eyes. "Whatever, Eli. Fine." Starting down the stairs, she slowed as she went past me. She pointed to me as she said to him, "You have some cred now. You know Luke Skeet." She shook her head and said to me, "I'd stay away from him if I were you. Apparently, he stopped selling drugs, but I don't believe it." She raised her voice. "He wouldn't be the first douche who lied."

Elijah propped a shoulder against his doorframe and sipped his coffee. "You might want to poke your nose where it can do good. Pretty Boy here already hates my guts. He's hated my guts for about twenty-two years now."

"Give or take," I added.

"Whatever, Eli, whatever." The girl rolled her eyes at him, but sent me a smile full of promises.

"Hannah!" the girl from the car yelled. "Get over here. We have to go."

Elijah chuckled. "Your cousin is in a snit. She spent the night. She's emotionally traumatized now, all that holding and cuddling." He pretended to grimace. "All those things that fill up nightmares."

Hannah gave him the middle finger as she hurried to the car. As they took off, Elijah let out a small sigh and muttered, half to himself and half to me, "What is it with me and emotionally unavailable women?"

I stepped up onto the patio. As he led the way back inside and to the kitchen, I followed and suggested, "You do have a screwed-up mother. That might be part of it."

"Maybe." He grunted and went to the coffee pot. "You want some?"

I was still feeling it from the two hours of sleep I got. "Yes, unless you're going to slip something in it."

Elijah shook his head. "You know me. I've been biding my time until I got you alone. Now, I can have my way with you, even if I am straight."

"I was referring to alcohol, but if you want to go that route, I've been reading your signals wrong for years now."

He barked out a laugh and leaned back against the kitchen counter. I leaned against the opposite doorframe, and we both eyed each other over our cups.

With the coffee and the slight jokes, we'd both been stalling. We couldn't anymore.

Elijah plunged first, "What are you doing here, Skeet? You don't need to be concerned if this is about Bri. She hasn't really been a part of my life since you left." *She hasn't?* Then he added more, "And I *have* stopped selling. Haven't you heard?" He flashed me a grin, but it was empty. "My mom went and got herself pregnant a while ago. Who will support the kid after she screws up and loses custody?"

"So, *you're* going to take care of him?"

He shrugged. "Gonna try. Whether they let me or not is another thing, but you didn't come over to talk to me about my problems. You're here because of Bri? She sent you?"

"No." *Why would she?* "I'm here about Emerson."

"Oh." He scratched behind his ear. "What about him?"

"He's still buying. I'm wondering if you'd help us to deal with him?"

He barked out another laugh, and his shoulders loosened. "Deal with him?" His green eyes narrowed. "How exactly?"

"Tell us how to stop him? We're open to suggestions."

He looked down at the floor and held his breath. He seemed to be thinking it over, but he looked back up. A resigned look was in his eyes. "You can't. I know enough about this shit to know you can't stop him until he hits rock bottom."

Well. That wasn't helpful. Glancing around, I didn't see any of his stuff. I asked, "Is he here?" I began moving down the hallway to the room Emerson always used. "Still sleeping?"

"No," he called after me. His body snapped to attention. "I mean." He scratched behind his ear. "Don't go down there. He was an ass last night. I'd steer clear until he's in a better mood."

I stared at him. Hard.

Eli didn't look away. There was no flicker of hesitation or question in his eyes. He didn't move at all, holding my gaze the whole time.

He was lying.

I'd grown up with Elijah Turner. Not many knew when he was holding something back, but I did. I had studied him all my life. That's what I did when he had the girl I loved. And I knew he was bluffing. I wondered if Elijah had even seen Emerson last night.

When I got into the truck, I called Braden. "We have a problem."

CHAPTER
TWENTY-ONE

I wanted the guys to meet at The Shack, but Braden mentioned it'd be better if we met somewhere Peter and Priss wouldn't know about. My old house it was. Pulling into my driveway, I looked at my house—my dad's house—and heaved a breath. Getting out of the truck, I could tell it'd been freshly painted. The last step had been fixed. The crack was gone from the middle of it. Heading up to the back door, I noticed the knob was secured back into place. Skimming an eye at Braden's house, I saw the curtain from Bri's old room had fallen back into place. A second later, her light switched off, and the knot was back in my gut. I had started calling the damn thing the Bri knot.

"What am I going to do with you?" I muttered under my breath. I wasn't sure whom I meant, the knot or the girl.

"Yo." Braden had come out of their back door and jumped over their patio steps. Landing smoothly on his feet, he stuffed his hands into his pockets and hunched his shoulders over, darting over to me. "Did you stay at The Shack last night? Bri said you never came back here."

Of course, she would've known.

Had she been watching for me the whole night? I grimaced. I wasn't sure how I felt about that. "I had to air out the place, didn't figure on driving back. It was too late." After I unlocked the door, we filtered inside. *Shit.* I stopped abruptly. The air was heavy, and there was an undercurrent of stale booze. I could smell it all. Tears, blood, screams, crying, my dad's cursing. Even now, I flinched because I could imagine the scrape of his boot when he stood from the couch. I never knew if he would head to my room and decide to beat me or if he would leave me alone. *Fuck.* That fear was still there; it had a death grip on me.

Braden mused beside me, "The place hasn't changed much."

I wanted to burn the place down. "No, it doesn't seem like it."

We heard tires on the loose gravel outside as someone else pulled into the driveway. The stairs creaked loudly underneath Gunn's weight. He looked freshly showered and relaxed. Giving us a wink, he said, "Hey there."

"I see you had a good night with the girlfriend."

"Yeah, man."

Braden frowned, hopping onto the counter. "We need to meet this chick."

"She's no chick. She's a woman." Gunn went to the kitchen table and sat down. He shook his head. "And no way am I letting her meet you. You and Luke are too pretty. The girls go crazy over you. You can meet her on our wedding day. Too late to leave me then."

Braden grinned. "Aw, sweet, controlling love."

Gunn gave him the middle finger, remarking, "Nah, that's called being smart."

I barked out a laugh. "Something you don't know, huh?"

"Hey!" Braden swung his head from Gunn to me, then back. "Pick on Braden Day? Is that what this is?"

"Stuff it. Like you can't handle it." Gunn leaned back in his chair, trying to restrain a smile. "You start it half the time."

Braden laughed. "You're right, I do. Okay, carry on. I wish you many nights of sex and blow jobs." He gave me a look, and just like that, I knew the joking was done. It was time for our unofficial meeting.

This was going to suck ass. Emerson was a pain, but we had grown up with him. He was like a brother to us. However, it was time, and feeling like I was about to hang a friend out to dry, I started it off. "Emerson relapsed last night."

"He uses every night," Gunn said so matter-of-factly.

I asked, "Every night?'

He shared a look with Braden who nodded and added, "It's been every night."

"Then it's worse than I thought."

"He's going to be a liability." Gunn seemed to hesitate. "We need to cut him from the band."

"I agree," Braden said quickly. His head was down, and his shoulders were tense. "I love him. He's family, but he's going to bring us down. It's only a matter of time."

"I'm down for Bri coming back." The suggestion came from Gunn. Both Braden and I swung our heads around, and he shrugged. "Like we're not all thinking it. I know you two have had words about her, but the girl is magic behind those drums. We all know it."

Fucking hell. I could feel that tsunami getting closer and closer, and I didn't know if I was ready for it or not.

Braden murmured quietly, "I think the decision is Luke's. We all know my vote on that one."

Gunn lifted his hand in the air. "I vote we ask her," he added, "I fucking love this band. This is my livelihood, too. I know I hit the lottery when she dropped out. Emerson's like a brother now, but he's going down a bad road, and we all know it. We've tried for a year, more than a year for you guys, and he won't stop. We have to cut him loose. She'll make the band better. It's a clear-cut decision."

Braden's eyes were getting bigger and bigger as Gunn talked. "Is this a yes? Should I talk to her? Is this really a go?"

I could feel Braden's excitement. Gunn grunted in approval.

"What about Emerson?" Braden asked both of us.

Emerson was family, but he was going to hurt us. "We'll figure something out with him."

Braden didn't respond, and Gunn's tone turned soft. "I love the guy. This hurts me, too."

It was hurting all of us.

Braden spoke up, "Bri's got a gig tonight—some house party. I say we go. Talk to her there."

"Wait a minute. I haven't agreed, and we haven't thought how to handle this with Priss and Peter. You know they're going to fight it. Priss won't want a girl in the band."

"Who the fuck cares?" Braden shot back. He jumped to his feet and started pacing. "You'll handle her. You're the only one she listens to anyway. I say we just go for it. Bring Bri in, kick Emerson out, and tell the Twins this is how it is."

"That easy, huh?" He had no clue.

"Yeah, why not?"

"Why are you fighting this, Luke?" Gunn asked. "You called the meeting."

"I know." I wasn't fighting it. "I just want to go over it, so we know there's nothing more we could've done for him. No regrets."

"He won't go to rehab. The Twins got him in four times over the last year, and he always left within a day. He won't stick it out. They covered for him. *We* covered for him. I've been covering for him all my life, so has Bri, and he treats her like shit," Braden swore. "It's done. We've given him enough chances."

"Okay." It was done then. "How do we act until it's done?"

Braden quieted and glanced away.

Gunn said it for us, "We act normal. That's all we can do."

"So, we go to the house party then."

Fucking hell. Bri was coming back. Had I agreed to this? Emerson had to go. That was set in stone, but Bri...I wasn't ready for her.

"They're going to go crazy." A speculative gleam formed in Braden's gaze, and his smirk grew. "That Wes guy will hate it."

"Wes?"

Braden rolled his eyes. "The singer in Bri's new band. I met him last night. He seems like a douche."

Gunn grunted. "I suppose I'll have to be security for you two. Too pretty."

"Bring your woman. I still want to meet her."

Gunn leveled Braden with a shrewd look. "Right."

Braden laughed, and hopped back onto the counter. He was more relaxed now, and he teased back, "I think you're hiding something, Gunn. Is this girl even real? Come on..."

They continued to tease each other, but it was a mask. I didn't participate in the conversation. They might sound happy and light-hearted, but they weren't. None of us were. We decided to cut our friend, our brother, from the band. I hadn't officially agreed to Bri coming back, but I couldn't think about her yet. We had Emerson to deal with first. I did the dirty work for us, so that meant I would be the one to tell him.

———— ———— ————

She was hitting the bass with a strong and sturdy hand. Her head was bent down, and her back was folded over. She was feeling the music. I could see her heel moving with the backbeat, but her left hand was hitting the snares.

Fuck.

The sight of her took my breath away. Her head came up, and her eyes were closed. She was biting her lip, and the rest of her body began to move in a frenzy. She was building up the second beat. It was coming. She was raising the room to a crescendo, but it was so silent. Everyone in the room felt it coming, and they reacted. People fell still. They forgot their dancing. They forgot the person next to them. They knew something big was fixing to happen.

It was all Brielle. She was making them listen to her. She was controlling everything.

I let out a ragged breath. No one else could do what she did. She should've been doing this all along. She shouldn't be stuck playing in a crappy house party like this or some dingy bar. She belonged in a stadium. She deserved to pour this magic out over thousands, having millions love her. That's where she belonged. Not here…and I had been the reason for where she was.

My jaw clenched.

The lead singer, Wes, stood at the front of the stage, clueless to what she was doing. He wasn't in tune with her at all.

The feeling to yank him down and take his place clawed at me. Braden was restless beside me, and I knew he was feeling the same. His fingers were playing out the chords along with the other guitarist. He was itching for his old spot as well.

I pushed forward. We were dressed in black hooded sweatshirts. We had gone the Elijah route, but we added a baseball cap to pull low over our faces. A few girls stopped and watched us with suspicion when we parked and darted to the back door. Even then, I knew there was something familiar about us to them. It was only a matter of time before people spotted us and realized we were there.

As she stopped hitting the drums, everyone froze in awe, waiting for her to continue. It took all my strength not to jump up there and take the microphone. My blood was pumping. I wanted to play with her, sing to her beat. This was the first time hearing her in a year, and I didn't think I could stop myself.

Her hand raised.

The girls next to us held their breath, and then Brielle slammed it down. The bass guitarist struck his chord, the lead guitarist joined in, and the guy at the keyboard joined in with the melody. The room went nuts, except for the singer. The fucking singer. He was standing there like I did. He held the microphone. His head was bent. Even his heel was counting the beats, but he was wrong. He should've been counting the beats when the beats weren't playing. He was reacting *to* Brielle, not being *with* Brielle. I could see the frustration on her face. The singer wasn't her match, and she knew it. I watched her bite her lip—the little thing she did—but she bit down harder than normal, and I knew it was because of him.

It was then when her head flew up that she skimmed the audience as she reached for the snare. She never skimmed the audience, but she did now. Her eyes caught and held mine, and they widened. I saw the shock filter in. It made her pause a fraction of a second, and then she grimaced. I could see the curse leave her lips before she shifted back into playing mode.

Her band never knew. She was the ultimate professional.

"Holy fuck," Braden exclaimed beside me. "She's gotten better. She smokes me. She was good the other day at Rowdy's, but tonight." He whistled under his breath. "Man."

Memories of when she came to me and asked for my guitar flooded me. She had needed to play music to earn money. I had gone with her, and it was one of the best memories I had. She never had a set memorized. She went with the flow and made up new songs. She was talented. People stopped to listen to her. I sat next to her, and sometimes

I sang with her if I knew where she was going with the chords. Her voice was hypnotic. She pulled on them, and she was doing it now with her drums.

"It's Sustain!"

Another person added, "It is! Holy—Sustain!"

"Luke Skeet?"

"Whoa, it is them."

More and more people started to spot us. The ones closest to the stage turned around and began to move toward us. People began pressing into each other. We were going to get overrun, but Gunn came up behind us. He reached around both of us and began walking forward, herding us out of there.

Gunn grunted into our ears. "People are swarming from outside. There was a big rush from the kitchen to the living room."

"Sustain is in my house?" A guy was dumbfounded beside us, scratching his head with one hand and holding a beer in the other. "How cool is that?! I'm awesome!"

Braden looked around us. Worry lines appeared on his forehead, and his shoulders lifted, straining. "We have to get out of here. We're going to get crushed."

"Luke! Oh, my gosh. It's you. I want to meet you."

People grabbed for me. Someone reached for my hand as others went for my shirt. When I felt it rip, someone shrieked, and then there were hands touching my skin. Someone reached for my jeans. I felt one of the back pockets starting to rip off.

Enough of this shit. I pushed forward, growling, "Let's get out of here."

Suddenly, four large guys moved around us. Two went in front and began shoving people out of the way. Gunn brought up the back, and the other two were at our sides. They held people back as well, and slowly we were able to able to move out of the room in that formation.

One of the guys in the front called over his shoulder, "The front door's blocked. Too many people. We can go out another way."

They moved into the dining room and down a back hallway. As we walked into a bedroom, I caught sight of a couple making out on the bed, and they jerked upright at our appearance. "Hey!" The girl's protest died as she saw us. Her mouth fell open in the next second.

"Whoa! You're Luke Skeet." She pointed at me.

My head lowered.

There was a door attached to the bedroom that led outside. One of the guys opened it and gestured. "Follow me. This is my buddy's house. We can sneak you out and around the crowd."

Braden said, "We're parked out front."

"Braden!"

We looked over. Brielle was running for us. An idea came to me, and I held my hand out to Braden. "Your keys."

He handed them over, and I tossed them to Brielle as she got to us. "Drive his car down the road."

She nodded and caught the keys. Without breaking stride, she ran right past us and around to the front of the house.

One of the guys frowned at her. "Wasn't that the drummer from inside?"

A girl jogged around the side of the house, stopped, and pointed at us. She yelled to the crowd, "They're over here!"

He added, "You guys are too big to be here."

His buddy agreed. "No, shit. Let's go."

They led the way into a wooded area behind the house. As we got farther away from the house, we could see more and more headlights heading toward it. One of our guides commented, "Word's out. I just got eight tweets that you're at Fuller's party."

The first one cursed again, "The cops are going to get called. You better text the other guys so they scram. We can't get in trouble with Coach."

Braden's phone buzzed, and he asked at the same time he glanced at his screen, "Coach? You guys on a team or something?"

Their leader nodded, grabbing a branch and moving it up so we could pass by. "Yeah, we're on the football team for the university here."

"Really?" Braden was impressed. His phone buzzed again, and he looked at me. "Bri said she's on a road up ahead."

The fourth member, who hadn't said a word yet, asked now, "How do you guys know the drummer?"

Braden was texting her back as he muttered, "Uh, she's my sister, why?"

"She single?"

The first two guys laughed at their buddy. The third was watching me, but I kept my mouth shut. I had no claim.

Braden glanced at me, but answered with caution, "Uh...I don't know. She doesn't talk to me about that stuff."

"She's hot."

"Good rack," the first one added, winking at his friend.

Gunn stepped onto a heavy stick and broke it in one snap. The power of his leg caught their attention, and they quieted for a moment. He said in that silence, "You're not her type."

"Are you her type?"

The fourth football player wasn't as tall as Gunn or as solidly built, but he flexed his hands as if ready for battle. An amused glint appeared in Gunn's gaze. He replied, "Like I said, you're not her type."

The third player spoke up now, "Carson didn't mean anything by it. He's a man-whore. We keep hoping he'll get help, but nothing seems to fix stupid."

"Hey."

He threw back, "Chill out, man. These guys are Sustain. They can send one tweet out, and someone would vandalize your parents' house. People are nuts."

Braden laughed. "Not that we condone that behavior."

I'd been tense from watching Bri on stage, and it hadn't lessened as we ran through the woods. If there was another remark about her, I was ready to swing. I didn't care how big they were.

Gunn had been watching me. He moved close and said under his breath, "If it happens, I'll do it."

"Why?"

"Because we need your pretty face for the fans."

I looked up to see if he was serious. He was, but he relinquished,

"Kidding. If you have a busted face, I think Priss would piss her pants from excitement."

Braden had overheard him and laughed. "No, shit. That'd be leaked to the gossip shows in two seconds flat. I swear, she has all the numbers for the gossip channels on speed dial."

The football players had gone ahead, but stopped and waited for us. The third one asked, "What's going on?"

"Nothing." I shoved past him. I spotted the road through the trees and saw the headlights for Braden's car at the same time. When we cleared the trees and headed up the ditch, all of us spread out and walked in one line for the car.

When we got there, Bri opened her door and leaned against the car. Her hair was whipping behind her face and one hand was resting on her hip. She tugged her shirt and then adjusted it back, but it didn't stick. It fell down, showing her black bra. Bri was clueless, scowling at us. She was the picture of fierce and alluring at the same time.

We were greeted with, "What were you guys doing there?"

She took in the whole line of guys before letting her eyes find mine, making me feel seared from the inside out. My insides felt yanked out, but I still wanted to touch her.

I looked away instead.

"We came to see you." Braden motioned to the guys.

"Are you insane? How was tonight supposed to go down any other way? You guys are celebrities. You can't be coming to house parties anymore." There was a clipped bark to her voice, but it faded on the last word, and I glanced over at her. She sneaked a look at me.

"Yeah, we didn't think ahead." Braden threw a hand to the football guys. "Got some extra room?"

She shook her head. "There is no way this little car can fit all of you hulks."

The guys laughed and one mentioned, "We can wait here. A bunch of our buddies are coming. They can pick us up."

I should've thanked them for saving us from the chaos, and I heard Gunn and Braden doing exactly that, but I looked back at her. Her hand was still on her hip, but her shoulders were slumped forward. She was kicking at some gravel on the road.

The football guys headed farther down the road as Gunn and Braden got into the car. We were alone now, but we still had an audience.

She wouldn't look at me anymore. I wanted to turn those dark eyes to me. I wanted to say something, but I had no idea what. I ended up with, "You're still really good."

Her head lifted, and I saw it. There was so much there. Fear, caution, excitement, warmth, and another expression I couldn't place. No, I did. She was still haunted.

"Thanks."

She was mine.

No. She wasn't.

She had gone to *him* that night.

Ah, fucking hell.

"We should probably talk."

Her eyes opened at my tone, which was rough, and panic flared across her face for a moment. "Oh. Okay."

CHAPTER
TWENTY-TWO

'The Talk' never happened.

Over the last week, my new place had become the hangout for everyone. Bri came a few times, but neither of us made the first move. Tonight was The Feast, and I figured it was time. There'd be a party afterward. Lots of booze. Lots of music. Lots of loose tongues going around. I had a feeling this conversation with Brielle was going to be like taking a shot of acid while doing acid.

Gunn picked up everyone. The Feast was located farther back in the park than other years. As we wound our way through the woods and down the hill to the small clearing where a stage was set up, I could hear Bri's band already playing. It was the same thing as the house party. The singer was off a beat.

When we stepped out into the clearing, someone called out my name, "Skeeter! Over here."

Dustin Glass waved a flashlight in the air, making air traffic signals with it, as if we were a plane coming in for a landing. "Right here, guys." He lit up four empty lawn chairs set up with the rest of his group. As we got closer, I recognized Paul and some of the guys from Shifter, who held up a hand in greeting, and some chick...Ava?...came over to sit in Braden's lap.

I asked as I sat down, "You still get invited to this stuff, Glass?"

"Yeah," Braden added. "You quit being our roadie after six months."

"You know me, guys. I've got my fingers in a little bit of everything." He spread his arms out. "Behold the gloriousness of yours truly. And, Braden, I had to. My folks gave me my trust fund back, and my dad worked his magic. He got me back into Harvard. Living the life and touring with you superstar a-holes was fun, but real life came knocking." He winked at me as he skimmed his hand over a girl's ass in front of him. "But if you ever need another worker for a summer tour, Mr. Glass is signed up and ready for duty. Getting these benefits," he squeezed her butt cheeks, "on a daily basis is like the first circle of heaven. Or, at least, I hope it will be, if you know what I mean." As he finished, he swatted the girl with a resounding slap.

She laughed and swung her gaze to me. She licked her lips and tugged the front of her shirt down, just far enough so I could tell she wasn't wearing a bra. My gaze lingered. Being around Brielle and not being able to touch her had sent *me* to the first circle of hell. This girl was willing, and she had curves to hold onto, but even as I considered it, she wasn't the one I wanted.

I mouthed back to her, "No thanks."

She opened her legs even wider.

I knew this type. She didn't care. She'd be there whenever, wherever, and however I wanted. It was the same feeling afterward. Those girls left me with nothing, just emptiness. After too many times of feeling that cheap emptiness, the draw for a quick fuck didn't hold any appeal. It never had, but there'd been a few months in the beginning when that was all I wanted as I tried to chase Brielle out of my system.

Fucking Brielle.

I shifted and tried to readjust myself. *Now* he was a springboard. Just the thought of her sent him into full action mode.

"That's the end of Callen, folks," Wes said into the microphone.

Emerson swore, "We're not his paying fans. He needs to stop talking to us like we are."

"The next band up is Easter Midnight."

No one clapped as they left the stage. A few people called out to Brielle, telling her she did a good job, but that was the only response. The other two members scattered, going to different groups, and Brielle headed toward us. Wes saw where she was going and held back at the stage.

"He's not welcomed," Emerson growled. "Braden, if that singer douche comes over here, I'm going to punch him."

Wes hadn't heard. He decided to come over anyway.

Braden laughed. "Better get ready, cousin."

When he was closer, Emerson hollered at him, "Just warning you, if you try to sit with us, I'm going to punch you. No dumbshits allowed."

He wavered in his walking, and his foot went sideways, making him trip for a second. "What'd you say?"

Brielle caught my gaze.

Everything else melted away. With the weight of her gaze on me, the world centered again. For one moment, just one god forsaken moment, I wished all our problems away. I wanted to be with her. I wanted her in my arms.

I had a snowball's chance in hell of getting any of that.

"Luke."

I glanced to the girl sitting on Dustin's right. It was Candy Lake. She gave me a warm smile and patted the seat in front of her, spreading her legs for me.

I could feel Bri's gaze on me, but I headed over to Candy and sat down in front of her. Her hands went to my shoulders, and she leaned forward. Her lips brushed my neck as she murmured, "Could you look any better? Rock stardom suits you, Skeet." She leaned down and gripped my arms, giving me a slight hug before she started massaging there, moving back up to my shoulders. As her hands settled into my deltoids, her legs pressed against me, hugging me from both sides. She was warm and comforting. She was what I needed at that moment.

Bri was glaring. Her hand crushed her beer can, and she jerked her gaze away.

Satisfaction flared through me. Good.

"Hunt!" Braden said, waving.

Jesse Hunt came over to our group. When he caught sight of me, he shook his head.

I held a hand out. "Hey, man."

He slapped it and gazed around. "I didn't know we had to bring our own chairs."

"You don't." Braden hopped off his and settled in front of Brielle, poking her at the same time. "You can have mine. Is your woman with you?"

Jesse cursed as he took the seat. "Yes, and do not let her know you referred to her that way. We're still in the 'coming together' stage."

Candy kept massaging my shoulders. Jesse's gaze lingered on her, confused. To his unspoken question, I shrugged. She wasn't Brielle. Jesse knew the status of my feelings. I met him one night in a bar, drunk off my ass, and the two of us decided to fight the entire bar together. I had invited him earlier, but I wasn't concerned he would invite anyone else. Jesse Hunt had his own celebrity status. His father was a world-renowned director, and he could go pro in basketball whenever he wanted. He played for Grant West University's basketball team, but it was only a matter of time when Jesse would decide if he wanted to finish his degree or go straight to the professional league. So far, he seemed content with his university team.

It wasn't long until his woman joined the group. She stood, gazing around the group with a star-struck expression, but Jesse caught her hand and pulled her to sit on his lap. Hunt was a good friend. We weren't close, but I knew he'd be there if I ever needed him and vice versa. Emerson teased him, trying to flirt with his woman. Hunt handled him fine. Studying them, seeing the easy camaraderie between Hunt and his woman, had me glancing at Brielle. They reminded me of us. They were best friends, no matter what was going on between them. He loved her. It was obvious. The sight of them sickened me. I should've been happy for them, but in that moment, I wasn't the good friend.

I wanted what they had; I shot Bri another glare.

I protected the band. I did the dirty work, maintaining everyone kept on task. I brought us to where we were, and I had done it by being the better man, but I wasn't in that moment. I was the jealous man. I was the petty man. I wanted a love like theirs, and I wanted it from Brielle.

She mistook my glare and lifted her chin in defiance. Taking a drink, she let me watch how she swallowed it before gracing me with a smug smirk.

The desire to grab her and haul her off into the woods was more than I could handle. I was still fighting it when it was our turn for the stage, and as we took it, I signaled for our new material. She was still with me. She was in my mind. The feel of her, the taste of her, and the need for her were suffocating me.

I sang to her. I didn't give a shit who knew.

This song was for her. It was about her. I wanted her to know.

You promised the world with my hand in yours
We grew up beside each other
Together, never apart, and now I can't let go
Here I am, on all fours
Baby please, baby that's mine
Baby please
Bring me home
Bring me in to you
No matter where you go, how far you are, you're home
Home, home, home
Don't let me go

The emotion was in my voice. Everyone could hear it, and I even heard Braden swear softly behind me. He knew as well. I was laying it out. When I opened my eyes and found her, she was still there. She was riveted, and she made no movement to wipe the tears from her eyes as they flowed down her face. One fell into her beer. She still didn't turn away.

I held her in my spell, the same one she wove when she played. She couldn't look away the entire time. Even as we finished our set and headed down, she couldn't move.

"Luke," Candy called my name. She patted the space in front of her again.

Brielle closed her eyes. I watched her as she held her breath. Something broke in me then. She did care. A flood of love and hate washed through me.

"Luke?"

Candy was looking at me, her eyebrows scrunched together. I glanced around. Everyone else was watching me, too. I had stopped in front of Brielle's chair. She was the only one not watching me. Her arms were wrapped around herself, and her head was pushed down into her chest. She was closing herself off from the world.

She had done that when we were kids, when she was scared and hurting. I hated seeing it then, and I hated seeing it now.

"Bri."

She stiffened, but I ignored it. I stopped thinking about the past. I turned it off. Seeing her like this made all of that go away. I wanted her to stop hurting. Without thinking, I bent down and slid my hands around her. Lifting her, I moved so I was underneath her. I pulled her onto my lap and wrapped my arms around her.

Her body was like cement, as if she was scared to relax. I ran a hand down her hair, smoothing it out. Her entire body shuddered as she let a sob out. She swallowed it immediately and stared straight ahead. I could feel her body trembling, yet she was still so rigid.

I had made it worse.

Cursing in my head, knowing I couldn't do anything else, I held her while neither of us said a word.

I wanted to loathe this girl, walk away, and live my life unscathed by her. I couldn't. She was my other half, and no matter how hard I tried, I couldn't convince myself otherwise.

A few more bands played, and our group sat in our small circle as some people wandered over to talk. When the first ones came over, Braden glanced at me, but I shook my head. I wasn't the leader tonight, and he nodded, stepping into that role for the evening. Braden did the talking for us. Candy tried to get my attention during the rest of the night, so did that other girl, but I ignored them and tightened my arms around Brielle.

It was awkward, but damn, I'd do it again. And again. And again. I didn't want to let her go.

"Luke, my man," Dustin called out when The Feast was over. Everyone was picking up their chairs and coolers, but paused and waited. He pointed at me, a wide grin on his face. "I know you have alcohol at your place, and I can get some kegs. What do you say? Should we end this night with a party to end all parties at your new place? You're a rock god. Let's party like rock gods!"

"Hey, yeah." Candy perked up. "I'm game."

Others joined in with the same sentiments.

I glanced at Braden, who shrugged. "Fine with me. We're on vacation, right?"

I grunted. "Says you. It won't be at your place."

"Come on, Luke," Candy taunted. "You can afford to hire cleaners. I don't think you're hurting for money."

I didn't want a party. I didn't want strangers at my place. I wanted Brielle, and I wanted privacy. But…I took in all the looks. They wanted a party, and damn, I knew I was going to give in, even before I said the words, "Okay—"

Dustin let out a war whoop and smacked his girl's ass. He pointed at me. "You won't regret it. It'll be awesome. A rock god party. Let's do this!" His fist thrust in the air in triumph. "Who's going with me to get the kegs?"

Others called out to him, and he motioned up the hill. "The cars! Let's get this bitch going." He took off, and his girl giggled, running after him up the hill.

Brielle had crawled off my lap, and I stood, waiting as she collected her chair and blanket. There was no going back. We would talk, even if I had to throw her over my shoulder and lock her away from everyone else.

"Bri?"

I stiffened. Callen's lead singer was there. His hands were stuffed into his pockets, and his gaze lingered on me as he said further, "Can I get a ride home?"

What the—?

His shoulders tensed, reacting to my anger, but he added, "The others just left—"

"Hey, man." Emerson clapped a hand on Wes' shoulder. He jumped back, but Emerson tightened his hold on him. He added, "We'll give you a ride home. I was just joking around before. I wouldn't punch you."

Bri frowned. "Emerson? What are you doing?"

He gestured to me. "I'm being a good buddy." His hand tightened again on Wes' shoulder. "I'm taking one for the team here. We'll give your rocker a ride home. No sweat."

"Uh." Wes had gone pale. "I think I see a friend. She can give me a ride home. Never mind."

He took off, and Emerson started laughing. "I think he just shit his pants."

"Why are you always such an ass?"

He stopped laughing and glared at Bri. "For the record, I *was* going to give him a ride home."

"You were?" Gunn had joined the conversation.

Emerson amended, "I was going to have Gunn give him a ride home, so you two lovebirds didn't have to part." He fixed me with a glare. "You're welcome."

Bri rolled her eyes. "You weren't going to give him a ride home, and you know it. You just wanted to scare him, like you did before, so he wouldn't sit with us."

"Again," Emerson bit out. His scowl deepened. "I did that shit for Luke. That prick just wants in your pants, and he's using you for his band. You make that band. His band sucks. He sings off-pitch half the time and tries to cover it up, and the other two are hardly on beat. The only thing they have going for them is their hot drummer."

"If you're hoping to piss me off by insulting Callen, it's not going to work. I'm not attached to them, so I don't care what you say about them."

"You're right. We all know what band you're attached to—"

"This isn't happening." I stepped between them and said to Emerson, "Walk."

"I was trying to help you."

"I know, but you're not anymore. Walk away."

"Luke—"

I lowered my voice. "Walk, Emerson."

Gunn was waiting to the side, and I nodded my head at him. He took hold of Emerson's arm and began to drag him away. I thought Emerson would protest, but he didn't. He walked with him, his head hanging down. A defeated air settled over him.

I waited until they had disappeared over the hill and then turned to Brielle. She was still behind me, gripping her chair tightly in one hand. Her blanket had been thrown over her shoulder.

"Will he always hate me?" She sounded defeated, too.

I didn't know, but I took the chair from her. "Can I get a ride to The Shack?"

She closed her eyes and drew in a breath. Pain flashed over her face, but she nodded. "Yeah."

CHAPTER
TWENTY-THREE

It was right. Being with her and sitting next to her felt right. Having her sit on my lap and holding her felt right, too.

"I was the one who robbed your dad. I took the money—it was my fault."

"That's why you went to Elijah?"

Her head moved up and down. She whispered, with tears streaming down her face, "I'm sorry, Luke. I'm so sorry."

Three years.

That sat on the bottom of my stomach for a year, four months, two weeks, and one day. My hand curved around the door handle, and I held onto it tightly. Glancing at her as she drove, I watched as she bit her lip. She was always biting her lip. There were bags underneath her eyes, and her arm was rigid.

Three years. I didn't know if I could make that okay in my head. If she could lie about that, then... *What else was she lying about?* a voice whispered in my head, feeding the black hole inside me.

She skirted her eyes to mine, but then looked away just as quickly.

The guys wanted her in the band again, but fuck—how could I do that? How could I play with her and not have her? I let out a soft breath of air. No matter what took place, there was no happy ending for us.

I didn't trust her.

The drive to The Shack was made in silence. When we got there, I had her pull around to the back door. When we went inside, she went straight to the bar. I paused, heading for the front door to let everyone inside, but at the sight of her behind my bar, a force slammed into my chest.

She hesitated, seeing my reaction. "What?"

That was right—having her here—in my bar. I forced my head to move side to side. "Nothing."

"Oh." She frowned, but grabbed a pitcher and went to the sink.

I had to force myself to look away. Shaking my head, I cleared my thoughts and went to the door. Unlocking it, I stepped back as everyone filed inside. They greeted me as they moved past me. Some of the girls touched my chest or arm, and a few of the guys thumped me on the shoulder. After the last one entered, I let the door close again and trailed behind the crowd. A group had congregated in front of the bar while Brielle was busy filling drinks. One of the bands jumped onto the stage. A guy caught my gaze and pointed to the guitar. "You mind?"

"Have at it."

The rest of his band joined him, and soon they started playing.

Dustin came in and waved with a set of keys in his hands. "We got the kegs. #fastestkegrunever!" He asked, "You got a back door or something where we can roll these bad boys in?"

"Yeah." I started forward. "There's a door by the bar. Hold on."

Dustin disappeared outside.

Bri called out, "I got it."

"You sure?"

She nodded and disappeared to the other end of the bar. The door was located around the corner, and it wasn't long before Dustin's voice was heard again, loud and clear, when he hollered, "We got beer chicks here. They're rolling through. Watch out, folks!" Three kegs were rolled in. He had the first one, and two more guys brought the others.

Brielle went around them and showed Dustin where to put the kegs.

Candy came in, following behind the kegs. She and her friends hopped onto the bar stools, and it wasn't long before Brielle had the kegs hooked up and was handing out the beer. Dustin got the first pitcher and came over to me.

He filled a plastic cup. "Drink up, Luke. This is the time for you to relax and enjoy being a god."

"Dustin, how I've missed having you on tour with us."

He barked out a loud laugh before he drank from his own pitcher. He handed his cup to someone passing by and threw his free arm around my shoulder. "The lifestyle was amazing. I fucking loved it, but, man, I'll admit I was happy to get away from the Priss Bitch."

I grunted. I liked that name.

"Don't tell me they're still doing the same shit?" Before I could answer, he glanced around. "Where are the guys?"

"They'll be here."

"They better be. I only have so many days home. I want to party hardy with you guys, and I can't do that unless those guys are here, too." He paused, tightening his hold on the pitcher before he said, "Emerson seemed in his normal form. How's that going?"

Dustin wasn't stupid. I knew what he was referring to, but I shrugged a shoulder. "He's trying."

"He's sucking at it."

"What do you mean?"

"I don't know exactly what you're talking about, but if he's trying to be sober, he failed tonight."

Fuck. "What do you mean?"

Dustin snorted before he took another large gulp from his pitcher. "He was high as a kite tonight. I'm surprised you didn't notice."

So am I...but then again...I glanced at Brielle behind the bar. She felt it and looked up, pausing as she extended a drink to someone. I murmured to him, "I was distracted tonight."

He knew whom I meant. "I can see that. So, that's still going on?" He tipped his head back, finishing his pitcher. "You two dance around each other so much. I figured you would've moved on or decided to get hitched. One or the other, you know. Anyway..." He lifted the pitcher and shook it. Only a small amount of beer was at the bottom. "Looks like I need a refill." He winked before he headed toward her. "Don't worry, Luke. I'll put in a good word for you. We both know you need all the help you can get."

He went to Brielle and gave her his pitcher. Then he leaned over the bar and pointed to me. She stiffened. Her jaw clenched, and her hand tightened its hold around the pitcher before she finished filling it. As she shoved it at him, she clipped a response, and he reared back. A wicked look flashed over his face, and he leaned back to laugh before moving away. Instead of coming to me, he headed to a table that Candy and her friends had taken over.

Bri came over and threw a thumb over her shoulder. "He told me to give you a pity screw and put you out of your puppy-dog misery."

I laughed. "Thinking about it?"

She huffed out, "Right. What'd Emerson say before? 'No dumbshits allowed'?" She pointed between her legs. "My vajayjay has the same policy."

"I'm not the dumbshit."

We were laughing. We were teasing each other. My nerves stretched. I didn't want this to go away.

"No, but you just had one talk for you." She smirked. "She's not okay with that."

Barking out a laugh, I snagged a finger through a loop on her jeans as she turned away. *What was I doing?* I hauled her back. "I always thought your vajayjay was a man."

She was holding back a smile as she rested a hand to my chest. "You think I have man parts?"

That one touch.

I wanted to close my eyes and relish it.

This is wrong, but I was beyond caring. I pulled her so she was flush against me. "I think you have balls of steel. That's what I think you have."

Her head went down, but I could hear the laughter she was holding back. "Oh, really?"

"Yeah, really." I let loose of her waistband and slid my hands under her shirt. Then I raised them, skimming over her back, lifting her shirt as I did.

Her eyes closed, and she sighed in contentment. "Luke."

I pulled her closer and skimmed a quick glance around the bar. There were people watching us, but no one I cared about. Dustin nodded at me. I knew he would take care of things, so I took her hand and led her through the back hallway to the attached apartment. When I shut the door, the sounds from the bar were suppressed.

Bri lifted an eyebrow. "You soundproofed this place?"

"I figure it's my home, so why not?"

She turned away.

We'd been joking two seconds earlier, but that was gone. Her shoulders tensed again. Her hand trembled before she stuffed it into her jean's pocket.

"Your home?" Her voice sounded hoarse.

"Yeah."

"You're not going to your real home anymore?"

I sighed. "Bri, I hate that house. It's his house. It's…" *Where you left me and chose him.* "There aren't a lot of good memories in that place."

"You grew up next to me."

"Those are the only good memories. There's too much of *him* in there. I can't stomach the idea of living there again, not now since I don't have to. I can afford something better."

I looked at her for a moment, drinking in the sight of her.

Her jeans were always faded and ripped. She wore them like a second skin, along with her top. The shirt might've changed, but Brielle wasn't extravagant. She went for the simple and sexy look. A tank top or a T-shirt. It never mattered. She was slender, and her dark hair fell past her shoulders, matching her dark eyes when she looked at me. The curve of her lips was perfect when she smiled.

She was breathtaking.

"What's wrong?"

"What?" I asked, thrown by her sudden question.

She reached for a chair, but her hand paused in the air. It formed into a fist, and she forced it open. Her fingers curved around the chair and she held onto it with a death grip. Her bottom lip quivered a tiny bit. She was watching me, but I felt like she was seeing through me, to something behind me, or…I stopped. Was she?

I looked behind me. There was nothing there. "What are you seeing right now?"

She flinched like I had slapped her. "Nothing."

"Brielle."

"Stop."

I had taken a step toward her, but halted at her command. My hand went out to her. I wanted to help her so badly. I wanted her to let me in. "What happened to you?"

A tear fell from her eyelid. It trickled down, slowing over the curve of her cheek, until it dropped all the way to the corner of her mouth. Then it held there until more joined it. All of them fell together, and she let them be.

"Bri." My voice was raspy.

"I love you," she whispered.

I froze.

She said the words.

She said them again, "I love you, and that's why I have to avoid you. It hurts too much. I don't know why you keep finding me or why you held me tonight, but you have to stop. I get it. I hurt you. Don't you think I know? Don't you think I hurt myself, too?" She was whispering, and she gestured behind me. "I see him. Even now, he haunts me. It's because of him. All of this is because of him. If I hadn't listened to him—you know what I did. It doesn't matter. You left, and it's been over a year." Her eyes fell to my chest, and she came to me.

I held my breath.

She was coming to me. She was initiating this, and if I let myself breathe, she'd go away again.

As she stopped right in front of me, her hands went to my shirt. She touched me how I had touched her only moments ago. Her fingers, so soft and warm, caressed my skin. I wanted her. She lifted my shirt, her hands grazing against me, all the way up until she pulled my shirt from my head. But she wasn't looking at me. My chest rose up and down, and I fought to keep myself under control. Every part of me wanted to gather her in my arms, carry her to my bed, and be with her. She would go with me. I could always claim her body. She gave that to me. It was her weakness, but her heart... My gaze fell to her chest, and I pressed a hand between her breasts, under her shirt, and she let out a ragged breath at the touch.

"Bri—" I whispered, but she shook her head, stopping me.

"I love you." She was so quiet. Her head dropped to my chest, but her hands began to trace my scars. I had one that started from my arm and ran all the way down my side until it disappeared under my jeans.

"You took your shirt off for that magazine cover." She pressed her lips to my third and smallest scar. It was on my neck. "You never take your shirt off. I thought it was because you were ashamed."

"Ashamed?" I glanced down at myself. "Of the scars? Girls love them." Her finger kept outlining the one on my neck. I caught her hand. "I never think about them. Do they bother you?"

She pulled her hand from mine, falling back a step. Her eyes were glued to a fourth bird that I had tattooed. I saw the question forming in her depths. She was wondering if the new tattoo represented her, and it did, but not in the way she was thinking. I had left her, not the other way around.

Then she looked away, but I grabbed her hand again and placed it on the scar on my neck. "This was when he took a knife to me on my fourteenth birthday." She'd been there. She had helped to mend it. I pressed her hand to the second one. "This was *that* night." I held it underneath my jaw, so she could feel the third one. "When he knocked me unconscious the first time." The photographer for the magazine shoot had gone crazy when she saw my scars. "They sell covers, Bri. Priss Bitch told me so."

"Priss Bitch?"

"Our manager."

"I know. I didn't know that's what you called her."

"Braden hasn't told you about her?" It didn't matter. I didn't want to talk about my manager. I was holding Bri. She was touching me. She was right in front of me, and I didn't want any part of this moment to stop. I drew in a shuddering breath, and my forehead slowly lowered to rest on hers.

She looked up at me, seeing right into me, and her hands were gentle as they held on to my arms. She whispered, like she was afraid to ask, "What are you thinking?"

I couldn't answer her. I didn't want to break this moment. Closing my eyes, I just breathed her in. This felt so right.

"Luke," she murmured again, stepping into me so every inch of her was pressed into me.

"Hmm?" I ran my hands up her arms, then back down, letting them fall to her hips. I should be shoving her away, but I clasped her even tighter to me. Tonight. I wanted tonight.

"I…" She stood on her tiptoes, bringing her breasts higher up against my chest. She wrapped her arms around my neck, embracing me.

To hell with this. If she wanted a loving hug, I wasn't the guy for that. Bending down, I grabbed the back of her hips and lifted her in the air.

She gasped, but held on to me.

I turned and walked to the back bedroom, carrying her inside. Kicking the door shut with my foot, I placed her back on her feet at the foot of the bed. My eyes held her, and I wanted her. I wanted to push inside her. One night. I trailed a hand down from her neck, through the valley between her breasts. She closed her eyes, and her chest rose as my finger continued down, all the way to her stomach, and then I unclasped her jeans.

I knew one time wouldn't be enough. I would want her until the day I died. She was a drug to me.

Then, seeing the answering desire in her eyes, I turned for the door. Locking it, I went back and undid my own jeans. Bri's hands reached for her shirt, but I stopped her. "No, I want to." My voice was husky. Taking hold of her shirt, I ripped it off her and tossed it to the side. When she left, she'd be wearing my shirt.

She'd be wearing everything of mine. My scent. My taste. The feel of my hands on her. I would be stamped all over her.

Then she reached up, grabbed a fistful of my hair, and yanked me down. As our lips collided, I stopped thinking all together and rolled her underneath me.

She was mine.

CHAPTER
TWENTY-FOUR

I was in trouble. Waking up next to Brielle, hearing her soft breathing, feeling her skin next to mine, made me groan. I could touch her, kiss her, breathe her in, and I could see her wake with a smile. That had my heart pounding. Fuck. One night hadn't been enough. I gazed at her now, resting with her head turned into the pillow. She was facing me, with those damn soft eyelashes and lips that seemed to already be smiling back at me even as she slept. I didn't think one lifetime with her would be enough.

She had my balls in the palm of her hand. One squeeze and I would crumble. I gazed down her back to the arch of her spine until where the sheet covered her, and I already ached to slide back inside her.

Then her eyes opened, and that old feeling of my world clicking into place came over me. Everything lined up. Everything was right again. It was damn cheesy, but it was true.

Again. I was in trouble.

"Hey." She smiled at me.

"Hey back."

Her eyes were shining, but a shadow came over them, and she moved to sit up. Resting against the headboard, she pulled the blanket to cover herself and fiddled with her hands. "Luke…"

It was coming.

"Wait." I crossed the room to grab my jeans.

"You're getting dressed?"

"No, just the jeans." The corner of my lip twitched up. "If we're going to have this talk, doing it naked would make me feel weird."

"Oh." She looked down at the blanket.

I was an ass. I could grab her clothes and toss them over to her, but I liked having her naked. I liked having her in my bed. I should even the playing the field, but I didn't want to. She was mine. I made a vow to myself. Every chance I got, her clothes were coming off. That vow would stick, no matter how this conversation went. Being away from her for another year had been the worst thing I'd done in my life. It was time to rectify that.

"Bri, listen." I raked a hand through my hair, sitting on the bed beside her. "I have to apologize to you—"

"No." She surged forward. Her hand rested on my arm, stopping me. "What I did, I'm sorry. I'm so sorry. He…" she broke off. Her fingers curled around my arm and held on tightly. "He," her voice was guttural and full of emotion, "I shouldn't have gotten into that car, but I did. I shouldn't have done what he told me to do, but I did. I shouldn't have hidden it from you, but I did. I did so many things that I can't undo."

Tears formed in her eyes, and they slid down, one by one, as she talked. She ignored them, and I recognized the look in her eyes. She was back there, remembering every detail. The urge to crush her against my body and make her forget everything crawled up inside me until my hands were digging into the blankets. She needed to talk about this. I could see that. I had to let her, and if I stopped her, I knew that same demon would keep coming back and haunting her.

"I was a coward." Her head looked down. "I—"

I couldn't listen anymore. My hand reached for her chin, and I lifted it, making her look at me again. All of those tears were still there, just pooling on top of each other. She looked broken. Cursing inside, I knew some of that was because of me. "I'm sorry."

"What?"

"I'm. Sorry. Me." This was half my fault. "What I said to you, when you finally told me, was wrong. I was an asshole. I was hurt, but I was wrong. You don't have to apologize to me. I have to apologize to you."

She shook her head. "What are you doing? No, you don't. I do."

"No, you don't." I cupped the side of her face, my fingers sliding through her hair. "You already apologized, Bri. You did the night I kicked you out of the band. I'm sorry for what I did. What I did—I gave us another year apart—I have to apologize to you for that." I pointed at the fourth bird on my shoulder. "This is me. Because I left you, and I never should've done that. I'm so sorry, Bri."

"Luke—"

"Stop." I held her face with both of my hands and leaned forward, my eyes locking with hers. "You were a little girl. I remember your dad. He was an abusive bastard. Bri, how many times did I crawl into your room and sleep in the closet with you and Braden? How many times did you put Band-Aids on my bruises from my own dad? Both our dads were horrible. I get it. I do. You can't blame yourself for doing what your dad told you to do. What would he have done if you hadn't listened to him? That's what has haunted me for the last year."

"Luke?"

She wasn't getting it. She blamed herself for everything. I wanted to crush her to me, but I'd be so wrong, so fucking wrong. "Bri." I waited until her eyes focused on me again. They were still watering, and she had looked away. When they came back to me, I started, "You saved me. In a fucked-up way, you did. He *left* that night. He thought he killed me, and he left me. You gave me freedom, and I've never thanked you for that. If I knew that would've happened, even with the beating, I would've done it again. And again. And again. As long as I knew he was going to leave, I'd have done almost anything. Yes, it hurt me when you didn't come to see me in the hospital. Yes, it killed me when I found out you were dating Elijah, but now knowing why, thank you."

As the words were coming from me, I realized I had been so wrong about so many others things. Tears and emotions swirled in my gut. I was struggling from letting everything spill out. "Bri, I'm the one who is sorry. I'm sorry I got mad at you. I'm sorry I didn't push to find out why you were dating Elijah. I'm sorry I accepted it, and I didn't fight for you. I'm sorry that when you finally told me, I was stupid and blind. I'm sorry. Not you. You don't have anything to be sorry about."

Her entire face was coated with tears, and I couldn't stop myself anymore. I began kissing them, absorbing them one at a time. She gasped, her hands lifting to touch the sides of my face. I moved from one tear to another. I loved this woman. I loved her with every cell of my body, and I needed to show her.

"Ahem." Someone cleared their throat from the other side of the door.

Bri shrank down in the bed, but I turned toward the sound. An interruption, at this moment, had my blood starting to boil. When I opened the door and saw it was Elijah, looking smug in jeans and a sweatshirt, I growled. "*Not* the time."

He jumped back, holding his hands in the air between us. "I'm sorry. I'm sorry. I'm getting that. I…" His eyes danced back to Bri, and he cringed. "I'm sorry. I'm sorry, Bri. I thought," an uneasy laugh erupted from him, "I probably shouldn't say what I thought either."

"Elijah." His name was dipped low in a warning. "I don't care that you can handle yourself in a fight. I don't care what the magazines will say about my face. If you don't disappear in two seconds, I will be pounding that face of yours."

"Okay, but seriously, I wouldn't have interrupted if it wasn't life or death." He dropped his hands and shoved them into his pockets. "It's life or death, man. For real."

"Whose?" Bri asked from behind me.

He shifted to look at her. Fuck no. I moved, too, blocking him. When he looked at me, my lip curled up. Yeah, right. He wasn't going to see her like that, ever again. And, as if reading that message in my eyes, he held his hands up again and took one more step back.

"Bri," I called over my shoulder. "I have a shirt by the bed. Want to get dressed?"

"Oh, yeah."

I stared straight at Elijah as we both heard her moving around behind me. When she zipped up her pants, he continued to look at me and only me when he said, "It's Emerson. He's in trouble."

Bri let out a series of curses. We heard her hopping around behind us, and her voice was muffled before it became clearer. "Why am I not surprised? Emerson? Really? What did my cousin do, because it had better be good to interrupt this moment with us?!"

"He…" Elijah started to look over my shoulder at her, but stopped himself. He said to me, "He's wearing a wire, and Brute's about to find out."

One second.

Two seconds.

Three seconds.

The room was silent for thirty seconds before Brielle lit a fuse. She started yelling and cursing. "My stupid cousin. What the hell? I'm going to kill him!"

Elijah and I shared a look. I agreed with every word she said, but it was Emerson. We were going to kick him out of the band, but he was still family. He was still from Grant West, like the rest of us. I knew why Elijah had come to me. I'd help him, no matter what, with Emerson. I already had, and thinking back to that last time, I shook my head. We barely got out of Brute's alive. How was this going to be any different?

I said to Eli, ignoring Brielle's curses, "Tell me you have a good solid-proof plan this time."

Brielle stopped yelling. She was quiet for a beat, and then she started laughing. "Are you serious? Wait, you are. We all are. We're all crazy!" The bed squeaked as she sunk down on it. She was completely dressed, shaking her head.

"Look." Elijah stabbed his finger toward the ground. "I am aware of how stupid Emerson is. I'm aware of how much of an asshole he's been. I get it, trust me, but he's up shit creek if we don't help him."

"You're talking about walking into Brute's territory again and what?" There were so many things that could go wrong. "If Emerson's wearing a wire, there's going to be cops everywhere. Why can't he say the safe word and have them charge the place?"

"Because Emerson being Emerson didn't think everything through. If Brute marks him as a narc, he's dead. I don't think you get it either. Brute's organization is no joke. He's the reason I'm out of the business. I didn't want to cross the line of killing someone. That's what Brute does. Emerson can't say anything. He can't be searched. They'll find the wire, and he can't call for help. The cops will give it away. We have to get in there and do something to get him out." He ground out, "I wouldn't be here if I had someone else to ask. Trust me, I've stopped selling. People are pissed at me. You're it. You're the only ones I can ask for help." He skimmed an eye over Bri. "I didn't know she'd be here, and I figured I couldn't ask Braden, because—"

A growl slipped from Brielle.

Elijah added, "She would've killed me."

I held up a hand. "Wait, I still have to wrap my mind around this. Emerson went to Brute's, and he's wearing a wire?"

"The dumbass got cornered by the cops. They took him in for something, and this was their bargaining chip." He shared a look with Brielle. "They tried the same crap with Bri, too, but I'm guessing Emerson was on something. He's got a big rock star rep to protect. I'm sure they said do this or be incarcerated."

"But a wire?"

"Yeah, cops do this shit. It's not just in movies. They like to get people to narc on their friends, or in this case, on his own drug dealer."

"What's he doing now?" Brielle asked. Standing, she folded her arms over her chest and narrowed her eyes. "You said he decided against going through with it."

"He said they're searching people for a wire. He didn't say why or anything."

I recognized that look and started shaking my head. "No. No way."

"Shut it." She sent me a scathing look and turned her back to me. It was a deliberate movement, and she asked Elijah again, "What's he doing to keep them from searching him?"

Elijah glanced between us, but I caught the familiarity in his gaze. Oh, yes. He'd seen this side of her, too. He knew exactly what was going on. Bri was going to help, and she was doing it no matter what I or anyone else said. If I forced her to stay… I wished I owned some handcuffs.

"He's taking a shit."

Brielle cocked her head to the side. "Say again?"

Elijah repeated, "He's taking a shit. He's pretending to have massive diarrhea. Once he figured out they were looking for wires on people, he took a dump in his pants. He can shit on command."

"You're serious?" Brielle swung back to me. "Is he serious?"

I nodded. "He used to practice on the back of our tour bus." I grimaced. "He thought it was hilarious. No one else did."

"Oh my god," she muttered. "My cousin is an idiot."

Elijah's hand shot up, and he snapped his fingers at her. "Yes, you're getting it. He's an idiot, but we all love him." Brielle's eyebrows arched high, and he amended, "We all feel some form of obligation toward him. How about that?"

She rolled her eyes. "Yeah, whatever. Wherever you guys are going, I'm going."

Her tone sounded flippant, but her teeth sank deep into her bottom lip. Brielle was worried, just as much as Elijah. This was Emerson. He was in trouble, *again*. I should've been worried, but she was coming. I was livid instead. I cared about him, but I loved her. And he was going to put her in danger.

Elijah had been watching me, his eyes shadowed.

I clenched my jaw. Fine. I jerked my head in a tight nod. "Let's go."

That was all Elijah needed. He was halfway out the door before he called over his shoulder, "I have weapons. You don't need to grab any. I have enough."

"Weapons," Bri murmured to herself. Her head was bent, and she pressed her hands against her side. "Okay. Weapons. We can do this." She started forward, but I grabbed her arm and pulled her back.

"You don't have to do this." *Please, don't do this.* "He has treated you like shit for years. You really don't have to go."

Her hand paused in the air and closed over mine. She gave me a reassuring nod. "I want to go. You're going. Elijah's going. And, yes, even my dick cousin—I care about all of you." Her eyes were tracing my face as she softened her tone. "And I love you." Her voice was a caress. She cupped the side of my face. "I love you."

I leaned into her touch. It was tender, warm, and what I wanted to enjoy—not what we were about to do. "Bri…" Visions of locking her in a room, tying her to a chair, and finding something that resembled handcuffs all flashed in my mind. Anything to keep her from going with us. I had a bad feeling.

"What?"

I shook my head. She started to pull her hand away, but I caught it and held it there for another moment. We were going into a storm. Her touch would be the only shelter that would keep me going.

"Luke," she whispered, moving close. "I know things are weird. I have no idea what the plan is for us, but I love you. I do. I've never stopped."

My lips cracked a grin. "You're telling me now?" I couldn't do anything about it. All those same images of locking her in a room, tying her to a chair, and handcuffing her came tumbling back, but in an entirely different manner. "You're making this so hard. I want you to stay here."

"I can't." Her hand pressed against my face again. "You're going. I'm going. That's how it is."

That was how it was. She meant those words, and they coursed through me. I felt every single one of them and drew in a new wave of strength. She was my woman. She said it right there. Fighting it was useless, because I'd keep coming back to her.

Her eyes were searching mine.

I pulled her close. A gleam of relief appeared in her eyes as her other hand grasped my shoulder. "I love you," she whispered, her forehead resting against mine.

"I love you, too," I whispered back. Framing her face with my hands on either side, I drank in the sight of her. Her eyes were sparkling, and her cheeks were pink. Her lips opened, and I wanted to kiss her. I wanted to pull her in and get lost in her.

"Hey," Elijah called back, knocking on the wall. "Pepe and Penelope, get your stanky asses up here." He pulled back and headed to his car, but we heard him say over his shoulder, "We have an idiot to rescue."

CHAPTER
TWENTY-FIVE

BRIELLE

This was nuts.

As Elijah drove to Brute's house, I glanced over at Luke. I could feel the tension radiating off him. I knew he didn't want me there, but he had to understand. I couldn't stay back. I was there for him. I was there to make sure he walked out alive. What I said back at The Shack was how I felt. Where he went, I went. That resonated through me, more than anything now. I didn't know what was going to happen, but if we all survived, I was going with him. I was going to be at his side, and I didn't care about the logistics.

Elijah drove the car around the last turn and slowed to park. We were two blocks away from Brute's house.

I was going to be at Luke's side from now on, but we had to get through this first, I reminded myself.

We should've formulated a better plan. We should've thought of some way that didn't include walking into Brute's house, but as we got out and Elijah handed us each a weapon from his trunk, none of those things happened.

The street was quiet, and the air felt cold. I didn't know what time it was. I didn't know this street or if it was usually this quiet, but I felt it was odd. Brute didn't live in a great neighborhood. The houses were old and most looked like they needed to be torn down, but a few had toys in the yard. There were abandoned tricycles and bikes on the sidewalk. A dog leash was left in one of the driveways. People lived here. Children played here. Pets were walked here. There should've been sounds of life around us, but unlike the last time we walked to Brute's house, it was eerily silent.

As I glanced up at one house, I watched as a curtain fell back into place. A second house—the same thing. After the fourth house, I stopped looking. They were all watching. It was like they had known we were coming.

A chill went down my spine, and I gripped the knife in my pocket tighter. I walked shoulder to shoulder with Elijah and Luke as we made the two blocks to Brute's house. Before getting there, Elijah cut down a back alley. Emerson was wearing a wire, so there were going to be cops around. Once we started down the alley, he ran ahead. We needed to get to the house before the cops could stop us. There were three houses between Brute's and us. As we sped past the first house, a car turned down the alley from the other side.

"Come on." Elijah picked up his pace.

The car kept coming.

We were at Brute's fence, and Elijah launched himself over it. He opened the door just as the car approached us. I braced myself, not knowing what was next—if a bullet would hit us first or if we'd be thrown into the back of it and whisked away. Nothing happened. They slowed down, and a woman wearing a baseball cap pulled low looked at me. It was the cop who had taken me to the police station a year ago. She met my gaze. A warning was in hers, and her lips were turned down.

I was grabbed and pulled into the back lawn.

The car sped back up. As Elijah shut the fence, I was hauled to the corner to a clump of trees.

This whole thing was wrong. Something was going to go wrong. I felt it in my gut, but I didn't say anything. My body was in a cold sweat. It had been a discussion before, but now that we were here, it was real. Too real.

"Was that a cop?" Elijah asked me, keeping his voice low.

I just nodded. A big lump was sitting at the bottom of my throat. I knew I couldn't talk, so I wasn't going to try.

"Wait, what?" Luke grabbed my arm. His eyes were fierce. "That was a cop?"

I felt myself nodding again. My whole body was tense. I didn't know how my muscles could move.

He cursed under his breath. "You recognized her?"

When it was too late. I wanted to say those words to him, but my mouth didn't move. I couldn't.

"What's your problem?" Elijah asked him as he pulled out a gun—a *gun*. My ex-boyfriend had a gun, and he was checking it for bullets, taking out the clip like it was the most natural thing in the world.

I couldn't look away from his gun as I heard Luke say, "My problem? Are you kidding me? If I'd known that was a cop, I would've forced Brielle to go with her. She doesn't need to be here."

"Hey," Elijah snarled back at him. I still couldn't look away from his gun, even as he slid it back into the front pocket of his sweatshirt. He added, "Look, I didn't know she'd be with you. I needed back up, and you're good in a fight. I didn't know. I thought," his eyes darted to me, "I thought you had a different chick back there."

Luke growled at him.

"I didn't know the two of you were back on, but she's here."

They were talking about me. I was there, but it was like I wasn't. Elijah had a gun. I had a knife. I don't remember what weapon he gave Luke... We were all armed. Somehow that should've been the start of a joke, but I wasn't laughing. I couldn't even talk.

Elijah continued in a whisper, "And it's Bri. Yes, I could've figured out a way to talk to you without her around, but you know her. She would've gotten it out of us somehow or just followed us like last time. Remember last time?"

"Yeah." Luke surged forward, getting in his face. "I remember last time. I remember Brute holding a *fucking* knife to her throat."

"Yeah, and she found us then, like she wouldn't have done the same thing this time," Elijah argued back. "She's here. It's done. She's a good fighter. She can handle herself."

"I'm going to kill you," Luke snarled. "If Brute doesn't do it, I'm going to do it."

"Piss off. It's done. You were all about helping me at your bar. Now you're here, and you're crapping your pants? My best friend's in that house, and he's dead if we don't get to him."

Emerson was dead. Hearing those words centered me. All the fear started to ebb, and I could speak again. Moving between them, I touched a hand to both of their arms. They were like cement, glaring at each other. "Stop," I chided quietly. "Emerson's one of us. We have to get him out."

"What's the plan?" Luke asked the question, and both of us waited for Elijah to answer.

He hesitated and then shrugged. "It's still morning. Most of Brute's crew will probably be sleeping. I don't know who they have in there, but the plan is to go in, start a fight, and try to run out with Emerson. He's holed up in a bathroom. I told him we're close. Once he hears yelling, he's supposed to bolt out with us."

That was the plan.

I glanced at Luke. I could sense a storm rising in him. "So..." he drew that word out. "We go in, wave a gun around, and hope that works?"

"Pretty much."

Luke grabbed the back of his neck, his Adam's apple moving up and down, as he continued to stare at Elijah. "That's the worst fucking plan I've ever heard."

"You have anything better?"

"Yeah," Luke clipped out. His hand moved up to his hair, and he grabbed a fistful of it. "What bathroom is he in?"

"Uh." Elijah pulled out his phone and texted Emerson. A minute later, it buzzed back. "He said the second floor, south side of the house."

We all scrutinized the house, searching the second floor windows, and as we did, Emerson appeared in one of them. He was looking for us, too. We could see him, but he couldn't see us.

"Okay." Luke pulled our attention back to him. "Text him and ask if he can open the window."

"You're serious?"

Luke shot Elijah a dark look. "Your plan sucks, and you're questioning mine?"

"Okay, okay." His fingers moved over the buttons, and he hit *Send*. We waited. Another minute that seemed like an hour passed before Emerson replied. "He said he can, but he's on the second floor—"

"We'll catch him," Luke said before he could finish. "We'll go over there and form a human ladder. Emerson can crawl down us. It'll work. They just can't see us. Does Brute have watchmen at all?"

Elijah snorted. "At night, yeah, but not in the morning. His crew parties hard. Guaranteed most of them are still wasted and sleeping it off. Whoever's searching for wires is in the house. They're not going to expect anyone to sneak up to Brute's house. He's a drug dealer. If anything, people run in the opposite direction. I would know."

"Okay." Luke was nodding, his eyebrows bunched together. "This might work then. Text him again. Tell him to open the window, and we're coming to help him."

"Wait." I grabbed Elijah's arm. "What about an alarm system?"

"Nope, Brute's alarm is himself. His kitchen is stockpiled with guns."

That lump formed in my throat again. My eyes got big. He was going to make us go into that room? I retracted my hand. "Well, thank god for this second plan then."

Luke glared at Elijah again, and so did I. He looked between us and asked, "What?"

"Kitchen. Stockpile. Guns," Luke hissed. "If you were to take a guess?"

"I was planning on guarding where he has the guns. I know the cabinets, and if I had a gun, I figured they couldn't get to them."

"Oh, yes, that makes it so much better."

"Yes, my plan sucked, but this one's not that much better. It's a risk. Coming to Brute's house is a risk in itself. Do you want me to text Emerson or not?"

Luke gestured to the phone. "Get it done and let's start heading up there." He surveyed the back of the garage. "We can keep to the fence and move closer to the house this way. When we get there, we can crawl underneath the windows, staying as close to the house as possible, and then make the human ladder."

"On it." Elijah was already texting. After he hit *Send*, he put the phone in my hand and squared his shoulders back. "Ready. Let's go."

We started forward. Elijah led the way, and Luke went after me. As I moved forward, his hand touched my hip, and we shared a look. He was both worried and furious. He wanted to be anywhere but here. I got it. I did. Those same feelings were swirling inside me, but we were here, and Emerson needed us. There was no other way around it. He nodded, as if reading my mind and squeezed my hip before letting his hand fall away. I picked up my pace and hurried to where Elijah was waiting for us. The distance between where we were and where we had to go seemed to take forever. It would take one person to see us. One person to look out their window and notice our slow trek there. With each step, my heart pounded so loudly. I worried everyone else could hear it, but nothing happened.

When we got there, Elijah got on his hands and knees. Luke climbed on top of him, and then I started up. Luke was holding onto a window frame to help steady himself. Stepping on Elijah's back, I climbed up Luke and moved so I was sitting on his shoulders. Then I looked up.

Emerson was gazing down at me. Worry lines had formed at the corners of his mouth, and there were bags under his eyes. "Shit," he muttered under his breath.

I couldn't talk, and my hands were sweaty, but I motioned for him.

He nodded. "Okay, I can't believe we're doing this, but okay." Kneeling on the window frame, he paused as he looked all the way down and then started to fall backwards. His hands loosened their grip on the window ledge, but I reached up and tapped his hand. He was that close to me.

"Emerson," I choked out. "Don't look down." I waved to get his attention. His whole forehead had a film of sweat over it.

He jerked his head back to mine.

I pointed at my eyes. "Look at me. Look here. Don't look down."

"I just found out that I'm scared of heights, Bri," he rasped out. Gone was the cocky jerk. This was my cousin, the one who had come to check on me when we were younger because I left and didn't wait for them. He was the same cousin I used to love to horse around with. He was scared, and just like that, my fear was pushed down.

A calm overtook me, and I lifted my hand enough to grab Emerson's hand. I took hold of it and leaned close. "Emerson," I said, my voice firm and steady. "We've done this before."

"That was when we were in the seventh grade. Times change. We've gotten fatter."

"Stop it. Look at me. Come on. You can do this. Just like before. Trust us."

Trust us. Those words echoed in my head. I had to trust Elijah and Luke, and Emerson had to trust all of us. We would get through this. I started repeating that mantra in my head, over and over again. I didn't know if I believed it, but I had to. We'd be fine. We'd get through this. Then I could do bodily harm to my cousin, but only afterwards.

"Come on. Turn around." I waited as he did. His whole body was trembling. I said further, "Extend one leg, but keep a good grip on the window frame. You have to hold yourself steady. Use your back muscles. They'll keep your body steady."

As I said it, he started to do it. He followed every command, and his leg came out in the air. I wrapped an arm around it, feeling Elijah and Luke suddenly become more stationary beneath us. They were holding both of us. As one leg touched Luke's shoulder, his other leg did the same thing. Then Emerson lowered himself out of the window. Only his arms were resting on the window frame. Sweat rolled off him, and he started to shake again. He'd have to let go, but he was still holding on.

"Emerson," I murmured, holding onto the window frame myself. "Let go. You're good. We've got you."

He nodded, taking gaping breaths. He couldn't speak. Closing his eyes, he let go, and his whole body weight came down on us. Elijah groaned from the ground, but Luke reached up and grasped Emerson's leg, that was now wound around his chest. All of us swayed against the house and then back out, but my fingers dug in, and I kept a hold on the window. Luke did the same, steadying us. He called up, "Emerson, start climbing down."

"Okay." He moved slowly until he was close enough to leap to the ground.

I clambered down right afterwards. The climb up was hard enough, but after enduring Emerson climbing down on me, scooting down Luke's body until I was close enough to jump seemed like child's play.

Luke was slower getting off and Elijah needed a minute before he was able to stand to his feet. Emerson had to help him up, and he clapped him on the back. "I've never been so happy to see you guys as I am right now. I've never loved the earth as much as I do now either." He bent down and kissed the ground. "Seriously, I owe you guys my life."

Elijah shook his head, wrinkles forming in his forehead. He tried to pull up the hood of his sweatshirt, but his hands were trembling. It took two attempts to pull it over his head, and then he hunched back down. "We still have to leave."

Luke touched my side as he moved to stand right behind me. He spoke for us, "Let's go."

Then we heard something that made my blood go cold.

"Not so fast."

Brute was standing behind us with a gun pointed at Emerson's head.

CHAPTER
TWENTY-SIX

Breathe, little girl.

People started yelling. Brute was demanding to know why Emerson was sneaking off. He wanted to know why Elijah was there and why the rest of us had come with him. There were no cops in the backyard. Not yet. A haze came over me. There was chaos everywhere, but I felt centered. Maybe I couldn't handle what was happening, but I didn't think that was it. It was something else, something I couldn't explain.

A voice in my head whispered, *"Family. It's all about family."*

Ignoring the shouts, I left Luke's side and took two steps forward. Brute was frowning at me, but that gun was still pointing at Emerson.

"Yes, the cousin that hates me." My own voice came to me—when Luke picked me up at the police station—and then a second memory was right behind it—when I accused Elijah. *"It's because of you my cousin went to rehab last summer, wasn't it?"*

I swung my gaze to my ex-boyfriend now. He had denied my accusation, but I never believed him. I always blamed him. I'd been wrong.

"What are you so goddamn worried about?" Emerson glared at me.

"You might not want to start with me."

"Oh, really?"

"Really."

He folded his arms over his chest, turning the same loathsome focus back on me. "Why do you say that?"

"Because I'm fairly certain those guys are your drug dealers, and Elijah won't like finding that out since you're his best friend."

I'd been wrong. Again.

Elijah *had* known. There'd been no way he wouldn't have known. I thought I finally had 'something' on my cousin, but I hadn't.

"No! You don't even know, Luke. I'm sticking up for you. For you, man."

He jerked a hand to Elijah. "And my best friend, too." He looked to me. "Bri, it's gone on long enough."

I looked at Luke. Emerson had been fighting for him. His hatred toward me had been about Luke and his best friend. I'd been the one who had been hurting them, and he knew the whole time.

"I just found out that I'm scared of heights, Bri," he rasped out. Gone was the cocky jerk. This was my cousin, the one who had come to check on me when we were younger because I left and didn't wait for them.

"Emerson," I said. "We've done this before."

"That was when we were in the seventh grade. Times change. We've gotten fatter."

"Stop it. Look at me. Come on. You can do this. Just like before. Trust us."

He had. He listened to me, followed my instructions, and trusted me.

I looked at my cousin one last time. His eyes were bleak, swinging back and forth between Brute and the gun. It was still pointed at him, but he wasn't saying anything. There was yelling, either from Elijah or Luke. They were arguing for Emerson's life. I felt someone tugging on the back of my shirt, but I ignored them.

I didn't know what I was doing, but I had to do something.

Brute was yelling over my head at someone behind me. His gun was waving in the air, up and down as he kept shouting. A vein was bulging out from his neck. Then I took the last step and moved, so I was standing in front of my cousin.

I took his place.

Breathe, little girl.

It was my mother's voice in my head. I could hear her again as she whispered into my ear. Plates had been shattered. The kitchen table was flipped upside down. Doors were ripped off their hinges. With each crash and roar coming from the other room, my little fingers had dug into her arm. That was the night he left.

I thought nothing could get worse.

I was staring down the barrel of a gun now.

I'd been wrong.

Then the gun went off.

EPILOGUE

The crowd was cheering. They'd been chanting 'Sustain' for the last fifteen minutes. Our time was up. It was so close for when we'd take the stage, and I couldn't move. Playing with them for small town gigs or at house parties was one thing, but this stadium filled to capacity was another level. My hands were sweating and shaky. As a drummer, that was embarrassing.

"Hey." Luke slipped into the room, and the chanting grew louder. It was muffled as he closed the door behind him, but it didn't matter. I could still hear them. They were in my head.

I leaned forward, rested my elbows on my knees, and hung my head between my legs. I couldn't believe I was nervous. This—playing for thousands of fans, playing with Luke, with Braden, as a drummer— this was my dream, and I was close to pissing my pants.

Luke sat next to me, and his hand grazed down my back. "You okay?"

I shook my head. I couldn't talk. Even the sight of him wasn't enough to distract me. Dressed in jeans and a T-shirt that hung over his form, molding against him, it was like the shirt had been created to make him more beautiful. No. Not even the sight of him could distract me. I had tried, through the entire rehearsal. Even afterwards, I pulled him in a back room, but the butterflies were still buzzing in my stomach.

"Hey," he murmured, drawing me to look up at him. As I did, meeting those grey eyes of his, some of the butterflies settled down. Some kicked up, for another reason, but I couldn't control how my pulse kept racing. His hand cupped the side of my face, and his thumb caressed my cheek. He leaned down, his forehead resting against mine. "You're going to be amazing. I know you are."

"Easy for you to say." My lips brushed against his. "You're already loved by millions. I'm new. They only know me because I kicked their beloved guitarist out of the band."

He laughed, the sound and air coating against my lips. "They don't. The true fans know you saved his life. When you stood in front of that gun, Brute hesitated, and the cops were able to shoot him instead. That's public information."

I reached for his hand.

He added, "Yes, some social networks are villainizing you, but we can't do much about that. They're just mad Emerson isn't with the band. They blame you. They're going to say what they want no matter what. We know the truth. The general public knows the truth, and the real fans do, too. They're out there and they're excited to meet you. They know you're Braden's sister…" He stopped after that, pulling away from me.

I said what he couldn't, "They don't know about us, though."

The corners of his mouth stretched out, flattening his mouth. "Priss Bitch might think she has some control over us, but she'll soon find out she doesn't. Don't worry about it."

After a phone caught the entire confrontation with Brute on tape, it went public fast. Once we were cleared by a medic team, we were taken to the police station for statements. It was the same ordeal as when they raided Elijah's house, but there was no interrogation. Everything had been a whirlwind.

That'd only been the beginning.

Wanting to get ahead of the social media storm, since the video was already viral, Priscilla and Peter made a public statement that Emerson was going into a drug rehabilitation program, and yes, the girl on the video clip was Sustain's new drummer. I was officially introduced in an interview with Becky Walters and the rest of the band.

The public's response had been mixed. Some loved me, proclaiming I was a hero, and others hated me, blaming me for the entire thing. Even though I could hear only cheering from the stadium, I knew I'd walk out to 'boos'.

"Hey." Luke caught my chin again and made me look at him. "I mean it. Don't worry about it. Everything will be fine."

Priscilla hadn't been happy to find out about me, but she'd been forced to accept my position with the band. Luke, Braden, and Gunn threatened to walk if she didn't okay it. Even Emerson said he'd make a statement against her. I'd been shocked when I heard about his support. Braden reminisced telling me the story, how Emerson caused a scene in a board meeting about me. I heard the story once a week for the last month, but as Luke said—Priss Bitch was a battle for another day. My first battle, getting my hands steady.

Someone knocked on the door and shouted through it, "Five minutes."

"You going to be okay?"

No. I smiled at him. "Yes."

The side of his mouth lifted, and he shook his head, pulling me close to press a kiss to my forehead. "You're such a liar." His lips lingered there, and I felt him take a breath. He murmured softly, "I love you. No one will take that away."

He started to pull away. I grabbed his shirt and pulled him back. "Promise?"

"Promise." His eyes were fierce.

Luke had been wonderful during everything. He never left my side, staying with me at night, getting breakfast for us in the mornings, holding my hand whenever I needed the extra strength. The only time he wasn't allowed to be by my side was when we were in interviews; there'd been a few since the Becky Walters' interview. Priss Bitch thought the fans needed to find out later on, that there'd been enough changes for them to process. After I used a bathroom at a restaurant and found two girls crying, clutching Emerson's picture, I agreed with her. Luke hadn't. He'd fought with her the entire time, only obeying because she threatened to kick me out.

"Two minutes." That same person rapped on the door again. It was brisk and louder than before. Their impatience was noted.

"I suppose it's time."

Luke stood and took my hand. When we stepped out in the hallway, a crowd of people were waiting for us. I didn't know who they were, but they rushed us to the stage, and right before we got there, I heard my name being called. Elijah and Emerson were off to the side. Luke was pressing behind me. He had taken to walking like that, and I knew he was trying to protect me. He saw them too and pulled us from the group.

"Luke—"

He turned around, his eyes flashing a warning. "Stall. These are our friends."

The stagehand frowned, but pressed a hand into a walkie and relayed the information. As we drew closer to Elijah and Emerson, Braden joined the group. Gunn was right behind him. The same crowd that had been rushing us to the stage formed a wall around us this time. They turned their backs to allow us privacy, and as they did, I felt safe from their prying eyes, and I could breathe a little easier.

Emerson noticed my reaction. The side of his mouth lifted up. "It's a little shocking, isn't it? All the sudden attention."

I nodded, pressing my hand to my stomach. The nerves were still there, bouncing all around. "I think it's worse because I'm a girl and I'm the new drummer."

"Yeah." Emerson hit Braden's shoulder. "They sure loved this dumbass behind those drums."

"Hey." Braden's hand covered where he had hit, but his eyes lit up. He was beaming. He had been growing out his hair, and because there was enough length, he had the sides of it braided. The top of his hair was set in spikes. He ran his hand over it now, gently pressing down on the tips. "You like my hair?"

"Rocker Extraordinaire." Emerson smiled back, but he swallowed at the end of his statement. A hint of envy was evident. "You look awesome, like always, but you and Luke are the pretty boys of the band." He hit Elijah's elbow. "This guy's the other pretty boy. He and I will hold Grant West down."

Elijah bobbed his head up and down in one fell swoop. "Damn straight. We'll represent home now."

"Ha." Braden was pretending to hit the air, his head moving up and down, in rhythm with the music playing in the background. "You guys hold the fort down. We'll represent nationally."

The teasing, going back and forth was good-natured, but as Elijah and Emerson both looked towards me, I felt a serious undertone slide into place. The group felt it, too, and everyone grew quiet for a split moment. Then Emerson said to me, "You'll do great, Bri. I got a pass from treatment. They didn't know I was coming here, but I had to come and say thanks."

I was in the band. He was not, but he wasn't talking about that.

Feeling my throat swell up, I murmured, "Yeah. You'd have done the same…" My sentence hung in the air. No one commented, then everyone started laughing.

Emerson shook his head, grinning. "No. No, I don't think I would've. I was an asshole to you." His eyes skirted from Elijah to Luke who was standing behind me with a hand on my hip. "I love these guys. Even if I don't show it, I do, and I thought you were hurting them on purpose. I was wrong." His gaze lingered on Luke. "I learned more about what you had to do, and anyway, I'm sorry."

It didn't take a genius to figure out who told him. Leaning back against Luke, his arm moved around me, and some of those nerves started to melt away. "Thank you, Emerson." I meant it. My cousin was back. He was the cousin I always loved and who had loved me back. Glancing to Braden, who was watching the whole thing, I felt everything click into place. This moment was right. My family was here. Even our mom had been ushered to the dressing room earlier to wish me good luck.

I was ready for that stage.

As if he felt it too, Luke's hand slid down my arm, and his fingers entwined with mine.

I looked up over my shoulder. He pressed a kiss to my forehead, then whispered in my ear, "Don't worry about it. You're mine and I want everyone to know."

I wasn't sure what he meant, but it eased my calm into excitement. I was about to go and play with him. Hearing the crowd's chant of 'Sustain', instead of imagining their rejection, I let their cheers meld with me. They were buzzing. So was I. I started to feel the adrenalin in my body. My blood began boiling and the itch to slam my drumsticks down was beginning to fill me up.

I was nearing that intoxicated state. I was addicted. As Elijah and

Emerson said their goodbyes and headed for their seats, Luke led the way, holding my hand. Right before we took the stage, I tried to pull my hand free.

He tightened his hold.

We were announced next and then, flashing me a grin, he led me out onto the stage. Walking out to the deafening sound of their cheers, I didn't care that they saw us holding hands. Luke was right. They'd either love me or hate me. I wasn't going to hold anything back. If I heard any boos, I wouldn't care. Every cell in my body was ready to play. Hopping up onto my seat, I got ready. No matter what happened, no matter who came against us, no matter the fights between us, I knew we would be fine. We'd sustain, but now—I raised my drumsticks in the air. Luke looked back and nodded, and I slammed down on the bass—now, I was content to kick ass.

www.tijansbooks.com

ACKNOWLEDGMENTS

Oh my word. This book took forever and an entire team of people to help me with it. Thank you to Jay McLean for being the first person excited about this and chatting with me late at night over it. Thanks to my beta Celeste, for really taking the hammer to me in the very beginning. She pushed me to make it better, which resulted in a whole other version of the book. Thank you to all my betas: Heather, Cami, Eileen, and Kerri. I always drop things in your inboxes and you guys help me out, no matter what it is or even if it makes no sense! Thank you, thank you to always being honest. Then another big wave of thanks to my editors: Ami at aldjediting.net, Paige, Marla at proofingstyle.com, and Chris at parececonsulting.com. To Debra Anastasia for reading Sustain and letting me know I'm not insane at times and to Kelly and Teresa. I dropped stuff in your inboxes so much. Thank you for looking it over and reassuring me! Everyone in the fan group, I love you ladies. Thank you to everyone in the street team. All those shares helps so much. I don't think you guys have any idea. I'm beyond grateful! To my cover designer, Lisa Jordan. I always say it, but you really do 'put up with me.' Last, to Jason and Bailey. You both *really* put up with me during this book. Love you both.

BONUS
SCENE
(FLASHBACK)

"Luke." I laughed. "What are you doing?"

He grinned down at me and held a finger up to his lips. "Hush, girl. You're going to get us caught."

Caught. I shook my head. "Luke, you're not thinking this through." We were outside a recording studio at ten in the morning. It was the time we figured no one would be around. After scoping out the place for a few days, we got the routine down; the musicians and workers came in the early afternoon and stayed until three or four in the morning. Ten in the morning was the best time for us to break in and look around. The idea had been Luke's. He was itching to see inside a real studio. His father talked about it since he used to manage a band, but those days were long gone. Drugs had taken over both of our dads' worlds, but since forming our own band, the talk about seeing the inside of a studio became more and more common. After a night of getting into my mom's wine and making out, Luke figured today was the best time to go. Now, we were outside the building after discovering it was locked up completely. There was no way inside.

As Luke checked a window, I tugged on his sleeve. "Luke, come on. Let's go. We're not getting in this way."

"No way." Steel determination looked back down at me. "Even if it's just…" He stopped talking and frowned to himself while my alarm bells started going off at his look. He had an idea. I held my breath in anticipation, knowing some of his ideas weren't always great ones.

I started to say, "Luke," when he shook his head quickly and bent down and grabbed a rock.

He flung it through the window.

SUSTAIN

"Luke!"

The glass shattered, raining down on us. He muttered a curse, but clutched me quickly. Pulling me forward, he wrapped his arms around me and shielded me with his back. It was over as fast as it started. Luke let me go, but kept his hands on my arms as I stepped out from his hold. He asked, "You okay?" His eyes roamed all over me as he checked for himself.

I nodded, feeling for blood, but it didn't feel like I'd been cut anywhere. With a shaky nod, I said, "Yeah, I'm good." Then I looked up at the window. The hole was big enough to reach an arm through, but we'd still have to clear more of an opening, which meant more glass had to be broken. "I don't know, Luke. I think we should just go."

"Nah." He flashed me a grin, one of those rakish ones that always had my insides tingling. He added, "A quick look. Come on, Bri. We're so close. We'll be gone before any cops get here. I just want to see what it looks like inside."

Inside a real studio. I heard the plea in his tone and swallowed my argument. I couldn't blame him either. People made music in there. Music that launched careers and changed lives—all inside those sound booths. "Okay." I couldn't wipe the grin off my face now. "Just really quick. We can't get caught, though. You know my mom will ground my ass."

Luke laughed; the carefree sound of it made that tingle go into hyper drive, along with my heart rate. As he cleared out more of the glass and reached inside to unlock the window, I stepped back to admire him. Tall. Trim. His face had such fierce determination now, but when he turned that concentration on me, I sighed inwardly, knowing I couldn't ever help myself when it came to him.

When the window was opened, he turned, his hands finding my hips. He hoisted me up, murmuring into my ear, "This is what dreams are made of, Bri. One day, it'll be us. I promise. Trust me."

Lightning Source UK Ltd.
Milton Keynes UK
UKHW010033110521
383501UK00011B/604/J